Waltraud

A True Story of
Growing Up in Nazi Germany

TAMMY BORDEN

D1607738

Waltraud

A True Story of

Growing Up in Nazi Germany

TAMMY BORDEN

ISBN: 9798392221783

Additional photos, author's notes, and German translations in back.

To my mother, Waltraud, my inspiration
and the most extraordinary woman
I have known or will ever know.
I love you. I miss you.

"Whatever in our life is hardest to bear,
love can transform into beauty."

— Corrie ten Boom —

CHAPTER 1
Christmas Eve 1937

Snow and ice settled between the cobblestones, crunching with each step, and smoke hung in the air, weaving through bare branches and swirling above our heads. Did the smell of burning embers come from chimney tops, or was it clinging to my coat from the candlelight service we just left?

I didn't know. And I didn't care. I didn't care about a lot of things these days.

Werner ran ahead.

Every other day of the year, my younger brother lagged behind whenever our family went somewhere. But tonight, he cast his laziness aside and urged me to quicken my steps.

"Come on, Waltraud, hurry!"

I ignored him. He ran back and grabbed the sleeve of my coat, tugging me forward.

"Why are you going so slow?"

"Let go of me!" I yanked my arm away and slipped on the icy street, stumbling to one knee. "Look what you've done!"

Mutti interrupted. "Waltraud. Tonight of all nights is not the time to fight with your brother."

"But he knocked me over!"

Mutti gave a look only mothers can give and I knew to let it drop. I steadied myself, and my stride remained the same. Werner sulked, while Mutti carried my baby sister, Anneliesa, on her hip.

I knew why Werner wanted to get home, but I didn't share his excitement. Already ten years old, I knew deep inside this Christmas wouldn't be the same. But Werner was just six and thought only about himself. He didn't understand or care how this Christmas was different from all the others.

Werner was especially good since St. Nikolaus paid a visit a few weeks earlier. On the eve of December 6th, we both left a shoe on the windowsill in our bedroom. We shared a room, and when morning came, we slid from beneath our feather beds onto the cold floor and ran to the window to see what St. Nikolaus left for us.

I reached inside my shoe and found a small orange. The color was pale, almost yellow, and the dry green stem was still attached. I put my nose to the rind. The smell of citrus was strong. It smelled like summer. I decided right there I would sit at the kitchen table for breakfast and bite into each juicy piece. And when I did, I'd envision myself on a tropical island with swaying palm trees and warm sand between my toes—not the cold, barren landscape of northern Germany. I knew the exotic fruit was nearly impossible to come by in the middle of winter, but I supposed St. Nikolaus had his magical ways of making the impossible happen.

I pulled my shoe from the frosted window and something rattled inside. A chocolate bonbon was nestled in the toe. I unwrapped it and popped the milky sweetness into my mouth, savoring each swoosh as it moved from cheek to cheek. I didn't dare chew. Instead, I let it slowly melt in my mouth and took in the experience of each delicious morsel.

I was especially helpful to Mutti over the last few months, and St. Nikolaus was fully informed.

When Werner checked his shoe, he let out a scream of horror. Tucked inside was a cold, hard chunk of coal. His wails of despair came quickly, probably heard in the next town. Mutti came running and flung open the door expecting bloodshed. Instead, Werner flung his shoe, nearly hitting her as she entered. Next, the black, sooty chunk went flying through the air.

Mutti was not amused. Her face was etched with irritation, yet I could have sworn there was a hint of something else. Satisfaction maybe?

Mutti's apron was misted with flour and her hair was gathered in a bun behind her head. Tendrils of beautiful red hair escaped and cascaded over her ears like flickering flames. I loved Mutti's hair. It was the same color as mine. And I had her same hazel eyes.

She leaned against the door frame, a hand still grasping the handle.

"My dear Werner, why so upset?" she asked.

I couldn't believe how calm she was. On any other occasion, Werner would have gotten a spanking with no questions asked for displaying such a tantrum.

Through tearful whimpers, Werner exclaimed how St. Nikolaus gave him coal instead of candy. Mutti left her post by the door and sat on the edge of the bed, motioning for him to sit on her lap. She held him close and stroked his hair, smoothing down the tufts of blonde still tousled from sleeping.

"Oh, I'm sorry, little one," she said. "Perhaps if you're good until Christmas, you'll get something then."

It was hard for me to feel sorry for Werner. For months, he was nothing but trouble. Refusing to do his chores was the least of his offenses.

His greatest misdeed happened in summer when he went to the pond in search of frogs and tadpoles. He thought it would be a good idea to put them in the rain barrel for safe keeping. When Mutti went to gather water to wash her hair, she found the barrel filled with muddy water and hundreds of squirming aquatic creatures swimming inside.

I'll never forget that scream.

Her disposition changed over the last six months, and dealing with Werner's mischief only added to her foul mood. The only time I heard her humming a joyful tune was when she washed her hair with the sweet-smelling soap Vati—my father—bought for her before he left. When Werner filled the rain barrel with tadpoles, he robbed her of that joy, too.

Everything was changing. Maybe Werner noticed it, too, and was simply acting out. I didn't particularly care what the reason was for his actions, but I did notice he was especially good in the weeks between St. Nikolaus Day and Christmas. It's incredible how much power a little piece of coal held.

Because it was Christmas Eve, Werner wanted to get home to find out if his efforts paid off. I was thankful for his improved behavior, yet doubtful it would continue past December 25th.

Even Mutti was a little more cheerful than usual, and my baby sister didn't fuss as much. Perhaps it was the spirit of the season, or songs from the Christmas program filling their hearts.

Each Sunday during Advent, Werner and I joined other children from our little town of Rautheim to prepare for the Christmas program at St. Ägidien Lutheran church. When it came time for the program, the thick, stone walls, stately pillars, and vaulted ceilings echoed with our rendition of Stille Nacht while parishioners held their candles—*Silent night, holy night, all is calm, all is bright.*

I stood in the front of church with Werner and the other children, and Mutti sat toward the back with Anneliesa who slept soundly through the entire program. If I didn't know better, I could have sworn there was a glint of a tear in Mutti's eye, but she wasn't one to show emotion. It must have been the reflection from the candles.

Next to her sat an old man. His face was puckered

with wrinkles and his gray hair needed a trim. A permanent scowl was affixed to his face, and the skin on his jowls looked translucent, while thick spectacles made his eyes look twice their size. His worn, wool coat was too big for his small, hunched frame and it draped over his shoulders like a horse blanket. His raspy cough pierced through the moments of holy, reverent silence.

Tears trickled down my cheeks through most of the program. I missed Vati. How dare a wrinkly old man occupy the place where he was supposed to sit. How dare his failing ears hear our sweet voices as we read the second chapter of Luke and sang Oh, Tannenbaum.

The old man's frail stature was such a stark contrast to the youthful vigor of Vati. It was Vati who should have turned to Mutti to offer her the sign of peace. He should have been the one to hold open the door as we entered the expansive sanctuary. He should have been the one singing along about angels, shepherds, and wise men.

And as we walked home, he should have been the one urging us to go faster, not my annoying brother.

It was the first Christmas without Vati. It had been months since I last saw him. It was a cool, rainy summer morning when he sat me down at the kitchen table and showed me an official-looking letter with the crooked cross on top. It was the same symbol on the flag flying above the schoolyard and on all the posters hanging on the walls of my classroom. And next to them, a dark silhouette of a large black bird. I hated black birds. They were the bullies of the bird world, and the one on the school wall was ominous and threatening, as though it might spread its wings and swoop down from the sky with its large talons to snatch me away.

Vati read the letter and explained he was being called to serve in Hitler's army. The draft papers were sent to every able-bodied man under the age of thirty-five, and Vati was about as able-bodied as they came.

"Is it war? Are you going to have to fight with guns?" I asked.

"No, no. Don't worry, kleine Liebling." That's the name he always called me—his little love. "We're not at war. I'm only going for training. That's all."

"Training for what?"

Vati didn't answer. But I knew. I'd heard Hitler's threats on the radio about invasions and rival nations. War hadn't come yet, but I could tell Hitler was itching for a fight.

"I'll be gone for a while and then I'll come back," said Vati. "Everything will be as it was before."

I never had a reason to doubt Vati. He was always truthful and didn't hide anything as best I could tell. But I didn't believe him and burst into tears.

"Now, now," he said. "I need you to be strong and help your mother while I'm away."

His arms enveloped me.

"Yes, Vati," I said with as much conviction as I could muster. "Why can't you tell them you have to stay here and take care of us?"

"It's my duty to serve the Fatherland."

His words stung and my body stiffened. Every morning at school I recited my allegiance to this

Fatherland he spoke of. Every day we were subjected to literature and lectures praising the German nation and its people. And every night the only station on the radio told of the supreme compassion, vision, and moral excellence of its leader, Adolf Hitler.

I couldn't stop the words from tumbling out of my mouth. "What kind of Fatherland takes away its fathers?"

He gently withdrew, holding my shoulders at arm's length. Our eyes met.

"Waltraud, you mustn't ever say that." His voice was steady and firm, his gaze pleading.

The tears stopped. My eyes strayed from his and stared at the paper. Of course I mustn't. Everyone mustn't. No one was allowed to speak against the Reich. The look in my father's eyes confirmed it.

Was it anger? Was Vati upset with me for speaking out? Or was it fear?

It was.

You never know where there may be listening ears. That's what he told us.

Vati was given a week to get his things in order, and he was gone. He reported to the barracks in Braunschweig where he'd have to stay for nearly two years of training.

And now, Christmas.

I resented Werner's enthusiasm to get home. Home to what?

When we arrived, we removed layer upon layer of winter garb and put on our night gowns, warming ourselves by the kitchen stove.

Mutti heated some milk to make a special Christmas

Eve treat—hot chocolate.

"It was a wonderful program," she said as she added the shaved chocolate to the steaming milk. "Werner, you sang so nice and loud. I could hear you all the way from the back."

Werner sat taller at the table. He'd received more than his usual share of accolades from Mutti since the coal showed up in his shoe.

Mutti poured the sweet, chocolaty mixture from the pot into cups and placed them in front of us. She rambled on about the service, the decorations, the singing, and even the nice man who sat next to her. She was much more talkative than usual.

I wrapped my fingers around the warm cup and stared at the tiny bubbles swirling around the rim as they clung to the edges.

Mutti's voice broke in. "Aren't you going to drink it?"

"It's too hot."

"Oh, I'm sure it's cooled off enough by now."

I drew the cup to my lips. The cocoa was smooth and sweet.

"Do you think Vati has hot chocolate?" I asked.

"Oh, I'm sure he and all his new friends are having a lovely Christmas dinner."

"But does he get to have hot chocolate? We always have hot chocolate on Christmas Eve. If not, it won't feel like Christmas."

I watched the bubbles again. Mutti assured me Vati was having a fine Christmas and was thinking of each of us.

"Well, I suppose we should go into the living room," Mutti said. "I've warmed up the fire. We can sit in there for the rest of the evening."

The living room was reserved for special occasions and stayed tightly shut most of the year, especially in winter. It didn't make sense to heat an extra room that didn't serve much of a function other than to sit on fancier upholstery. It was the room where, each year, we gathered around the Christmas tree Vati cut down earlier in the day and brought home. We'd all decorate it together, and he'd lift me high to add the final touch. The star.

But this time, there was no tree.

There was no Vati.

Even so, Werner jumped up, eager to go in. Mutti moved quickly to cut Werner off at the door. I set down my cup and faced her. Mutti smiled.

It had been a long time since a smile graced her lips. Most days, Mutti looked like she'd eaten sour grapes and had a line between her eyebrows, especially when I'd talk about Vati being away. She didn't like when I asked too many questions about him, maybe because she didn't have the answers.

When she didn't want to talk about it anymore, she'd take a long breath and pinch her lips, then pretend to wipe imaginary crumbs off her skirt.

That's when I knew to let it drop.

"Waltraud, come on. Let's try to make the best of it."

I pushed away from the table, the chair moaning as it scraped across the wooden floor. Mutti was in good spirits, and while I hardly felt the same, I didn't want to take away from her rare moment of joy.

We stood at the door. It creaked at the touch of her hand, and a flickering light crept around the corner from inside. As the door swung open, I couldn't believe my eyes.

A beautiful tree sat on the table, lit up with glowing, white candles. Silver tinsel and white angel hair draped softly over the boughs. Glass ornaments and chocolates wrapped in brightly colored foil hung from the branches.

And next to the tree—Vati.

"Vati!"

Even Werner screamed as we both ran to him. The force of the two of us flying into his arms nearly knocked him over and he leaned against the windowsill to brace himself.

"Hold on, children. Hold on!" he said through his laughter. "You might knock me down, along with the tree, and burn the whole house down."

Mutti laughed too as she stood at the door holding Anneliesa, whose wide eyes were fixed on the sparkling tree.

"Vati, oh, we missed you!" I said.

"Oh, and I've missed you," said Vati. "Tell me. Have you been behaving yourself?"

Werner spoke up, "I have been very good, Vati. I even helped Mutti clean the table yesterday."

"Is that so?"

Vati and Mutti's eyes met with a smile, and she nodded.

"Well, Mutti agrees. Let's see if any gifts arrived for you."

Vati redirected Werner's attention to what sat tucked beneath the table with the tree. Werner screamed and ripped himself away, practically diving on top of a toy truck. He dropped to his knees and pushed its wheels back and forth over the rug while making sputtering engine noises with his lips.

"And how about you, little Liebling? I hear you've done your fair share of helping, too," he said.

I nodded with a big smile and gleaming eyes.

It was true. I was a good helper. I fed the pigs and gathered eggs from the chicken coop, helped cook, and cared for Anneliesa while Mutti ran errands. I matured far beyond my ten years on earth since Vati went away.

"Then let's see what there is for you," he said.

Stepping aside, I bent low. There it sat beneath the table, the box with the picture of a smiling girl and the words *Eine Singer für kleine Mädchen*—A Singer for little girls.

My eyes grew wide. I dropped to my knees, squealing with delight, feeling like a ten-year-old girl should. I carefully opened the cardboard cover to reveal a little black and silver Singer sewing machine. It was shiny and new.

I held it up, my eyes aglow, tracing the smooth, painted surface with my finger and feeling the soft, green felt on the base. I grasped the little knob on the round wheel, spinning it slowly and watching the needle go up and down, up and down in rhythm.

Vati knew I wanted the little machine, but I never dreamed I would have one to call my own. It called to me from a shop window nearly a year earlier and I told Vati about it then, and several times since.

"Vati, it's the most wonderful thing I've ever had!" I was shaking with excitement.

"First knitting, now sewing?" Vati said with the broadest smile I'd ever seen. "You'll be the finest homemaker in all of Germany. Maybe all of Europe."

The difficulties of the past months were forgotten and replaced with elation for the days ahead when I could begin new projects and get lost in the pleasure of creating something lovely.

Mutti had made herself comfortable on the fancy sofa next to the fireplace, and Anneliesa sat propped against the upholstered arm surrounded by pillows, chewing on the foot of a fabric doll she was given as her gift. Vati sat next to Mutti who melted into his side as he put his arm around her.

I watched them, wanting to capture the moment in my mind forever. She was beautiful sitting next to Vati, and different somehow. The lines between her eyebrows were gone and she had a softness to her. Without him, she wasn't whole.

"Now, where's my hot chocolate?" Vati jokingly chided.

Mutti smiled as she rose from the cushions and walked toward the kitchen.

"And waffles!" he called after her as he stood and clutched Anneliesa in his arms.

He lofted her into the air, nearly brushing the ceiling and catching her in a heap of laughter. The doll tumbled to the floor.

"It's not Christmas without hot chocolate and waffles!"

It almost felt like Vati never went away, and I had a sense of hope for the first time in many months. I was proud to say I was a daddy's girl. But for that moment, I relished in the joy of having my family whole again, of Vati's laughter, of Mutti's smile, and yes, even Werner's annoying mischief.

I knew Vati's return home was only temporary, but I didn't want thoughts of him going back to the army to cast a cloud over such a beautiful homecoming.

I couldn't help but secretly wish for a miracle, though.

I often thought up elaborate stories in my head, ones where uniformed officers showed up at our door with an official telegram to inform Vati the Führer no longer needed his services.

"You are to attend to the needs of your family at home," they'd say.

They'd salute, turn on their heels, and march away. The click of their shiny black boots would fade as they marched into a heavy mist, never to be heard from or seen again.

But that was only a fantasy.

CHAPTER 2
Spring 1938

I walked the familiar route to school, kicking stones with my shoe, attempting to strike imaginary targets with little success. I kicked another stone. Missed again.

The sun peaked around billowy clouds, and pink roses spilled out between the bars of a wrought iron fence along the path. The flowers were beautiful, and I breathed in their heady scent while stepping on soft petals that fell to the ground.

On any other day, I'd imagine myself a princess, walking the aisle of a grand ballroom scattered with rose petals to announce my arrival where I'd wed a handsome prince.

But the black metal posts of the fence cast shadows like prison gates, reminding me of the tall fence surrounding Vati's army barracks. It might as well have been a prison. He couldn't leave.

Five months passed since that pitiful day after

Christmas when he returned to the army. The long goodbye was filled with lots of hugs and tears, and promises of letters to be written and better times to come when we would all be together again. Our family, minus Vati of course, eventually got back into the mundane routine of life in Rautheim. Several letters arrived, but my longing to see him was overwhelming.

My walk to school was consumed with thoughts from a few days earlier when I convinced Werner we should visit Vati at the barracks. The place where he stayed wasn't far—a little more than an hour on our bikes—which made it even more unfair he couldn't come home for visits.

We set out early and arrived at the edge of the compound, propping our bikes against a tree. Hundreds of acres of fields and buildings sprawled across the complex as we walked alongside the tall metal fence.

"Which building do you think Vati is in?" Werner asked.

"Hard to say," I said. "Too bad he isn't in the ones across the street. Those look much nicer."

The army barracks were old, a combination of rusty metal and wood. Every building looked tired. But across the road, the buildings were new and clean. There were long airfields and training grounds for planes and paratroopers. A plane with a swastika painted on its tail fin was getting ready for take off just as we arrived. Werner insisted we stop and watch, and his eyes glowed as it effortlessly lofted into the air.

Hitler sure was proud of his Luftwaffe air force, and it

showed.

"I want to be a pilot when I grow up," Werner said excitedly.

"You get scared climbing trees," I said. "I don't think you're cut out for flying."

"You have a point," he said, and we laughed.

We got to the gate and a guard approached from a little hut on the other side. We clung to the black bars and peered inside.

"What do you children want?" The guard was gruff.

Instinctively, Werner and I stepped back from the gate, straightened our stance, and saluted with outstretched arms.

"Heil Hitler," we barked in unison.

Mutti and Vati told us if we see an official or a uniformed officer, we must always salute. Anything less could mean trouble. What trouble, we didn't know. But it wasn't the time to find out. Besides, we hoped our patriotic gesture might earn the sympathetic ear of the guard.

"I said, what do you want?" he repeated.

He didn't sound very sympathetic.

I spoke in as respectful a tone as I could muster. "We've come to see our father."

Werner didn't say a word. He stood at attention with his hands planted by his side, feet together, and his chest sticking out.

The guard eyed us with suspicion. He had a long rifle slung across his hip.

"He can't see you."

"But you didn't even ask us his name. How do you know he can't?"

"Visitors are not allowed," he grunted.

"Please, sir, we came all this way, and —"

"Silence!" he shouted. The sun glinted off his gun and blinded me. I gasped. I pushed too far by questioning the soldier and I knew it. Inside, I felt small and on the verge of crying from fear and disappointment. I stood firm. Werner trembled.

"Go home," he said.

Dejected, we turned away and took a step toward our long journey back to Rautheim.

"Halt!" It was the guard. We froze.

His voice was low, "Aren't you forgetting something?"

Werner looked at me, frantically searching my eyes, hoping I knew what it could possibly be.

"Salute," I whispered through the corner of my mouth.

We spun around, thrusting our arms to the sky.

"Heil Hitler!"

We turned and ran as fast as we could, and the long shadows of the metal fence flickered as we passed by. I got to the corner first, but Werner wasn't far behind. When we rounded the corner, we collapsed in a heap near the big oak where we left our bikes.

Werner cried. I was too angry to cry. That was no soldier. That was a bully.

I couldn't help but repeat the incident in my mind over and over as I continued walking to school. I was still mad at the soldier, and mad we couldn't see Vati.

I kicked another stone. Another miss.

"Waltraud, Waltraud! Wait up!" Liesa's voice jolted me back to reality.

"Why didn't you answer?" she said as she ran to greet me.

"What do you mean?"

Liesa slung her book bag over her shoulder and laughed. "Oh, Waltraud, you're always daydreaming. I called after you three times to wait for me. Didn't you hear me?"

I didn't. I was too lost in my thoughts.

"Oh, sorry. I was just thinking about stuff."

"You sure think a lot. Must have been pretty important. What kind of stuff?" she probed in her cheerful tone.

Liesa Weber was a good friend, although she could be oblivious at times, asking a lot of questions bordering on interrogation. It was all innocent enough. She didn't understand why I occasionally got lost in thought or was in a contemplative mood.

After all, Liesa's family was larger and she was the youngest of ten children. We often joked how she was lucky she was a girl; otherwise she'd have been named Adolf after the chancellor. It was another of his stupid rules. Hitler wanted mothers to have as many children as possible, and if the tenth child was a boy, it would be his namesake and Hitler would be the godfather. But she was thankfully born a girl before Hitler came to power.

As the youngest, Liesa was a bit spoiled if I do say so myself. She didn't have to do as many chores, and her papa was older, so he didn't have to go for training in the army. Secretly, I was envious of Liesa's carefree life. But she was the dearest friend and confidante a girl could ever ask for, and we had many fantastic adventures together.

"I said, what are you thinking about?" she asked again.

"Nothing too important, I guess. Just how much I hate bullies."

Liesa's smile faded and she stopped, placing her hand on her hip.

"Is Bruno bothering you again after all this time? I thought for sure he'd leave you alone after what happened. You sure showed him!"

The story of my encounter with Bruno Adler grew to legendary proportions on the school yard—me, a small-statured school girl versus the Goliath of a boy named Bruno. He was a couple years older, and why he targeted me, I didn't know. His incessant teasing and intimidation were unbearable.

When Bruno sat behind me in school, he pulled my hair and dipped the tips of my long, red braids in the ink well. Once, he even splashed ink on the hem of my dress on purpose. And after school, he'd wait for me and threaten to beat me up while calling me names.

The breaking point came when he cut off one of my braids with his pocket knife. The teacher barely scolded him. After school, I ran home crying and Mutti cut the other braid off to the same length. I didn't particularly care for short hair, but I had no choice in the matter, thanks to Bruno.

The next day in school I pretended not to care about

my hair and tried to convince others my new hairstyle was all the rage in Paris. Deep down I hated it, but I couldn't bring myself to show it. I did my best to avoid Bruno all day, but when Liesa and I walked onto the playground after classes, there he was with mocking words spewing from his mouth.

"Hey, ugly," he said with a nasty grin. "Nice hair."

"Leave me alone, Bruno." I turned to walk away.

"I've seen mangy dogs looking better than you. You know what they do with mangy dogs, don't you?" he threatened. "They hold them down and shave it all off."

I stopped in my tracks. I'd had enough.

"Here, Liesa." I handed her my book bag.

He looked at his friends with a smirk as I stomped toward him. The boy stood at least a head taller than I, but I could reach his nose, which I punched with all my might.

Bruno was stunned. As he tried to avoid the second blow, he tripped backward over a stone and fell to the ground. I pounced on top of his stocky frame and scratched his face with my fingernails, pulled his hair, and kneed him in the... you know what.

He curled in a ball and begged for me to stop.

A circle of children gathered, cheering me on. Many of them were subjected to his harassment, too, and they relished the thought of Bruno getting what he deserved.

By a girl, no less.

I kept swinging. Kept scratching. Kept kicking. I willed myself to not stop until there were tears. To my surprise, it didn't take long, and the giant whimpered like a baby and promised in between sobs he'd leave me alone.

"Next time, I'll do worse if you don't," I said, towering over him.

I brushed the dust off my skirt, smoothed my hair and straightened the pin Mutti put in it to hold it back from my face. Bruno was cowering in pain, but I gave him one last shove with my foot for good measure.

Even giants fall sometimes.

I walked home with my head held high and a sense of victory and pride. It felt good to fight back. But when Bruno's father showed up at our doorstep to complain, I second-guessed my act of bravery. Thankfully, Vati wasn't sent away for training yet and he was there to answer the door.

Herr Adler was well known in the village for how he spouted off at town meetings, reminding everyone about all the rules to follow and the consequences for failing to do so. He was a small man with slicked-back hair that looked like he combed it with grease. And his sharp nose and close-set eyes made him look like a rodent.

As a block warden, he prided himself on being fully informed about the latest regulations announced by the government. There were new ones each week, and he was more than happy to enforce them.

Vati greeted Herr Adler politely enough, and I hid behind the door to listen. When I peeked through the crack between the hinges, I didn't understand why Herr Adler didn't bring Bruno along. Instead, he brought along his other son who was a couple years younger than I was.

When Herr Adler told Vati what happened on the

school yard and the way I bloodied his son's face, Vati was confused.

"I'm not sure I understand. I don't see any scratches," he said, gesturing to the small, healthy boy who stood beside his father.

When Herr Adler explained it was his other son, Bruno, who was much older than I was, Vati stood silent.

How would he respond? Would Vati reach behind the door to pull me to his side and ask me to make an apology? How would I face Bruno again?

"Herr Adler, I suggest you leave," Vati said.

The tension in the air was thick.

Herr Adler protested, insisting on an apology and strict punishment for my actions.

"She needs to heed the Führer's instructions to be obedient and submit to the authority of her fellow countrymen!" he snapped.

"Your beloved Führer also instructs girls to grow strong and to stand up to tyrants, dear sir."

Herr Adler's face grew red and his nostrils flared as he spoke through gritted teeth.

"What would you know about the Führer's instructions, Herr Michaelis. Last I checked you weren't even a registered member of the Nazi Party."

There was a cold silence and Vati folded his arms over his chest.

"Last I checked," he said. "A person's political affiliation was not public record. Auf Wiedersehen."

"I demand you bring that girl out here immediately! She needs to—"

Vati interrupted with words more glorious and eloquent than I'd ever heard.

"What do you mean coming here and accusing my little girl of beating up your brute of a son who is, no doubt, twice her size? If I were you, I'd be embarrassed to admit it."

Herr Adler's pointy nose twitched like a mouse and he tried to get a word in edgewise, but Vati didn't hold back.

"If what you say is true, I have no doubt he deserved every bit and more. Instead of telling me how to raise my children, you should teach your own to not be tyrants, and to treat their fellow German citizens with the decency they deserve. I bid you a good evening."

Herr Adler stood open-jawed, and before he found the words for a rebuttal, the door swung shut in his face.

My anxious eyes looked at Vati.

"I'm sorry if I caused trouble. Will he take you away? Or me?"

Vati pursed his lips. "He's not going to send me or you to a labor camp over a schoolyard scuffle."

I couldn't tell whether Vati was angry at me or Mr. Adler. Maybe both.

"Bruno is the boy who cut your hair, isn't he?" he asked.

I nodded.

"I figured as much."

His tension eased and he let out a breath, one he held for the longest time. He knelt on one knee and held me squarely by the shoulders, his stare piercing through me. But instead of a reprimand, his lips unleashed with a smile that spanned his entire face.

"That's my girl," he said.

My anxiousness dissolved and my soul swelled as I absorbed the pleasure of his approval.

Turns out, Vati hated bullies, too.

CHAPTER 3
Spring 1938

W hen Liesa and I walked into the classroom, Bruno looked down, pretending to straighten something on his desk. Liesa shot me a knowing smile.

Our conversation on the way to school ended in uproarious laughter as we retold the story of Bruno's fall from power. He never bothered me since, and made sure to avoid me at all costs. And the knot that once formed in my stomach at the mere sight of him went away.

I knew to keep an eye on Bruno, though. He couldn't be trusted.

The teacher, Frau Langer, called class to order and everyone saluted. We stood at attention and pledged allegiance to the flag mounted on a stand in the corner, the one with a Hakenkreuz—a swastika. Next to it was an easel with a large portrait of Adolf Hitler, looking as stern and mean as ever.

We started our morning routine with a song. I liked

singing but preferred the classic folk songs we used to sing in school when I was younger—songs about the beautiful countryside, edelweiss flowers, and the legend of the mysterious Lorelei maiden who sat on a tall cliff on the Rhine River. She'd distract merchant sailors with her enchanting beauty, causing them to run their ships ashore onto the jagged rocks.

But ever since Hitler came into power, those beloved tunes were replaced with patriotic songs and anthems about battalions, the hope of the swastika, comrades and, of course, Hitler himself. They all had morbid lyrics about wars and death. The melodies were upbeat and happy-sounding, but didn't match the words.

After all the fuss about flags, the Führer, and the Fatherland, the day went on as usual with teachings about arithmetic, geography, spelling, and science, not to mention home economics and sports. Sports was my favorite part of the school day. I loved running.

After the 1936 Olympics in Berlin, the emphasis on health and fitness in school was heightened, and all the children were required to participate. It was one new rule I didn't mind so much.

Before Vati left, he coached me about my running form and how to pace my stride, and he entered me in competitions at the city sports festival each summer. He was athletic, too, and played on the town's soccer league. But that all changed when he left for army training.

I took to heart what he taught me each time I knelt to start a race.

"Get low," Vati would say. "Then, when you hear the

starting signal, use your legs to spring up and get a head start."

The other kids thought I looked silly crouched like a tiger when I was ready to start a race, but Vati said he saw a picture in the newspaper during the Olympics, of a runner poised for the start of a race doing the same thing.

"If it works for Olympic athletes, why not for my little Liebling?" he'd say.

It did work, and I won many races.

The Olympics were a source of great national pride for Germany, and we were reminded often about how we won the most medals of any country in the world—more than three-hundred. We won lots of medals in gymnastics, wrestling, track and field, and swimming.

Swimming wasn't exactly my favorite sport, especially after I fell through the ice when skating on a local pond a few winters earlier. Thankfully, there were others there to throw me a rope, and it was the last time I ever went skating. I did catch my death of cold, though.

Was my mind playing tricks on me or was my daydreaming getting the best of me again? Recalling the fall through the ice sent a cold chill crawling up my arms, and it settled in my throat with a tingle.

When it was time for gym class, I didn't win any races, no matter how hard I tried. I was even slow by my own estimation, and my heavy head clouded my thoughts.

The school day couldn't end soon enough, and I trudged my way toward home. The thought of doing chores when I got there sounded dreadful. And how did the weather turn so scorchingly hot since morning? The earlier chill was replaced with a flush of heat rising through my chest and up my neck. Every joint ached.

Mutti wasn't there when I walked in the back door. She got a job at a greenhouse to earn more money after Vati left. During the day, Anneliesa stayed with Oma and Opa Michaelis, my grandma and grandpa. And Mutti picked her up on her way home each evening.

Werner sat at the kitchen table doing nothing at all except eating a piece of bread with some butter on it.

"You're not supposed to eat before Mutti gets home, and especially not before doing your chores," I said, setting my book bag on a chair.

"I need strength to do my chores," he said with stuffed cheeks. Crumbs tumbled out of his mouth.

Werner had an excuse for everything, and it annoyed me more than usual. I snatched the roll from his hands and thrust it on the table.

"Get up and go in the shed to get some wood for the stove so Mutti can make something to eat!"

"All right, all right. I'll go. Why are you in such a mood?"

"Because you're always so lazy, and I'm tired of doing all the work around here."

Werner slipped from the chair and sulked his way to the door. He took his time gathering the firewood and eventually returned with an armful, only to find me sitting in the same chair he occupied earlier.

"If you're so worried about my chores, how come you're not doing yours?" Werner griped.

He dumped the wood into the wood box and brushed

off pieces of bark clinging to his shirt, leaving them scattered at his feet. I stared at the dirty floor, angry at Werner for making such a mess for me to clean up, but I lacked the energy to scold him.

My head tilted back on the wooden chair and I closed my eyes. The burning in my throat had become much worse and I let out a short, soft moan.

"You don't look so good," said Werner, grabbing the hunk of bread on the table and popping it in his mouth.

Mutti walked through the door with Anneliesa in one arm and her empty lunch pail in the other. The squeal of the door hinges and the clanging of the metal pail reverberated in my head.

"How was your day at—" She stopped mid-sentence at the sight of me.

"Waltraud yelled at me!" bemoaned Werner.

"Take your little sister and go play," Mutti said, handing Anneliesa off to Werner.

"But—"

"Take her, and don't argue with me."

She set the pail down and rushed to my side, pressing her hand to my forehead.

"You're on fire. Come on, let's get you to bed."

"I haven't done my chores yet." I caught a glimpse of the concerned expression on her face.

"I'll have Werner help me, now let's go."

I didn't protest at the idea of Werner doing a little extra work for once. Mutti slid her arm beneath mine and led me to the stairwell in slow motion. I stood at the bottom and looked up the long expanse, unable to take a step forward. The stairway stretched before me and might as well have led to the top of the Swiss Alps. The thought of climbing them was just as impossible.

"Come on, up you go," she said with a tug on my arm.

But her voice was a million miles away. I sighed and leaned against the wall to steady myself, looking down at the wooden planks. They were moving like rolling waves lapping on a sandy shore. The floor shifted beneath me. I wanted to speak but no words came.

"Waltraud... Waltraud..."

Mutti's voice drifted beyond the mountains and I slid down the wall.

Sinking.

Falling.

Darkness.

* * *

Hushed voices spoke in the hallway outside my bedroom door. It was already dark outside and it was too late to have visitors, especially on a school night. Was it still Wednesday? How long had I slept? It didn't matter much, it wasn't a restful sleep.

My waking moments were filled with coughing fits and my dreams were consumed with visions of demons with gnarled fingers holding me down while they poked, probed, and prodded.

My tongue was rough and felt three times its size, and my throat was raw and blistered, as though it might collapse and suffocate me. The skin on my neck and arms were like sandpaper, and tender to the touch. I'd never felt so miserable. It hurt to move.

I listened closely to the voices. One of them was Mutti and the other, I wasn't sure.

"She'll need more bed rest. And she likely won't be able to eat solid food for a while," said a man.

"I've got some chicken broth and apple sauce in the pantry for when she's able," said Mutti.

"Good, good, that will do fine," said the man. "Clean the bed linens every day and wash them in boiling water for ten minutes. I'll leave you with some medicine, and I'll have a nurse stop every couple of days to check in."

Medicine? Nurse? Of course. Now I recognized the voice. It was Doctor Opitz. He was a kind, older man with round spectacles who always had a smile on his face. And even if his lips weren't smiling, his eyes were.

He was Jewish, but he wasn't at all like the Jews I learned about in school. He was one of the smartest people I knew. Our family always went to see him if we had any small ailments, but he never had reason to come to the house before. In fact, he kept to himself most of the time and didn't venture out much anymore.

"And how long must we be quarantined?" Mutti asked.

Quarantined? My heart pounded in my chest so loudly it drowned out the voices and I couldn't hear the answer.

"Mutti," I tried to cry out.

But it wasn't a cry. It was barely a whisper. My throat was so sore the words wouldn't come.

What's wrong with me? Why did demons visit my dreams? Am I going to die?

"Mutti," I tried calling again.

The murmuring voices kept talking, unaware of my whimpers. I tried propping myself up on the pillow and barely budged an inch. But it was enough to reach the nightstand. I lifted my arm and let it fall on the hard wooden top.

The voices stopped, but no one came in. Again, I lifted my arm. Thud. To my relief, the door swung open and light from the hallway spilled into the room. Doctor Opitz peered in.

There was that smile.

"Waltraud, it's good to see you," he said.

I didn't feel the same, considering the circumstances. I knew he wasn't there to socialize with Mutti in the upstairs hallway.

"We're glad you decided to join us. It's been two days, after all," he said

Was I in bed for two days? It wasn't possible. Mutti approached and dipped a rag in a bowl of water, dabbing my forehead. The coolness brought relief to the inferno inside my aching head.

"Don't strain yourself, sweetheart," she said.

Mutti wasn't prone to calling me sweetheart. Something was wrong. Terribly wrong.

"What's wrong with me?" My voice was raspy and faint, and it took a great amount of effort to squeak out those few words.

Mutti looked at Doctor Opitz, hoping the answer coming from his mouth might be more convincing.

"You'll be fine," he said. "You're a strong girl, and in no time you'll be back at school playing with your friends."

It was reassuring to hear him say so. He was a doctor, after all. And I could only assume he was sharing his professional opinion.

"It appears you have a case of scarlet fever, Waltraud," he said. He wasn't smiling anymore.

I gasped, lifting my hand in front of my face, turning it slowly from side to side, examining the tell-tale red blotches on my wrist and arm. There were lots of sad stories of distant relatives and other children in town who died from the dreaded disease.

My arm fell limp across my abdomen.

"I don't want to die," I whimpered with a squeak. My throat seized.

The pain from the resulting coughing was unbearable and sucked what little breath I had inside my lungs into an imaginary abyss. I panted. Doctor Opitz took a step back into the doorway and kept his distance. Mutti reached for a cup of water and held it to my lips while lifting my head off the pillow. I took a sip, the liquid cooling my blistered throat.

"Oh, don't talk silly, now," she said in soothing tones as she rung out the rag and pressed it against my forehead once more.

She glanced sideways at the doctor.

"He's leaving us with some good medicine, and a nurse will check in to make sure everything is progressing as it should."

"Now, you haven't eaten a thing. I'll go warm up some chicken broth."

I groaned, turning my head away. The thought of anything in my stomach made me nauseous.

"No?" she relented. "How about some chamomile tea then? I've got some brewing."

She set the rag back in the bowl, got up, and headed for the door, motioning for Doctor Opitz to follow. Before he walked out, he turned to me.

"You'll need to eat to keep your strength up," he said. "Even if you don't feel like it. Doctor's orders."

The smile was back.

He and Mutti left the room and closed the door behind them. There were more hushed whispers as they walked down the hallway. Their footsteps and voices descended down the stairwell. I sat in silence, scanning the room.

The angel of death. That's what the teacher at school called the disease when we studied it in class. Maybe that's who visited me in my dreams. Maybe he was trying to snatch me away.

Mutti returned with the tea. "We'll have to let it cool a bit before you drink it," she said as she sat next to the bed.

Normally, there wasn't a chair in the room, and I imagined her sitting there for some time attending to me when I was unaware. I liked the idea of her nurturing me. It was a tender side I rarely saw.

"He visited me," I whispered.

"Yes, it was very nice of Doctor Opitz to come to the house, wasn't it?" she said.

Mutti held the cup in her hands and blew on the tea to

cool it. Steam rose from the rim.

"No, not him. The angel… the angel of death. I saw him."

She stopped blowing mid-breath. Her eyes lifted from the tea cup and stared at me.

"Oh? When was this?"

"I don't know, but he was here."

"I'm sure it was only a dream, sweetheart. You were delirious with fever."

There it was again. She called me sweetheart. Something inside told me Mutti did, in fact, believe me about the angel, but she didn't want to admit it out loud.

"Did Doctor Opitz leave?" I asked.

She didn't answer. Instead, she gently propped up my head and lifted the cup to my lips.

"You shouldn't be talking so much. Here, drink some tea. You must be terribly thirsty."

I was, and the herbal tea felt good going down and calmed my churning stomach.

"Is he gone?" I asked again.

"Not yet." She hesitated, wiping fake crumbs off her skirt, then clasped her hands in her lap.

"He's checking on your little sister."

Our eyes met. "No, Mutti. Please, don't tell me she—"

She looked away and I knew the truth. My eyes welled with tears. It was one thing for me, a resilient eleven-year-old girl to fight off the deadly angel, but poor Anneliesa was only a toddler, barely two.

"I'm going to check in with the doctor before he leaves," she said.

I stared at the cracks in the ceiling. A tear trickled from the corner of my eye and ran down my temple. Mutti dabbed it away with a cloth and left the room, shutting the door behind her. I lay silent, alone in the dim light.

It's my fault. I brought this disease into the house. If Anneliesa dies, it will be my fault.

I loved Anneliesa. There were many times when it was my job to take care of her while Mutti was away. I even made a little dress for her with the sewing machine Vati gave me. When I played peek-a-boo with Anneliesa, she bubbled with the most infectious laughter. I wasn't sure what motherhood might be like, but I imagined the way I cared for my little sister and the love I had for her was as close as I could know for now.

The thought of losing her was heartbreaking. It wasn't outside the realm of possibility for Anneliesa to die. After all, it wouldn't be the first time the angel snatched someone from our family.

The faint memory of a baby still came to mind once in a while. It wasn't of Anneliesa, but of another child, a second younger brother whom I never got to know because he died of whooping cough when I was only three-years-old. His name was Günther, and my only memory was of him cradled in Mutti's arms crying loudly, and a deep, guttural cough, a cough that grew more and more fragile with each hour, until one day, the coughing stopped and there was silence in the house.

And Mutti wore a black dress.

I wasn't much for praying, but I silently begged God to save my baby sister. Wrestling Bruno on the schoolyard was one thing, but wrestling with an angel was another. I needed to call on someone who fought harder than I could. I didn't have the strength, and I knew Anneliesa had even less.

We used to pray every day in Kindergarten and first grade. The teacher would start out each school day with a prayer of thanksgiving and a petition for the Almighty's mercy. But not too long after, the teacher said it was no longer allowed, and the prayers to God were replaced with praises for Hitler.

I regretted not engaging in many conversations with God since then, and feared my indifference might dissuade Him from coming to my aid when I needed him most, when Anneliesa needed him most.

The angel's presence lurked in the hallway, waiting for his opportunity to steal me and Anneliesa away. I could sense it.

But I also sensed another presence even more powerful, and imagined God bending low to listen to my prayer with open ears while holding the angel at bay with a mighty, outstretched arm. A sense of peace came over me, and I closed my eyes and fell asleep.

The next several days were filled with more feverish fits, visits from the nurse, Mutti trying to spoon feed me, and me trying to keep it down without throwing up. The blisters in my throat made it difficult to speak, so I wrote on a piece of paper when there was a pressing need or a question needing answers. I asked about Anneliesa's condition several times a day.

Mutti simply said, "She's still here."

And although I'm sure she doubted whether she could say the same the next time, in the end, Mutti's black dress hung limp in the closet.

CHAPTER 4
November 1938

The quarantine lasted four weeks. Werner slept on the daybed in the kitchen and never caught the fever. He was happy to be quarantined and out of school for so long. But even he started getting bored as the days dragged on. He wasn't allowed to play with friends, after all, and a boy can only invent so many stories to keep his mind occupied.

Eventually, I could eat solid food without choking and heaving, and my strength was returning. It would be fine if I never ate another bowl of chicken broth, apple sauce, or milk soup again.

Mutti knew I would be okay when I asked for potato dumplings. With gravy, of course.

My skin was still tender in spots where the layers peeled off from the rash, but the salve Mutti applied from Doctor Opitz each night helped ease the incessant itching.

As for Anneliesa, Mutti said she came very near death in those first few days. But thankfully the angel didn't take another baby from her arms, and Anneliesa grew stronger, too. I thought back to my prayers to God and thanked him many times since.

Another prayer went unanswered, though, the one about bringing Vati home. When I thought I might die, I worried about never seeing him again and how sad he would be if Anneliesa or I passed to the other side while he was away.

But we both made it, and Vati's letters kept coming with hopeful promises he would be home soon.

Meanwhile, the leaves turned to shades of orange, copper, and gold, and the heat of summer gave way to the chilling winds of November. I kept doing my chores, going to school, and participating in sports.

But I couldn't run as fast as I used to before I got sick. It was like a pair of bellows from the wood stove sucked all the air from my lungs and I could barely catch my breath.

My legs wanted to run, but my lungs couldn't catch up.

I was determined to get back to my old self, though, and practiced every chance I got, sometimes even running home from school. I wanted to be strong when Vati came home.

The time for thick, wool coats and mittens arrived and I pulled my winter boots out of the wardrobe, tipping them upside down and shaking vigorously to make sure nothing was inside. I didn't want a repeat of the time when Werner slipped his foot inside his boot for the first time without looking, only to have his toes plunge into a mouse nest.

I loosened the laces and squeezed my foot inside as far as I could. I loosened them some more. And some more.

I descended down the stairway, stepping sideways on each step, and hobbled to the kitchen table.

"Looks like someone needs a new pair of boots," said Mutti.

She set down her dishtowel and knelt on one knee, pushing her thumb on the brown leather. It didn't give way.

"I could wear thinner socks."

I tried to wiggle my toes without much success. Money was hard to come by, and I didn't want to burden Mutti with another expense. The boots weren't nearly worn enough to justify needing a new pair. But I didn't look forward to walking to school with pinched toes and blistered heels.

"Nonsense," said Mutti. "We'll go into the city to look for a new pair. Wear your other shoes for today."

I was relieved. And pleased. The idea of going shopping amidst the hustle and bustle of busy streets and abundant storefronts in Braunschweig was thrilling. Unlike our small town of Rautheim, Braunschweig's streets were lined with dozens of shops and storefronts.

The next day, we all bundled up and rode our bikes to Braunschweig. Anneliesa was wrapped in blankets and tucked snugly in the basket on my bike. She always rode with me ever since last summer when Mutti lost her balance while riding along a stream. Anneliesa was in the front and came tumbling out, rolling down the hill right to the water's edge. I sprung from my bike and ran to save her. She wasn't hurt, but Mutti insisted my little sister ride with me ever since.

We parked our bikes and walked the streets of Braunschweig. It was a medieval city dating back to the eighth century, and it had some of the oldest half-timbered buildings in all of Germany. The city center had narrow streets and tall, stately architecture. Ornate window storefronts were filled with clothing, jewelry, pocket watches, and every trinket imaginable.

The wonder-filled buildings looked like they came from folklore, and in the height of summer, every window box was filled with billowy red geraniums that spilled down the sides of buildings like honey.

Storefront signs read Deutsche Kaufmann—German merchant—and hung on some of the windows. Those stores were filled with shoppers, many more than the businesses without the sign.

A shoe store appeared before us and I pressed my face against the glass. A pair of fancy boots with smooth, shiny black leather the color of licorice called to me. They had a row of embossed metal buttons down the sides, and dainty lace trim peeked above the top.

"I really like those," I said, pointing with hope-filled adoration.

Mutti looked at the price and sighed. I hadn't paid attention to the tag tied to the laces with a piece of string. They were among the most expensive in the window.

"But I'm sure they wouldn't be very warm," I said.

Disappointed, I looked back in the window at the other boots.

"Those are much more practical." I pointed to a pair of plain brown boots tucked to the side for half the price.

The lines on Mutti's forehead softened. "Those look good and sturdy."

Sturdy. It wasn't exactly the fashion statement I hoped to make in school.

"We'll have to see if there's a pair that fits you," she said as she turned to go inside. She reached for the door. She hesitated. It didn't have a German merchant sign, only a name painted in gilt letters. "Goldmann's Shoes."

But Mutti paid no mind, grasping the handle and standing tall. The door swung open to the chime of a small copper bell.

Two ladies walked past on the sidewalk and gave Mutti a haughty glance as she stood holding the door. But she gave them a look of her own right back and ushered us inside, closing the door behind her.

"Come in, come in!" a man said as he stood from behind a desk.

"I take it you are Herr Goldmann, the shopkeeper?" said Mutti.

"Yes, yes, of course."

His hands beckoned us inside and he listened as Mutti asked about the boots. I sat on a stool and slipped off my shoes while Werner spun round and round in a wooden swivel chair behind the desk.

The shop owner measured my feet, then slipped into a side room behind a curtain. His animated voice spoke to no one in particular while shuffling items back and forth on a shelf.

"Ah, here we are," he said, emerging with a a pair of boots. "These should do the trick."

He grabbed a boot and laced it up as nimbly and quickly as I could cast stitches onto my knitting needles. The boot slipped onto my foot effortlessly, and he pressed on the toe with his thumb, just like Mutti.

"Now, how does it feel?" he asked.

I stood, shifting my weight. The leather was stiff and needed some breaking in, but my toes wiggled with a little room to spare.

"Can I try on the other one, too?"

"Ah, a smart girl. Never buy a pair of boots without walking in both."

Herr Goldmann laced the other boot and slipped it on my foot.

"Walk around the shop a bit," he said. "That's the only way you can tell."

Mutti stood to the side holding Anneliesa, observing as I walked to the front of the store. When I reached the display window, the finely buttoned boots with lace trim beckoned me to draw nearer. I stared. They were even more beautiful up close, and I had to stop myself from reaching out to touch them.

No. They couldn't be mine. I turned on my heels.

"I think these are just right," I said.

The walk to school the next morning was much better in my new boots. When I went in, Bruno and a group of his friends were gathered to the side. They were up to no good, as usual.

Bruno, who turned fourteen, had a new group of friends who all participated in the Hitler Jugend—Hitler Youth. Not that they had a choice. It was mandatory for boys of his age to join, and every Wednesday after school they dutifully attended their meetings, and many outings in between.

Bruno's arrogance strengthened since he started attending the meetings, despite his humiliating run in with me a couple years earlier. He liked pointing out when a classmate broke the rules or failed to hoist their hand up quickly enough or high enough to salute when an adult entered a room or passed by in the hallway. He was a smaller version of his father.

Bruno still left me alone. He had, no doubt, moved on to more noteworthy exploits to impress his friends than terrorizing a red-haired girl with freckles and sturdy new boots.

I caught myself staring at the group of boys. Bruno scoffed.

"What are you looking at?"

I turned to go inside. Something was up.

The school day carried on with the typical subjects. Much more time was spent learning about geography and the government. Seemed like every other day there was a new map of Germany on the wall.

And the essays.

Every time Hitler gave a speech on the radio, our class had to write a report about what we learned. The unfair demands of the Treaty of Versailles. The aggression of

Poland. The superiority of the Aryan race. He sure talked a lot.

I hated essays. It didn't make much sense to write everything down. Everywhere we turned, the message was there—the radio, lectures, text books, pamphlets, posters, and schoolyard conversations. What was one more piece of paper with the same information going to matter? It didn't matter, and I knew it.

There were new text books in school, too, and Frau Langer was strict about completing the lessons. There were entire chapters in social studies and biology dedicated to teaching how corrupt other nations and people groups were, especially the Jewish people, and how they were genetically inferior.

Even the arithmetic books had a way of belittling the Jews. I stared at the mathematical equation on the page.

> *The Jews are aliens in Germany. In 1933 there were 66,060,000 inhabitants in the German Reich, of whom 499,682 were Jews. What is the percentage of aliens?"*

I dare not admit my disagreement and confusion. Not because of the math problem, but the Jew problem. I didn't understand how they were a problem. Doctor Opitz came to mind every time someone said how uncivilized and cruel the Jews were. But he was a kind man, especially when I had scarlet fever. And so was the shopkeeper in Braunschweig.

I studied my new boots. Maybe I'd sew some lace ribbon to the top of my socks to help them look less boring. Less sturdy. What I wouldn't give to own the enchanting pair in the shop window.

Mutti wasn't supposed to buy things from Jewish shops, but she didn't think much of all these new rules either. Herr Goldmann expressed extreme gratitude for the business. He even gave Mutti a little discount when she mentioned we couldn't stop at the cafe on our way back home because there wasn't enough money left in her coin purse.

The school day ended, and on my way home, Bruno and his group of friends walked ahead. Something wasn't right.

The next morning, I shuffled into the kitchen with a yawn. A crackling voice on the radio greeted me, and Mutti sat at the table. She reached for the knob to turn off the news like she usually did when there were children in the room. But her hand suspended in the air, and only turned down the volume.

I suppose she decided right then and there I was old enough to hear the news. All the news.

"Did something happen?" I asked as I walked to the stove to warm my back.

Mutti held a dishtowel, and if it were a living thing, it would have had the very life squeezed out of it for as tightly as she wrung it in her hands.

"Our beautiful Braunschweig," she said with a mournful sigh.

"What about it? Is everything okay?"

She sat silent. I tuned my ear to the announcer on the radio.

The streets of all Germany and Austria are on fire, and synagogues lie in ruins as noble citizens lashed out against the parasites of the Jewish community in solidarity overnight.

"Why, Mutti?" I listened in disbelief.

...people took to the streets. Every Jewish shop has been looted, and many Jews have disappeared, further cleansing the population of Germany.

It's being called Kristallnacht—the night of the broken glass—because of the windows of Jewish stores that are now shards of glass, littering the sidewalks...

I was as mute as Mutti. I stared at the radio, too, envisioning Herr Goldmann's beautiful storefront windows shattered by sledge hammers and crowbars, with dozens of shoes scattered on the ground. I thought of hoodlums and hooligans ransacking his shelves and taking off with merchandise as mementos of their cowardly deeds.

Our eyes met.

"Are we at war?"

"No, no." She shook her head. "Not yet."

"The whole country? Every city? Every shop?"

I was afraid to ask, but already knew the answer. Tears came, accompanied by a vision of Herr Goldmann in terror.

"The German merchants didn't get damaged," Mutti said. "To happen across the entire country can't possibly be a random uprising of thugs. There must have been some coordination from the government to do something so horrible, so despicable, so—" she stopped herself short, realizing she allowed her thoughts to escape her lips.

"Waltraud," she said. "You must be very careful about what you say about this, about anything involving the government. Keep to yourself. Don't criticize. Don't do anything to stand out."

Mutti said it as a warning to me as much as it was a reminder for herself. She couldn't carelessly comment about her misgivings about Hitler or his policies as she was prone to do on occasion. Times had changed, and the days of having casual conversations with neighbors about this or that involving the Reich were no longer safe. Not now.

What did it all mean? Fear and growing tensions surrounded us at every turn. This I did know—I'd most certainly have to write an essay about it when I got to school. But I didn't dare write what I really thought.

The mood was somber when I arrived at school. Children spoke with hushed whispers and wary eyes to make sure no one outside their small group overheard their rumblings.

Bruno and his friends were huddled off to the side. Their mood was decidedly different with bursts of boastful laughter and comradely pats on each other's backs.

Even so, they looked a bit haggard as they walked by. Their Hitler Youth meeting the night before must have put them through extra marching routines and athletics. I couldn't pull my eyes away.

Bruno walked by and sneered at me with a familiar, menacing look, as though he might break his restraint and rekindle his aggression toward me. The principal of the school appeared in the doorway and Bruno and his group snapped to attention, thrusting their arms up with hands held high.

"Heil Hitler," they chimed in unison.

Others quickly saluted. Recalling Mutti's warning, I joined in.

That's when I saw it. Bruno's hand. It was raised as a symbol of unwavering devotion and allegiance, and on it, a fresh wound covered with a bandage. The shadow of a bloody gash seeped through the white gauze, and he held it high like a red badge of honor.

I knew in an instant what it meant. He was one of them. He was there among burning buildings and shattered glass. He was far more dangerous than I gave him credit for. His threats of the past weren't as improbable as I made them out to be, and I was no match for his growing strength and confidence, nor his zealous band of teenage comrades.

From then on, my words were more guarded, and I never met eyes with Bruno again. I didn't want to find out what kind of harm he was truly capable of on the schoolyard when I knew what he did in the early morning hours under the cloak of darkness while roaming the streets of Braunschweig.

In fact, I wouldn't be surprised one bit if Bruno's mother wore a beautiful new pair of boots with buttons and lace.

CHAPTER 5
May 1939

S torks returned to glean kernels from the fields outside town. Spring bulbs of yellow, pink, red, and white bloomed where snowbanks once lined the streets, and fresh air lofted into homes through lace curtains fluttering in the breeze.

The sight of new life was a pleasant distraction from the tension and stress of the months since Kristallnacht. The small town I lived in didn't experience many problems, but the city of Braunschweig had terrible damage. Many shops were boarded up and, as suspected, Mutti found out the shoe store was among them, with no trace of Herr Goldmann or many other Jewish shopkeepers. Even their synagogue was turned to rubble.

Where did they go and what happened to them? I didn't know.

Despite growing tensions, there was hope in the air. It wasn't merely the emerging tulips, daffodils, and crocuses bringing a promise of change, nor the May Day celebrations a week earlier where we gathered around the maypole decked with ribbons and wreaths.

Vati was coming home. The waiting was over and the day finally came.

The house was buzzing with excitement, and Mutti was awake before daybreak to prepare for Vati's welcome home dinner. I peeled potatoes and carrots and gathered eggs from the chicken coop, and I measured the flour for making bread. I placed it in the wooden bread trough, broke off a piece of sourdough starter, added some water and a pinch of salt, and kneaded away.

"You'll have to get it to the bakery early," Mutti said. "We'll want fresh-baked bread for dinner."

"I can't believe he's coming home," I said as I worked the dough. "I feel like I've been waiting my whole life!"

Mutti chuckled. Nearly two years certainly was a substantial portion of my time on earth. Perhaps she sensed I was growing up quickly, especially since my twelfth birthday would arrive on May 26th. For now, I relished in the innocence of childhood and the girlish delight of Vati's homecoming.

"If you knead that dough anymore we'll have to use it for bricks instead of bread," she said.

Laughing, I separated the dough into two loaves, patted each into a soft, round ball, placed them in a basket, and covered them with a damp flour sack.

"Don't we bring our bread for baking on Fridays?" I asked.

Normally, each family was assigned a specific day to

bring their bread for baking in the large brick ovens at the bakery. How they kept all the loaves straight was beyond me.

"I talked to the baker and he said he'd fit us in for our special occasion," Mutti said.

She thought of everything.

I walked to the bakery with my cloth-lined basket and left the dough, returned home for more chores, then headed back to retrieve the freshly baked bread.

Mutti was trimming the ends off white asparagus spears and spring onions when I returned with the warm loaves. I loved this time of year when asparagus was in season. There was something about the smell of the earth and seeing the fields outside town with the deeply furrowed rows. The farmer mounded dirt over the asparagus so sunlight wouldn't reach the sprigs and turn them green. Once that happened, they became tough and bitter and were only good for pig fodder.

A roast was in the oven and a hearty smell filled the house. It reminded me of the glorious dinner on Christmas Day when Vati surprised us. A lot changed since then. Anneliesa was more than two years old and was walking and talking, and Werner grew ten centimeters, but he was still lazy as ever. Mutti grew too, but in a different way. She became stronger, learning to carry on without Vati around.

Not only had I grown in height, but I took on more grown-up responsibilities. And there were a lot of activities and lessons on homemaking in the Jungmädel group, a branch of the Hitler Youth for young girls I was a member of since age ten.

The leaders of the group were intent on teaching us about being mothers, and preparing us for when we'd turn fourteen. That's when I'd graduate from the Jungmädel and have to join the BDM—Bund Deutsche Mädel—the League of German Girls. But it was still a couple years away.

I didn't want to join the Jungmädel, but I didn't have a choice. Every German girl was required to sign up. It was one of those new rules.

For the most part, though, I liked the meetings with craft times, sports, and social events. And there were plans to take outings during the summer into the foothills of the countryside. I was willing to put up with a few more boring lectures to go on adventures and spend time with new friends. Liesa joined, too, so it meant more time together.

Mutti also signed me up for confirmation classes at St. Ägidien. There were only five of us who went—three boys and one other girl. I wasn't thrilled. Most of my friends in the Jungmädel were being confirmed in the new way organized by the Führer, under the flag instead of in the church. Children pledged their devotion to him and Germany instead of God, and the classes only lasted a year instead of the two years of religion classes.

I endured a lot of teasing for being so old-fashioned when I told friends I wouldn't join them for the state confirmation and had to go to church instead.

But Mutti insisted on a proper Lutheran confirmation. Aside from religious reasons, I suspect it had as much to do with her feelings toward the Führer. He may control what people say and do outwardly, but in her mind, the soul was off limits.

But none of it mattered on this special day. I pushed the events of the past and the uncertainty of the future from my mind to focus on Vati's return. We hummed along to a folk song on the radio, a nice break from the blathering speeches.

"Isn't anyone going to welcome a soldier home?"

Vati slipped in the back door while we were unaware. How long was he leaning against the door post with folded arms, silently watching before making his announcement?

I spun around, almost knocking over a pan on the stove.

"Vati!" I ran into his open arms.

Werner wasn't far behind and embraced Vati's leg, while Anneliesa stood at a distance, confused at the commotion, wondering who the tall stranger might be. And Mutti smiled wide with relief.

I didn't want to let go, but Vati gently pulled away and reached to hold Mutti close. She returned the embrace and buried her face in his chest, and they hugged for an awkwardly long time.

"Welcome home," she said softly.

Mutti looked different in Vati's arms. It's like she was a different person when he was there.

He held her face in his rough hands, looked her in the eyes, and kissed her right there in front of everyone. She blushed and playfully pulled away.

"Oh, Gustav," she said flustered, then bent to grab his rucksack next to the door.

"I'll take this into the bedroom so we can sort through it and wash your clothes."

"There won't be much to wash other than underwear and socks," he called after her. "I don't plan on wearing that uniform anytime soon."

"Good! I have a mind to burn it!" she called out as she exited the room.

Vati laughed and walked through the kitchen. At the sight of Anneliesa, his eyes lit up and he rushed to hold her.

"Anneliesa, my sweet girl!"

Panic overcame her and she turned to run. Her eyes darted from side to side in search of an escape, but she found herself trapped in a corner and fell to the ground, tears streaming down her cheeks. I ran ahead to pick her up.

"Oh, Anneliesa, don't be afraid. See, it's Vati."

I bounced her up and down to console her and turned to face Vati. His outstretched arms fell to his sides, hanging like string from his slumped shoulders, a sad look of disappointment on his face. Poor Anneliesa didn't even know her own father, and Vati's happy homecoming was dampened by the reminder of all he missed since he went away.

He looked to me with questioning eyes, as though seeking permission to hold his own child.

"Here, Vati," I said, nudging Anneliesa toward him. "It's okay," I reassured her.

Vati hesitantly held out his hands and I slipped an anxious Anneliesa into his arms. He held her gently and kissed the top of her head.

"Oh, my little one," he said. "You'll grow to love me soon."

Mutti re-entered the room. "Dinner's almost ready."

"I don't think I've ever smelled anything so wonderful," said Vati.

Anneliesa fussed and reached for Mutti as she walked by. He held her out.

"Here. I think she's a little undecided about me."

"Oh, she'll be fine," she said as she took her from his arms and set her on the floor.

Anneliesa ran back to the rug to play with her doll.

Werner approached Vati. "When do you go back this time?"

"Never!" he said boisterously. "This time, I'm here to stay."

Mutti spoke under her breath. "Unless Hitler gets any big ideas."

"Now, Emma," he said. "I'm sure it's all rumors."

"He's already taken over half of Europe. First Austria, then Czechoslovakia," she spoke coldly. "And there are rumors of Poland being next. Chamberlain from Britain said if Hitler doesn't stop the invasions, they'll make him stop."

"Ah, all talk, my dear," he responded. "You do have to admit there's a lot of good he's done for Germany. Before Hitler, there weren't any jobs and the economy was in ruins. It's easy to forget the days when we didn't have any food on the table."

"I haven't forgotten," said Mutti. "But at what cost?"

I didn't forget either. When I was little, Mutti sometimes made meals out of thin slices of stale, dry bread with water and sugar sprinkled on top. Even the chickens didn't want to lay eggs back then. And Opa Rose, my Mutti's father, sold his animals because there wasn't enough food for them either.

As much as I didn't care for Hitler, he did come through on his promise to put bread and butter on every table, and people started working again to provide for their families. He earned the people's trust. But when I listened to his speeches now, he didn't talk much about the people anymore, only power.

"Oh, my dear. You worry too much," said Vati. "Let's hope Hitler doesn't call Chamberlain's bluff."

"I'm not so sure it's a bluff," said Mutti, followed by an awkward silence.

The mood shifted. Hitler didn't only invade bordering countries. He invaded our home, too. He was everywhere, and he found a way to slither his way into our happy moment like the snake he was.

Vati sensed it, too, and tried to lighten the mood.

"I will not have talk of Hitler ruin a perfectly wonderful homecoming. I've had enough of him to last me quite a while."

Everyone did. But I was sure Vati put on a happy face for the sake of the moment. I didn't want to admit it, but I knew deep down he wasn't convinced of his own words. Hitler was unstoppable in his thirst for more.

More land.

More acclaim.

More power.

More.

Something was stirring. It was in the air and on the streets, showing itself as unsettling rumors of war and impending invasions. Even children whispered back and forth about stories from older siblings, distant cousins, and outspoken uncles.

"I'll tell you what I haven't had enough of." Vati broke in. "Good home cooking. What have my girls made for dinner?"

I quickly set the table and everyone gathered around to enjoy the feast. Mutti placed the roast in the center of the table with the asparagus and other side dishes in separate bowls. Vati looked around the table at all of us, together again after such a long absence.

"I think this is an opportune time to offer a blessing, don't you?" he said.

He interlocked his fingers and bowed his head. There was a hush around the table, a reverence. When Vati spoke, his voice cracked.

"Lord," he said, clearing his throat. "Bless this food to our bodies and those who prepared it. Thank you for the love around this table, and the love you've shown us. May we forever be grateful. In thy holy, precious name, Lord Jesus. Amen."

It wasn't an exceptionally long prayer, but I'm pretty sure God stepped inside the room. The earth stood still, and Vati's head stayed bowed a little longer, as though he were continuing on in a silent conversation. Everyone waited for Vati with anticipation. He lifted his head and unclasped his hands.

Earlier, I considered how everyone changed since Vati left for training in the army. I didn't think to consider how Vati might have changed, too.

He had. How, I wasn't sure, but I hoped I would have all the time in the world to find out.

CHAPTER 6
Summer 1939

A light summer breeze drifted across the open field as I stretched my legs.

"You'll never beat me," said Herbert, a swollen-headed boy who was my age. "I've been training, and I'm much faster than you. Besides, you're a girl."

I stood with other children on the side of the track at the Sportplatz, annoyed at Herbert's words. He was a stocky boy with ears that stuck out too far from his head. And he was always spouting off about something. I rolled my eyes and turned away.

Earlier in the week, Vati said he entered my name into a competition at the annual summer sports festival. I was twelve now, and it was my chance to show Vati all my hard work and training while he was away, and prove any trace of weakness from the scarlet fever was gone, too.

The weeks since Vati's return were among the happiest in my life, and the gloomy thoughts that once filled my head dissipated like the morning mist. With each passing day, my heart grew lighter, and a newfound hope bloomed within me.

When Vati returned home, he went back to work as a foreman for Herr and Frau Gerbe in their livery stable, taking care of the work horses and maintaining their harnesses and equipment. Sometimes he dispatched laborers into the fields with horses and plows, or he'd send them to work on the new highway being built. The Autobahn.

Occasionally, he'd go along to help build the giant motorway, guiding the horses as they pulled a massive contraption behind, sputtering and spewing black smoke as it went. He'd come home filthy and smelling of asphalt. There weren't nearly enough cars to justify such a big road, but Hitler had a lot of grand ideas.

When he wasn't working, Vati spent time with us and planned small outings. It was only the two of us on this glorious summer day at the Sportplatz. He sat on a bench with other parents and onlookers, and I sought his advice about Herbert's challenge.

"Vati, do you think I can beat that boy over there?"

I pointed at Herbert. He was parading back and forth along the edges of the track like a rooster.

"Hmmm. He looks like a formidable opponent," he said, stroking his chin and being a bit over-dramatic.

"What do you think? Can I beat him?"

Vati surveyed the boy, then nodded his head.

"I'll tell you what you need to do."

I listened intently for his advice.

"Don't run too fast."

I laughed. Was he joking? No, he was entirely sincere. I tried to reason with him.

"But he'll surely win then. That doesn't make any sense."

"Ah, but I didn't say to run slow the whole way. Only at the beginning."

"But he'll get a head start."

"Oh, yes, he certainly will," said Vati with a wry smile. "Let him think he's beating you. Stay behind the whole way. He'll think he's on world record time and run even faster to make it look like he's winning by leaps and bounds. But he'll use all his strength in the beginning and run out of steam."

Vati got a determined look on his face.

"Then, in the last leg of the run, go as fast as you can and sprint past him!"

I wasn't so sure about this plan, but Vati's advice never let me down before.

"Okay. I'll give it a try."

I returned to the starting line. Herbert stretched his legs from side to side and stared me up and down.

"You might as well withdraw from the race now," he said. "You don't have a chance."

"Well, I'm going to try," I said. "Besides, what if I do win?"

"Ha! That will never happen. I've been training."

"Oh, really?" I'd heard him say it a hundred times. "Well, if that happens, you'll only beat me by a hair then."

"Oh yeah? Just wait and see. You'll be lucky if you get

within fifty meters," said Herbert.

I acted concerned and turned away so he wouldn't notice the smile forming on my lips. Herbert's ego was far too inflated to avoid such a challenge, and he played into my ploy perfectly. Vati's idea might just work after all.

A whistle blew and someone called out through a megaphone for the runners to gather at the starting line. Herbert and four others took their places alongside me for the four-hundred meter race.

I crouched low and glanced at Herbert poised with one foot forward. He jutted his chin and stuck out his tongue at me. I was compelled to return the sentiment, but held my tongue and looked ahead instead.

"Ready... on your mark..." One of the event organizers stood at the side of the track and raised a cap gun into the air.

Bang!

The shot rang out and I sprang from position, almost forgetting Vati's words. Herbert bolted forward, too, and took the lead. I, instead, stayed behind the pack of runners and paced myself with steady, even steps.

As predicted, Herbert ran faster than all of us and took a sizable lead early on. At the half-way point, I rounded a corner and ran past the small crowd of onlookers where Vati sat. His cheers and chants rose above all the rest.

"Now!" he yelled. "As fast as you can!"

Vati's words spurred me on. My breath steadied. My stride lengthened.

One. Two. Three. Four. Each runner was behind me

now except for Herbert, but the distance between us became shorter and shorter.

The finish line was only fifty meters away and Herbert gulped at the air as I approached from behind. My feet struck the pavement and he glanced back, his red face punctuated with wild eyes. He pumped his arms harder, but his pace steadily declined.

The crowd cheered. My lungs burned. My legs ached. But I pushed harder and harder.

We were neck and neck. I dared not look at him and focused only on the finish line. Every muscle, joint, and tendon worked in unison to propel myself forward. I no longer heard the crowd, nor Herbert, only my own steady, controlled breathing, and the wind passing by my ears.

With one final push, I leaned forward. The ribbon, once held taut across the track, broke free. It spun and twirled into the grass, and the small crowd cheered at my comeback from last place.

Vati was among them, jumping up and down like a school boy, shouting, "Did you see that? Did you see? That's my girl!"

I stood catching my breath. Herbert, however, was on the ground on all fours, his chest heaving in and out in between coughing and spitting the mucous clogging his lungs.

"Hey, Herbert," I called.

He turned his head and eyed me with scorn, unable to speak for lack of oxygen. I didn't say another word, only stood at a distance with my hands on my hips and stuck out my tongue. Herbert rolled over onto his back, huffing, puffing, groaning.

"You did it!" Vati grabbed me from behind and lifted me in his arms with a big hug.

"I told you it would work!"

It did, and I relished in Vati's elation and pride. Had I ever felt so happy? So free?

"That was more exciting than the Olympics," he beamed.

I hugged him close and drank in his delight. Oh, how I loved him. Oh, how I wanted to stay in that moment forever.

I received a first place ribbon for the race during the awards ceremony, and also won a ribbon for the long jump competition. Vati and I walked across the field to head home, and I was still flying high.

"Did you see when I ran past him? You were right. He got tired fast."

Herbert was kneeling on the ground stuffing something into his knapsack when we strode by.

"Better luck next time, Herbert." I smiled.

"You're the one who's lucky, he said at the sight of the two ribbons pinned to my chest. "I'll beat you next time. I'm in training, you know."

I rolled my eyes. "Yes, Herbert. I know."

Vati and I kept walking as he wrapped his arm around my shoulder. He replayed in great detail the day's race and the look of horror on Herbert's face when I sprinted past him.

"I'm surprised Herbert runs out of breath so quickly and doesn't win more races," said Vati.

A smirk formed on his face.

"You'd think with all that hot air, he'd practically float to the finish line!"

We burst out laughing and walked hand in hand. It was so good to have Vati back home.

CHAPTER 7
Summer 1939

Mutti slathered a chunk of butter on a small roll. "Why don't you eat another piece of bread," she said. "You'll need it for the long trip they have planned for you today. And take a sweater. It's colder in the countryside."

Vati's voice came from the hallway. "Cold? It's been terribly hot all summer."

He was ready to head out the door to work on the big road again with a team of horses, but not before he pulled on his boots and gave Mutti a peck on the cheek.

Life became extraordinarily normal since Vati came home, and the mundane routine of seeing him lace his boots before giving Mutti a kiss was something I looked forward to each morning. It grounded me, bringing a calming sense of security and comfort.

Life with Vati home was a kind of wonderful hard to describe, like the feeling you get when walking through tall grass and brushing your fingers across the blades, listening to the buzz of honey bees hovering over wildflowers, and the hush of the wind through a grove of aspen trees. The world was lighter and our family was whole again.

Even so, a darkness loomed, casting a shadow over our world. The radio broadcasts and speeches kept talking about how war was the only way to ensure the annihilation of the Jewish race in Europe. Vati didn't want to talk about it, only saying there was nothing to worry about. But I was worried. Everyone was.

I picked up my rucksack and headed for the door. "I've got to get to my Jungmädel meeting."

"Take some rolls in case you get hungry," said Mutti.

I grabbed the rolls wrapped in a dish cloth and hopped on my bike, leaving thoughts of war behind. The meeting wasn't a normal meeting, but a field trip to the forest, and I'd been looking forward to it all week.

When I arrived at the town hall, I searched the group of girls. It was hard to tell them apart sometimes. After all, every Jungmädel girl wore the same uniform—a white shirt, black skirt, and a red kerchief with the leather knot.

I craned my neck.

"Here I am, Waltraud!" Liesa emerged from the group and ran to greet me. "I'm so glad you made it!"

"I wouldn't miss it," I said. "It probably won't be as adventurous as our field trip last winter, though."

I hopped off my bike and propped it against a tree.

"Besides," I gave Liesa an over-exaggerated smile. "It's mandatory, remember?"

Liesa and I burst out laughing. The forced enthusiasm about activities like marching, singing, listening to speeches, and essays became the butt of many joking remarks between us.

The trip last winter was a great adventure. We stayed at a large youth hostel in the snow-covered foothills of the Harz Mountains in central Germany. I'd never been so far from home. In between lots of lessons and training, we got to try new activities like snowshoeing.

I recounted the story for Liesa as we walked toward the group of other girls, mimicking the clumsy way we lifted our feet in the deep snow.

"They might as well have tied tennis rackets to our boots," laughed Liesa. "Our faces were in the snow more than our feet!"

But there was no hint of snow on this beautiful summer day. More girls arrived and the volume of our collective chatter was silenced by a piercing whistle.

We scrambled to form a line, youngest to oldest, and stood tall with arms at our sides, chin up, and eyes watching an unseen landmark in the distance.

We saluted our troop leader, Fräulein Baumann, who held a clipboard in her hand. She referenced it several times as she examined the line of girls. She began roll call.

"Elsa Feurling."

"Here," the youngest girl's voice called out.

The leader read off several names down the line with the same result.

"Waltraud Michaelis."

"Here!"

More names were called off.

"Gretta Schilling."

Silence.

"Gretta Schilling," she called out again more loudly.

Eyes flitted back and forth. Where was she?

The Fräulein's jaw clenched. It wasn't the first time Gretta missed a meeting, and the thought of skipping such an eventful day was a slap in the face. She moved her pencil toward the clip board and started writing.

"Here!" A desperate cry came from the distance.

Gretta rode furiously on her bicycle and dismounted in a frenzy, leaving the bike in a twisted pile on the ground. She ran to her place in line, disheveled and out of breath.

"Here!" she repeated through gasps, snapping to attention.

Fräulein Baumann approached with steady, calculated steps.

Gretta's eyes looked straight through her in utter panic. Her stockings were scrunched around her ankles and her leather tie was askew. Wisps of blonde hair clung to the sweat on her forehead, even though the morning air was cool, and the flush in her face grew increasingly red.

The leader stared at her, slipping her clipboard under her arm. She reached a hand toward the young girl's throat. Gretta's eyes grew wider and her lip quivered as she braced herself.

With a swift jerk, Fräulein Baumann grabbed Gretta's leather lariat and pulled her toward her. A wave of terror flowed through the line, but no one moved.

"Your tie is crooked," seethed the leader. "It is disrespectful to the Führer and the Fatherland."

Gretta stood silent, her eyes welling with tears. The leader loosened her grip and methodically straightened Gretta's tie, flattened the fabric of her shirt, and stood back.

Donning a plastic smile, she spoke. "Now, I suspect this will be the last time you hold up our proceedings and present yourself in such a state of disarray."

"No, I mean. Yes. I, I—"

"Silence!"

Gretta was shaking now. Fräulein Baumann scanned the girl up and down.

"Get back in line."

Gretta took a step back and let out a controlled and silent breath.

I felt sorry for her. Gretta struggled in the group. She wasn't athletic, and her timid nature made her an easy target for some of the more mean-spirited girls. And Fräulein Baumann didn't stop them. In fact, I think she found a twisted pleasure in terrorizing the weaker girls.

I tried to put the incident with Gretta behind me and focus on the day ahead, but I knew our troop leader would jump at any opportunity to put a girl in her place. I'd seen my share.

We mounted our bikes and headed for the Elm Forest. The woodland countryside was a welcome refuge from my chores, and I found solace there when Vati was gone. The ferns and moss-covered rocks whispered to me in our own secret language, telling me everything would be all right and they'd forever be my friend.

Sometimes I lay on the forest floor, watching clouds float by through the leafy canopy of trees. I doubted the famed cathedrals of Cologne or Berlin compared to the reverent beauty of the towering oaks, maples, and beech trees arching overhead.

Yes, I was glad to return to the forest, and glad I didn't have to spend my time there thinking of Vati being gone.

Our bikes rode in single file. On either side of the road were fields dotted with small herds of cattle put out to pasture, and the bells around their necks clanked like tone-deaf wind chimes as they grazed. They watched us with curious faces and ruminating jaws as laughter and carefree conversations flowed among our caravan of girls.

The Elm Forest sat on top of a large ridge, and our conversations slowed as we pedaled harder to climb toward it. I was glad Mutti sent the rolls along and I nibbled on one as we rode.

We reached our destination and walked into the forest to a natural spring gurgling from the earth. It formed a small stream that trickled down the hillside, meandering between knobby tree roots and dispersing into a sea of ferns. It was captivating, and I actually enjoyed the short science lesson about the underground aquifers and the forest floor.

We were released with instructions to search for unusual plants or other items and bring them back to the group to report on what we found. Young girls ran through the woods, each hoping to discover something rare to impress Fräulein Baumann.

I found myself engulfed in the shady forest, serenaded by songs of the robins and larks. I inhaled the smell of decomposing leaves deep into my lungs, a sweet, earthy mix of soil and organic matter steeped in spring rains and baked in the summer's heat. My fingers traced the rough bark of a pine tree and its needles tickled my face. The spongy moss was soft underfoot, more luxurious than the finest Persian rug to ever grace a queen's palace.

I turned over a fallen log with my foot, hoping for something unusual among the trees. But the plants and flowers were no different than those in the woods near home, yet just as wonderful.

There were few flowers this time of year. The hepatica, trilliums, and other ephemerals of spring already went to sleep. Only the violets remained.

Though the forest was abuzz with girls running this way and that, I barely noticed. I leaned back against a log and flicked at the rough lichen clinging to its bark, filling my senses, absorbing a quiet peacefulness only the forest could bring.

It was Vati who taught me the ways of the forest. As far back as I remembered, he'd take me with him when he walked among the trees and wildflowers.

My tiny fingers curled around his as he led the way, occasionally lifting me high over a log or rock, pointing out native plants he foraged and dried for tea, like wild nettle or the sweet-scented flowers of linden trees. He'd stoop low to turn over a log in search of a salamander, or hold me high on his shoulders to see the nest of a song thrush made of grass, twigs, and mud tucked into a bush. The eggs looked like jelly beans.

They were as blue as Vati's eyes.

"Aren't you coming?" Liesa interrupted.

"What?"

I had lost myself in creation.

"She blew the whistle. Didn't you hear it?"

I didn't. I wanted to stay where I was, but I forced myself up.

"You're not bringing anything?" asked Liesa, holding a handful of old acorns. "You're going to get in trouble."

I sighed and followed her back to the group to stand in line, empty handed.

Fräulein Baumann asked each girl to show and tell about their discoveries, and I was bewildered with each one. To me, they weren't unusual at all, except for the beautiful feather Gretta found. From a woodpecker, I think. I was glad she redeemed herself with such a fabulous find.

The Fräulein told one girl some wild mushrooms she found were poisonous, and the girl threw them to the ground like they were on fire.

Everyone laughed.

She moved down the line. How could I be so stupid? What was I thinking to not have anything to show? I should have pretended, but it was too late. She stood in front of me.

"And you, Waltraud? What did you find?"

"I, I—There wasn't—"

"Nothing?"

I confessed. "No."

"You mean to tell me that in all the forest you couldn't find a single thing to share? A leaf? A stick? A rock? Nothing?"

Some girls snickered, and a hot flush of embarrassment traveled from my stomach and rose to my cheeks. A vision of the Fräulein's hands reaching for Gretta's throat flashed through my mind.

"You asked us to find unusual things," I said. "I've seen all those things before. To me they weren't anything special."

She was not amused.

"Those there," I pointed to the discarded mushrooms on the ground. "They're not poisonous. We eat them all the time. They're the same ones growing in the woods near home, and—"

"Do you think you're smarter than all the girls? Than me?"

I should have known better. My mouth always got me in trouble. On the one hand, we were taught to be strong and confident in our Aryan identity. On the other, any expression of independent thought or challenge of authority was considered defiance.

I hated the hypocrisy.

"Pick them up," said the Fräulein, referencing the scattered mushrooms.

Bewildered, I stepped out of line and gathered them in my hands.

"Now eat them."

Gasps of concerned whispers echoed through the

group. I grasped a mushroom between my fingers and examined it carefully. They were the same as those I found growing in the mossy patches beneath mature beech trees not far from home. I was sure of it. I brushed it on my skirt and popped it in my mouth.

"See, they're good, just a little chewy when raw," I said. Some girls giggled and Fräulein Baumann's head jerked toward them with shifty eyes and nostrils flared. The giggling stopped.

"They're Pfefferling mushrooms—wild chanterelles—the best kind. And those there," I said, pointing to the smooth, round mushrooms in another girl's hand, "are Steinpilze—porcini."

The displeased look on her face said it all, but I couldn't help myself. My explanation, however true, pushed the boundaries of her patience.

"Next time, you will follow my orders. Do I make myself clear?"

I nodded.

"I said, do I make myself clear?"

"Yes, Fräulein Baumann."

"Now, get back in line!"

I did as she said and she moved down the line. I leaned to the girl who stood next to me.

"Don't eat your mushrooms," I whispered. "You'll probably die."

The girl looked down at the pretty red-capped mushrooms in her hand and slowly bent to the ground, placing them in a pile and wiping her hands on the grass.

I bit my lip, trying not to smile. She was one of the

mean girls in the group, and I felt great satisfaction in causing her unease.

After our time in the forest, we got on our bikes and rode on winding roads to a clearing bordered by perfectly manicured boxwoods and colorful rose gardens. An old house with an outdoor seating area was there, bigger and more stately than any I'd ever seen in Rautheim.

"What is this place?" a girl asked.

Our leader pointed to a small sign affixed to the side of the building.

Tetzelstein.

"It's a historic site with a monument," she said. "In fact, I have another lesson for you."

Liesa's rolling eyes met mine.

"After the lesson, we have a special surprise."

Rumblings of curious excitement trickled through the group, each girl trying to guess what the surprise could possibly be. But first, we marched along a woodland path where we came upon a small stone steeple.

What, exactly, was a tiny church doing in the middle of the woods?

Fräulein Baumann explained the history of the monument and how there once lived a religious monk named Tetzel in the 1600s. Folklore suggested he built the small chapel as part of a scheme to swindle local villagers out of their money.

"He sat inside the steeple holding a copper bowl," said the Fräulein. "And as people walked by, he'd shout to them from inside."

In an instant, she transformed into an endearing

creature, like a famed actress who might have graced the stage of the Deutsches Theatre in Berlin. I was amazed at how quickly and effortlessly she could switch from a stern dictator to a theatrical performer. All the more reason not to trust her.

With voice booming, she summoned the words of the long lost monk from ages past, pausing dramatically between phrases and gesturing with her hands.

Wen das Geld
Im Kästen klinkt
Die Seele aus
Den Fegefeuer springt!

Laughter bounced off the narrow stone walls of the steeple and into the rustling leaves of nearby trees. I laughed along, too, reciting the words in my mind.

When your money in the kettle clinks,
your soul will from the hellfire spring!

The Fräulein's exuberant impersonation switched to a critical rant about the hypocrisy of the church and its many failings and offenses.

"Ultimately, religion is for stupid people. A ploy to get your money," said the Fräulein. "The only one you can trust is Hitler, our faithful Führer."

Girls sat somber-faced as they listened. I cringed at the mention of his name.

"What about Martin Luther?" I asked. Liesa shot me a

warning glance. "My catechism teacher said he spoke out against those kinds of things and—"

Our leader's glaring stare was back. Why couldn't I keep my mouth shut? Her eyes penetrated through mine, trying to reach my soul to pluck any thought of religion from it. The old Fräulein was back in a blink, and I sensed her smoldering anger.

I crossed the line again. But I couldn't sit idly by while Hitler was praised as a faithful Führer, to be trusted more than the faithful Father I learned about in church.

I didn't like the confirmation classes and found them boring, but I still felt a still, small voice inside telling me it was true.

"And this type of nonsense, children, is why it's better to be confirmed beneath the flag instead of in the church!"

Fräulein addressed the others, ridiculing my words and extending her rant. I tuned out her droning voice. My stomach turned and I wanted to cry.

Was it shame? No. I knew in the depths of my soul I was right. Was it because I couldn't speak freely and defend my beliefs, however weak they were? Yes, that was it. We had no choice but to conform as the venom from her mouth slowly seeped into our veins.

I'd forgotten about the promised surprise. But when we returned to the big house, each girl took a seat at a table outside. Several women emerged with trays full of fancy cut crystal stemware containing a dollop of something white and frothy.

One by the one, we were served a dish and given a

small silver spoon.

"Pudding!" shrieked one girl with delight.

She dug her spoon into the creamy dessert and put a large scoop in her mouth. Her eyes swelled to twice their size and she stood with a start, dropping her spoon which rang like a bell against her crystal dish.

At the ping of the clinking glass, one girl chided, "What's the matter? Trying to get the hellfire out?"

Everyone laughed as the girl coughed, unsure if she should spit or swallow.

What in the world caused such a reaction? What kind of surprise was this? Maybe it was a cruel joke. Horseradish sauce? I wouldn't put it past Fräulein Baumann. I didn't trust her.

"Ice cream!" shouted another girl.

Everyone's eyes lit up and they dipped their spoons inside their dishes, tasting the sweet concoction. Sounds of rapture replaced the prior commotion as they treasured each spoonful.

I'd never had ice cream before, but heard about how good it was. I scraped the tip of my spoon across the top of the dish, picking up a tiny scoop. I licked it off. It was wonderful, and the tiny silver spoon and crystal dish made me feel like royalty as I savored every creamy spoonful.

Had I ever had a more decadent dessert? Velvet silk with a hint of vanilla swirled around inside my cheeks. The disturbing events from earlier melted away as quickly as the frozen treat.

"As a special prize, you can each keep your silver

spoon," said Fräulein.

Excitement trickled through the group and we tucked our spoons inside our rucksacks for safe keeping. It was just the right size to stir honey in my tea.

We mounted our bikes and coasted effortlessly down the hills toward home. Before long, Rautheim came into view and the dirt road merged with cobblestone streets.

Aside from Fräulein Baumann, I enjoyed the day. Any day spent in nature was a good day in my opinion, so I tried to fix my thoughts on my time in the forest instead.

When I got home, I told Vati all about the day's activities and the ice cream, avoiding the disturbing parts about our troop leader. Mutti was making dinner, and the glorious scent of mushrooms frying in butter filled the kitchen.

It was the smell of home.

Everything was perfect. I wanted to suspend time and the feeling of contentment I felt at the sight of simple things I once took for granted—Vati relaxing and reading the newspaper, the stain on Mutti's apron she tried to blot with a damp towel, Werner playing peek-a-boo with Anneliesa.

I wanted the carefree days of summer to go on forever, for our family to always be together.

Little did I know, life would never be the same.

CHAPTER 8
September 1939

Our family walked to the center of town. A dozen or more soldiers gathered at the town square. Scenes of young men hugging their mothers, and fathers holding their children and kissing their wives unfolded before my eyes.

Soldiers. I thought I'd never have to think of Vati that way again, but it was true. He was one of them again. Only this time it wasn't for training.

It was war.

He clutched his canvas bag filled with fresh, clean clothes and a small supply of home-baked goods, boiled eggs, and dried meats—enough to last a few days and to supplement the monotonous rations of army life. He slipped his free hand inside the crook of Mutti's elbow as we walked in silence, eventually joining the others who stood along a stone wall.

My stomach turned at the thought of him leaving

again. It was a lifetime ago when Vati left the first time. I didn't fully comprehend how long the separation would last back then.

As days turned into weeks turned into months, I came to understand the painful reality of his absence. As time passed, the ache and longing grew deeper, and I resolved if I ever had to say goodbye again, I would be more fully aware.

And I was.

He returned from his military training only five months earlier, and spring's beauty was erupting all around then. It was a hopeful time of new life and, much like the yellow daffodils swaying in the breeze, Vati's return brought with it a cheerful outlook on life.

As spring turned to summer, there were more and more radio broadcasts about how Poland did this or that to pose a threat to Germany and its people.

Hitler already took over all of Czechoslovakia. Why did he need Poland, too? Maybe I was naive, but I pushed away any thoughts of what it might mean for us at the time. I reasoned we were far away from those borders, tucked away in the quiet, northern region of Niedersachsen—Lower Saxony. Surely, we'd never see battles fought on our own streets.

But Mutti's suspicions were right. Before long, Hitler pushed the boundaries of Chamberlain's patience and the rumors became a frightening reality. Germany's army invaded Poland on a rainy Friday in early September. Poland's forces were no match for thousands of tanks, bombers, and Luftwaffe fighter planes dispatched in a surprise attack. Hitler's Blitzkrieg, his lightning war, didn't take long to overwhelm them.

Great Britain, led by Churchill's army, and France kept their promise, declaring war. Vati was immediately summoned to report for duty with only a few days' notice.

The leaves turning from green to yellow reminded me change was inevitable. Just like the linden trees fighting the autumn winds to hold on to their leaves, I wanted to hold on to Vati and fight, too.

But I couldn't.

A big truck arrived. Wooden benches lined the sides, and men started boarding, throwing their sacks into the belly of the truck bed.

Vati knelt to Werner and gave fatherly instructions, something about being the man of the house. But Werner couldn't bring himself to look up from his shoes. Vati stroked his cheek and lifted his chin.

"You'll be a good boy, yes?" Vati said. Werner nodded.

I fell into Vati's arms and a river of tears streamed down my cheeks.

"Oh, Vati. Please don't go," I begged.

"Believe me. Everything in me wants to stay. But I have no choice."

It was true. Little by little, I was told what to do, what to think, and what to believe. So many choices were being taken away. And now, Vati was being taken away, too.

He whispered in my ear. "I will miss you so much, my little Liebling."

The lump in my throat grew. Even though I was

already twelve years old, practically a young lady, I was still his little love. No one could take that away.

"Be brave now," he said as he caught a tear on my cheek with his thumb.

I felt anything but. He gave a final embrace as I wept, then stood and hugged Mutti for a long, long time and gave her a tender kiss.

"I'll be home soon," he told her as he brushed a wisp of hair aside from her face.

Her eyes searched his for reassurance and found none there. With a final kiss on the cheek for Anneliesa, he boarded the truck. It roared to life and lurched forward as the driver shifted into gear and engaged the clutch. The men held tightly as it sped away.

Everything in my soul screamed for it to stop. When it didn't, I bolted from Mutti's side and ran after the truck, barely able to see through the flood of tears. If Mutti yelled for me to stop, I didn't hear.

"No, Vati! Wait!"

I screamed as I ran. But the accelerating engine drowned out my voice.

"I love you, Vati. I love you. Don't go!"

I called out after the truck. How did I forget? I'd rehearsed it a thousand times in my head. How did I not tell him how much I loved him in those final moments when I had the chance? Surely, he knew. He must. But I didn't say the words.

I ran as fast as my legs could carry me, faster than when I raced Herbert, following the truck down one alley and around the corner. But the distance between us grew greater and greater with each stride. It passed the bakery, the butcher, and the school. It slowed at an intersection and I thought I might gain ground and catch up, but it raced forward again.

I wouldn't stop running. I couldn't. Huffing, heart pounding, I willed myself to keep moving. But no amount of training or Vati's coaching made me run fast enough or far enough. The truck gained momentum and rounded another curve.

It was gone.

With burning lungs, I slowed to a stop. The street was empty, quiet, except for my breath. In a daze, I looked at the streets and yards around me. Everything was going on as it was before. A cat walked through a yard. A woman hung her wash. A leaflet blew across the street. Why were things carrying on as though the world didn't stop spinning, as though nothing at all was wrong.

But everything was wrong. Terribly wrong.

A raven landed in a tree overhead. I glared at it with seething eyes as it nervously hopped from branch to branch, watching me, mocking me. Its silhouette looked like the eagle in Germany's emblem perched on twisted branches in the shape of a swastika. It let out a raucous caw.

Something welled up inside, an anguish and disdain so raw, so intense, I couldn't hold back. I picked up a rock and flung it with all my might at the bird while screaming at the top of my lungs, an indecipherable wail of simultaneous hatred, horror, and sorrow.

The crow took flight in the direction of where the

truck disappeared, scolding me in its retreat. I collapsed in a heap and wept among the fallen leaves. A single, black feather lofted from the sky and landed at my feet.

Night fell by the time I got back home. I roamed the streets for hours, unable to bring myself to walk in the back door to the cold reality of a house void of Vati's presence.

CHAPTER 9
Spring 1940

When the truck disappeared around the corner, life changed.

I still attended school every day and the Jungmädel meetings twice a week, but field trips became few and far between—considered frivolous in a time when all the men were off to war. Any joy surrounding the gatherings was replaced with more intense training, marching, saluting, and listening to speeches.

I dreaded the time when I'd move on from the Jungmädel and join the BDM. I'd have to go away for Pflichtjahr then—a mandatory year of service to the Fatherland.

Pflichtjahr was all Hermann Göring's idea. He was Hitler's right-hand man and decided every teenage girl should work for a year in agriculture or as a housekeeper to make sure she was prepared for her role as a wife and mother. And if girls didn't go to Pflichtjahr, they'd be penalized and couldn't continue their education.

From what I heard, it was more like forced labor. But it wouldn't happen until I turned fourteen, more than a year away.

Surely the war would be over by then. The radio said so.

The only thing good about school? Bruno and his band of hooligans finally graduated and moved on, so I didn't have to live under his watchful eye.

I walked into class. It was Monday—the day each student brought something from home to donate to the war effort to make bombs. A piece of paper. Old tin foil. Plastic. Even hair and bones.

It didn't make any sense how those pieces of trash were going to make a bomb, but after saluting the teacher, I dug in my rucksack and dutifully placed a single page from an old newspaper on the teacher's desk. Mutti had the great idea of not bringing the entire newspaper at once to make it last longer.

"Only a single page?" said Frau Langer.

I had to think fast. "My mother used the rest to start a fire in the stove."

With a wave of her hand, Frau Langer dismissed me to my desk and relief swept over me. I didn't dare mention Mutti holding back from the war effort, no matter how small. I glanced across the room at a particular girl and our eyes met. She quickly looked down, her hands clasped in her lap.

Ursula was once a boisterous and devout girl, eager to please, but her demeanor changed dramatically since the day she stood in front of the class and told the teacher about her grandfather and how he refused to give her any of his old catalogues to support the war effort. He even went so far to say Hitler was a bum and a scoundrel. It wasn't long after when the Brown Shirts showed up at his door and he was sent away to a labor camp. Ursula deeply regretted her words and had since transformed into a quiet, withdrawn girl who mostly kept to herself.

The pressure to inform our teachers or Jungmädel leaders about neighbors who might be doing something remotely suspicious was intense and reinforced at every turn. We were even told to denounce our own parents, saying our real father was the Führer and our devotion should be for him above all else.

I doubted Hitler had any clue what it was like to be a father. He wasn't even married, and he didn't know how to take care of children, let alone provide for his own country. He even issued ration cards because he couldn't keep us fed or warm.

Some father he was.

Last winter, we all slept in the kitchen near the wood stove to keep warm and conserve coal and wood because it was in short supply. We closed off other rooms and stuffed rolled-up towels and sweaters at the bottom of the doors to keep out any drafts. Mutti and Anneliesa slept on the daybed while Werner and I slept on piles of blankets on the floor, enveloped in feather beds.

Our ration of three cords of wood and four-hundred pounds of coal briquets for the year dwindled quickly. I was glad when spring decided to show up.

The war was already taking its toll, and while most people enthusiastically supported the war, some people were growing weary. But no one dared say so or complain out loud. Instead, they boasted about their sacrifices, as if hunger and cold were a noble thing.

Hitler didn't stop at Poland to the east. He set his sights on Norway to the north and Belgium and France to the west. The map on the wall in front of my school classroom had pins to mark new borders and his conquests. I swear it changed every time I looked at it.

I studied it hard and sometimes found myself lost in thought, daydreaming about where Vati might be.

All we knew was he was sent to France. But where in France? What was he doing? Was he in danger? When would the war be over?

Hitler was the boy who cried wolf in every speech, promising victory was at our doorstep and insisting the war would be over soon. Very soon.

But it dragged on.

When Vati's last letter arrived, it looked like the envelope was opened and resealed. Sure enough, when we read the pages inside, portions were crossed out with a thick, black line. I held it up to the light, hoping to see what he wrote. But it was no use.

About the only words left on the pages were Vati's musings about the rugged terrain and wishing he could indulge in Mutti's cooking again. And his love for all of us, of course. Anything written about cities he was near or details about his troop was crossed out.

Nothing was sacred or secret anymore.

Vati was a courier in the army, delivering orders and messages between military headquarters and the front lines. Couriers usually used motorcycles, but Vati rode a horse instead. He was issued an army horse, but said it didn't compare to Minna, his own mare back home.

It strangely brought comfort to envision Vati on top of a sure-footed mare or stallion. Maybe it's because it brought back memories of him working as a stable master in town. He surely knew his way around horses.

I searched the map on the wall again when the teacher placed a piece of paper on my desk. I stared at it, pencil in hand. I was supposed to write a report on the latest speech Hitler gave on the radio the night before, but Mutti turned it off as soon as he started talking. At the time, I didn't protest, but I questioned whether I should have spoken up, knowing I'd have to write an essay the next day.

The only time Mutti tuned in to the radio anymore was late at night when we were already in bed, when folk songs reminiscent of another time played softly through crackling speakers.

Sometimes I would quietly walk downstairs and peer around the corner to find her sitting in the dark. In moonlit shadows, I watched in silence as she stared out the window into the blackness, into nothing.

I longed to run into her arms. For her to embrace me and promise everything would be all right. To take me by the hand and lead me back to bed. To tuck me in as if I were a little child, and offer the assurances of peace and security I desperately longed for.

But as I watched from the doorway, I sensed a coldness. As each day passed, the colors of her soul faded into a muted palette of gray. And even though she sat only a few steps across the room, the expanse separating us felt insurmountable, as did my longing for things to return to the way they used to be.

So, I turned away and quietly went back to bed.

Meanwhile, the paper still sat blank. I scribbled something about the supremacy of Germany, the aggression of neighboring countries, and disparaging remarks about inferior races and Britain's new prime minister, Winston Churchill.

There. That should do it. Hitler's speeches usually mentioned those things in some way or another.

The teacher strode past each desk to collect the papers and I held mine up warily, meeting her eyes as she took the page. Could Frau Langer read my mind and detect my anxious thoughts and uncertainty with a single glance? She read through the paper and turned it over only to find it blank.

"The Führer had much to say in his address yesterday. Are you sure you captured it all in your brief report?"

"Have I forgotten something?"

The teacher glanced through my report once more and looked at me with pursed lips and a stern gaze, then quietly added it to the stack of papers in her hand and moved on to the next student.

I let out a quiet breath. Even if I had listened to his speech, it was hard to focus with the pang of hunger in my stomach. Mutti traded some of our ration cards for more coal.

"We'll freeze to death faster than we starve to death," she reasoned.

The color-coded ration cards allowed for staples like milk, cooking oil, flour, bread, barley, sugar, and a little meat. The meat was most useful for bartering because it was in such high demand, so I was disappointed when Mutti said she traded those ration cards. But she promised we would have meat soon enough because Opa Rose was raising rabbits in his basement again.

I couldn't tell anyone about it, of course. Having undocumented livestock—even soft, cuddly rabbits—was strictly prohibited. But Opa was a clever and shrewd man, having some inside information about when the inspectors would come around next time.

A household was permitted to have only two rabbits. No more. So, he always kept a male and female. And everyone knows what happens when you have a boy and girl rabbit.

Unlike other livestock, rabbits grew quickly and, more importantly, were quiet. Neighbors were completely unaware. When word spread the inspectors were coming around, he would quickly butcher all but two.

Mutti said it was about time for us to pay him a visit. It was risky, but Opa Rose insisted he had things under control.

I watched Ursula again and shuddered to think what would happen if Opa got caught. As my stomach rumbled, the thought of Hasenpfeffer stew almost seemed worth the risk.

But to cook it, we needed more wood to make a fire. That's why Werner and I planned to go to the forest that afternoon to gather old branches and fallen logs for the wood stove. We had to secure a permit for that, too.

How ridiculous. We couldn't even gather sticks without government permission. What next? Rocks? I could see the headlines now—"Girl arrested for undocumented rocks."

After school, Werner and I set off with a small saw in hand and a wagon in tow.

When we got to the forest's edge, we took in the sight of the bare trees. They were eager to release winter's grip. Their branches swelled with dormant buds ready to announce spring's arrival, like last year's spring when Vati came home and everything was new, alive, hopeful. This spring felt different, though. The wildflowers that pushed through lingering patches of snow didn't look as cheery. Even the birds didn't sing as much.

"Come on, Werner. Let's get this over with." We stepped into the forest.

Werner searched for kindling while I used the saw to cut through larger fallen logs. The angled sides of the wagon bowed under the weight.

I cut through one last log and rolled it over, ready to lift it on the wagon when I saw them. It couldn't be. The fawn-colored treasures glowed like amber and I swore if I'd found an actual chest full of jewels, I wouldn't have been happier.

When Werner saw them, he squealed.

"Morcheln!"

It was true. Wild morel mushrooms. A harbinger of spring.

"Shhhh! Don't give them away," I whispered.

"Oh, the thought of mushrooms fried in pork fat. I can almost taste it!"

"Quiet! If you keep talking, the whole town will know."

I scanned the forest. There was an older couple about fifty meters away busy at work gleaning their own wood, but they probably dismissed Werner's squeals as typical childhood nonsense.

"Here, hold the saw and keep a look out."

Werner took it and stood behind me, looking terribly conspicuous. I dropped to my knees and plucked the mushrooms from the moist, hummus-rich earth.

"Werner, give me your hat."

"But I—"

"Don't argue, just give it to me."

He handed me his hat and I nestled a few mushrooms inside, then carefully placed it on his head. I placed a few more in my dress pockets for good measure.

"Now, don't squish them or you won't get any for dinner."

Werner pushed and I pulled. I forgot the ranger would be waiting at home to check our wagon when we got there. When we approached, we saluted, and Werner stood frozen, teetering on the edge of a nervous meltdown.

The ranger inspected the wagon, looking underneath branches to make sure there weren't any freshly cut logs from live trees hiding on the bottom, a strictly forbidden action.

"You've gathered a nice load of wood here," he said. "It's good to see our young folk willing to work so hard. True Germans."

"Thank you, sir," I said.

He handed me a piece of paper. "Be sure to give this receipt to your mother. Heil Hitler."

We responded with a salute and he rode away on his bicycle.

We did it. We hid our glorious mushrooms. I wasn't sure if we weren't supposed to pick them, but I was convinced if they regulated gathering sticks, picking mushrooms would be a far greater offense and land us both in prison.

Werner relaxed and we rushed inside the kitchen to find Mutti, spilling our magnificent bounty onto the table. Her eyes lit up like candles and a smile drew across her face, along with a chuckle of delight.

Oh, how good it was to see Mutti smile.

CHAPTER 10
August 1940

Nearly a year passed since Vati left, and life was a drudgery of daily chores, school, homework, Jungmädel meetings, and trying to make ends meet.

All I wanted to do was sleep, but a strange, howling cat woke me from my dreams, starting low and rising in pitch. How dare that feral creature keep me from the only respite I had from reality.

The groggy fog of my awakening began to lift and the howl grew louder, spilling through the open window and leaping off the walls, drowning out the purr of Werner's breathing. He could sleep through anything.

The door burst open, slamming against the wall, startling me and even Werner who sat up in a start. Mutti shot through with Anneliesa in her arms.

"Get up! Put on your shoes. We have to go. Now!" she yelled in a panic.

Was this happening? Or was it another drill? No, it

couldn't be a drill so late at night. A false alarm?

We jumped out of bed and felt in the dark for our shoes, grabbing for our shirts hanging on the bed posts.

The air raid siren faded to a low moan. Maybe it was a false alarm. But it swelled again, wailing like a woman giving birth and rattling my brain. We scrambled down the stairs, almost tumbling over each other in the darkness. Anneliesa wailed, too, confused and frightened, adding to the ear-piercing siren.

"I'll get the lantern," said Werner as we stumbled toward the door.

"No!" yelled Mutti. "All lights out. Now go!"

"Who would see us?" he asked as Mutti dragged him by his shirtsleeve to the moonlit street, joining the throng of others in housecoats, night shirts, and sleeping caps.

How could Werner forget about keeping all the lights off? Didn't he pay attention to the picture books in school and participate in practice drills? Of course he did. He was in a daze like the rest of us and still half asleep.

There was chaos on the street, people running every which way, and shouts of mothers calling for their children. But most remained surprisingly silent as they ran along cobblestone streets. One family climbed down a steep embankment of a ditch, disappearing beneath the street into an ancient dungeon turned root cellar. I imagined them shutting the door behind them, huddled among carrots buried in sand and grabbing for racks of dried sausages hanging from the ceiling, as if having a picnic.

Who was I kidding? No one had that many ration

cards.

The siren rose and fell, rose and fell. But there was another sound, like a swarm of angry bees. Was it thunder? No, it was a starry night.

We arrived at the bunker and were hurried along by shouts from the air raid warden.

"Keep moving! Keep moving!"

There wasn't time for saluting.

I stumbled over a small child who cried in fear in the dimly lit, windowless expanse. There were only a few benches lining the walls, occupied by elderly men and women. Cots in rows were already claimed, leaving the cool slab floor for the rest of us.

Thick walls made of concrete and steel encased us as we packed in tighter and tighter. The heat of summer was amplified by the confined quarters and bodies strewn here and there. The concrete floor was strangely soothing. Practically the whole town was there, maybe as many as one hundred. Maybe fewer. I couldn't tell for sure.

The stream of people dwindled and the air raid warden latched the heavy door behind him. The outside world was shut away and the siren's wail and approaching planes became muffled. His whistle blew a long, drawn-out trill, and the crowd grew silent but for a few mothers trying to hush their crying infants.

"There's no need to worry," shouted the warden. "The Führer's forces will protect us from the enemy."

He read off procedural instructions as a reminder of the training we received in school and the announcements made on the radio, after which he shifted to his own dissertation about the state of the war and how Hitler's army was poised to win any day now.

Great. Another speech.

Thankfully, it didn't go on very long, and we sat among the low murmur of whispered conversations.

The droning hum of planes buzzed directly overhead, bringing gasps of concern. Were they the Royal Air Force coming with bombs, or the Luftwaffe coming to shoot them down? Both?

We learned about bombings in school and the destruction they caused, setting entire cities on fire, killing innocent civilians, and leaving others with horrific burns and contorted faces.

There was a low thud in the distance, or was it close? It was hard to tell.

The earth beneath us trembled in unison with my nerves, then settled. My nerves did not. I sat with knees pulled tightly to my chest and my head down. The few lightbulbs hanging from the ceiling swayed and flickered, hissing and spitting like bacon frying in a cast iron pan. Audible whimpers of children and even some adults set me more on edge.

Mutti held a sleeping Anneliesa close to her chest while covering her head with her hand, leaning her in as if to protect her should any debris fall from the ceiling. Werner leaned against Mutti, nervously fidgeting with the buttons on his shirt.

It's no surprise they'd target Braunschweig with its factories and military airfield, but would they bomb our little town of Rautheim only a few kilometers away? It wouldn't take much for a quick-fingered pilot to jump the gun and miss, sending a parade of bombs to rain on our sleepy town.

Another thud. Another tremor. And another. The night dragged on. Was it morning yet? I hardly noticed when the hum of planes subsided. The wail of sirens transitioned to a long, sustained growl and I knew what it meant.

The attack was over.

Relief swept through the crowd and mothers began rustling their sleeping children.

"We've been spared!" a voice called out.

Cheers erupted and everyone started getting up, some groaning as they stretched their aching joints and tingling feet. The air raid warden unlatched the door and I peered above the crowd to see what the outside world looked like.

Were buildings turned to rubble? Was there fire? Would my school still be there? Would we find bodies in the street? To my surprise, it was still dark outside, barely past midnight.

We exited the bunker and walked quietly with steady steps, so unlike the frantic dash earlier. In the dark, it was difficult to see whether any buildings were bombed, but there weren't any bricks in the street. A good sign.

The faint smell of smoke filled the air and a pink glow glimmered in the sky over Braunschweig to the north. It was hit.

We arrived home, too tired for conversation yet too awake to sleep.

"Can we stay here in the kitchen on the daybed?" I asked.

"Yes," said Mutti. "I'll make some tea. Maybe it will calm our nerves."

Werner and Anneliesa were already asleep by the time the tea kettle came to a boil. Mutti poured the hot water over the dried chamomile flowers, casting a soothing aroma into the air.

"Well, we survived our first bombing," she sighed. "Next time we should have a satchel packed with some clothes, and we should each have our shoes by the door so we're ready."

She looked so weary. I sat at the table across from her, holding the hot, steeping cup of tea to my chin, allowing the steam to caress my cheeks, breathing in the sweet scent.

"How many next times do you think there will be?" I asked.

Mutti sighed.

CHAPTER 11
May 1941

I stood silent on the platform of the train station with Mutti by my side, a train ticket in one hand and a suitcase in the other. I stared at the open door.

Aside from the field trip with the Jungmädel group a few years earlier, I'd never spent much time away from home.

But my time in the Jungmädel came to an end and I was inducted into the BDM. The admission ceremony took place a few weeks earlier at the community hall on Hitler's birthday, April 20th.

There was plenty of fanfare. Triumphant music blared from a loud speaker, assaulting the eardrums of those who sat too close. The hall was decorated in flags with red and black festoons draped across a small stage with a podium.

And, of course, there was another speech.

Each of us recited the oath in unison, promising to offer our devoted love and loyalty to the Führer and the flag. Liesa and I thought to only mouth the words, but we decided against it. The beaming girl next to me would have told the leader in a heartbeat. I was sure of it.

A handful of mothers sat stiffly with thin lips pursed in straight lines as they watched their daughters go through the procession. Mutti was among them.

But most of the girls were excited, and so were their mothers who gushed over the new milestone. I had long grown tired of the forced allegiance and constant pressure to become the perfect Hausfrau with a gaggle of children.

Instead of nurturing their children, most women worked in factories or odd jobs to help the war effort as more and more men and even teenage boys were drafted and sent to the front lines.

Hitler forgot it's hard for women to become mothers with hardly any men left to father them.

Not long after the BDM ceremony, the dreaded day came when I turned fourteen.

But instead of having a party, I stood at a train station ready to leave for Pflichtjahr, my compulsory year of service to the Fatherland. I wasn't afraid of work. Being the oldest, I certainly did my share at home. But I had a bad feeling about this.

Someone announced the final boarding call. I felt anxious yet strangely numb at the same time.

Mutti placed her hand on my back, "Go on, now. If you wait any longer, the train will leave without you."

If only it were an option.

"I don't want to go."

I turned to face her. When did I grow tall enough to look her straight in the eyes? Or were her slumped shoulders bringing her down to my height?

"You need me at home," I said.

It was true, but it didn't matter now. Mutti gave me a hug and kissed my cheek, a loving gesture I wasn't expecting.

"You can visit for Christmas and we'll be together again."

Christmas was an eternity away.

The whistle blew and steam spewed out of the locomotive. I held my breath and stepped on the train.

The screech of metal on metal echoed through the train cabin. I slouched in my seat near a window and gazed outside. The squeal eventually transitioned to a steady chug and churn as scenes of the northern countryside came into view. Small villages and pastures of fresh green grass dotted the landscape.

Gently rolling hills eventually turned to flat prairies and misty bogs kissed by the sun. No bombs. No army trucks. No signs of war. It looked mythical, like a silent film at the cinema, only in vibrant color.

I had so many questions.

Where would I stay?

What would I do?

Would I get along with my host family?

Unlike Liesa and some other girls my age who were sent to stay in camps and then dispatched to work on the land, I was being sent to a farm on my own. I didn't have a choice of where I would be sent, but it sounded like a better assignment to stay in a home with a nice family rather than a work camp.

Maybe I was overthinking this whole thing and believing the worst. Maybe I would stay with a grandmotherly woman who treated me kindly, or I'd get to play with farm animals in between chores. In fact, I might actually enjoy my time in the countryside. I did love nature, after all.

The entire train ride was occupied with a swirl of unknowns in my mind, and I almost missed my transfer in one town. I arrived at the final train stop and stepped onto the platform.

A man, a little older than Vati, exited the station wearing trousers, a white shirt, hat, and open vest. He stood out among the others. There weren't many men his age left, aside from those who returned with missing limbs or battle wounds. He looked whole and I wondered how he avoided the draft.

He approached me. "Waltraud Michaelis?"

"Yes, sir."

"You will call me Herr Schäfer," he said matter of factly.

"Yes, Herr Schäfer. Pleased to meet you."

"And when you address me or any of my family, you will salute." His eyes blazed. "Do I make myself clear?"

"Yes, Herr Schäfer. Heil Hitler!" I swallowed hard.

He eyed me up, scaling my small frame with his gaze, a scowl on his face.

"They're certainly not sending their finest stock, are they?" He grunted. "Come along."

I chased after him, wrangling my suitcase as he stomped with long strides toward a horse-drawn wagon.

"I'm stronger than I look," I said, the suitcase batting against my ankles.

I only weighed a little more than one-hundred pounds, but I wasn't about to accept the insult. He hopped onto the bench seat as I stood beneath holding my suitcase.

"Well, let's see how strong you are," he said. "Toss it in the back."

Grabbing the handle with both hands, I swung the suitcase and flung it onto the boards of the wagon. A plume of dust and straw ascended upward. I climbed onto the bench seat, and we were off.

The wagon ride was silent but for the clicking of hooves and the wooden wheels spinning on sun-baked dirt roads. We drove to the edge of town to a farm surrounded by fences and fields.

Frau Schäfer was a well-endowed woman with a perfectly pressed apron and a ring of light brown braids swirled perfectly atop her big-cheeked head. She didn't look like a farmer's wife and I knew she didn't do any work on the farm by her uncalloused hands and fresh, clean clothes.

I saluted, and she greeted me with about the same enthusiasm as her husband, but at least she carried my suitcase as she led me to a small, stuffy room in the attic. It had a single bed pressed against the wall, an old dresser, a lamp, and a woven rug. She left me to unpack my things with instructions to come downstairs in the kitchen within ten minutes for a meal.

Dinner was awkward. After a quick introduction to their son, about the same age as Werner, and a younger daughter, I sat at a long table beside them. Two older sons were absent, apparently drafted and stationed somewhere near the North Sea.

Maybe I'd help with the two young children or spend time with them. That wouldn't be so bad.

"What grade are you in school?" I asked the young boy.

He looked at me with disbelief and then to his mother, as though the mere asking of the question exposed a deep, dark family secret. Frau Schäfer looked at me, too, with bulging eyes.

"There will be no talking at the dinner table," she said.

"Entschuldigen Sie, bitte," I responded.

But I wasn't sorry. It was a stupid rule.

"And you will not engage with the children," she said, as though she read my mind. "I am quite capable of rearing my children. You're here to work."

Silverware clinked on porcelain and pricked my skin with each ping. No one spoke a word, except to ask to pass the butter. I wasn't accustomed to so much food, but I guess farmers had plenty to eat. The Schäfers, including the chubby-cheeked children, clearly had their share of meat and potatoes.

The Nazi ideology of "blood and soil" served them well.

The strange dinner habits of the Schäfer family

weren't the only awkward presence in the room. There was a thin, young man at a small table in the corner, his clothes worn, his face gaunt.

How old was he? I studied his face. Maybe twenty, maybe a little older. His dark blonde hair was disheveled and he needed a haircut. His eyes were deep set and cornflower blue. Instead of the spring carrots, bread, and stew set before me, he only got bread and broth. No butter.

No one acknowledged him or introduced him. It was so odd, but I dare not open my mouth to ask who he was. I couldn't pull my eyes away, and Herr Schäfer spoke sharply.

"You are not to speak with him."

His words startled me, and I jolted my gaze away. I swirled a chunk of pork around my bowl of stew with a spoon. My eyes drew upward again to see the man.

"He's a prisoner of war, a filthy Pole," said Herr Schäfer.

The young man didn't flinch at the crass words and kept sopping broth with his bread.

"He's lucky he wasn't done away with. But they figured he was better put to work than put to death."

Who were "they," and why couldn't he sit at the table with us? With a clean shave, a haircut, and a change of clothes, he'd have looked like any other German who walked the streets. Yet, because he was from the other side of an invisible line on a map, he was considered the enemy.

"Pay him no mind and leave him be," said Frau

Schäfer. "Eat your dinner and help me clean up. Then you will stay in your room for the rest of the evening. We'll give you instructions on your duties in the morning."

I forced myself to finish my meal and did as I was told. As I climbed the stairs to the attic, a heaviness loomed.

This wasn't going to be easy.

CHAPTER 12
Summer 1941

The days were grueling. Waking at six each morning, I was given a light breakfast and dismissed to do my work. I fed the pigs and cows, dropping hay from the loft and hoisting it into their feeding troughs with a pitchfork. After giving each a scoop of grain, it was time for milking.

But I never milked a cow before. There were seven of them and they were milked twice a day. Herr Schäfer and the farm foreman had no patience for a skinny, red-headed girl turned farmhand who sat on a wooden stool. I tried to master the skill quickly, yet not quickly enough.

Their motivation tactics consisted of lots of wild-eyed yelling and belittling comments, putting both me and the cows on edge.

Stupid.

Useless.

Weakling.

Schreckliche!

Terrible summed it up pretty well.

I recoiled from their berating insults, which only made them heap on more.

Squeeze. Pull. Squeeze. Pull.

I struggled to find the right rhythm to get the milk to come out. The cows gawked at me with their big, wild eyes and I was afraid they'd kick me or conspire with neighboring cows to crush me between their massive torsos. They sensed my inexperience and nervousness and shifted their weight from one hoof to the other, flipping their manure-soaked tails from side to side and slapping me in the face.

It took as long as forty minutes to clumsily milk a single cow, but my technique slowly improved to half the time.

It didn't matter, though. The overlords hovered over me with their insults nonetheless. I learned to drown out the foreman's yelling, but I couldn't escape the whip hanging from his belt loop. He fashioned it out of a piece of thick rope, and anytime I made a mistake or didn't move fast enough by his estimation, it slapped across the back of my legs or backside. He was a menacing monster who treated me and the POW like disobedient dogs who had no choice but to cower in submission.

Once milking was done and the pails of milk were emptied into large milk cans, I'd lift them onto a cart and wheel them outside. Herr Schäfer took them into town to sell, only after his wife skimmed off the cream and reserved some milk for herself, of course.

Every morning was the same. At lunchtime, I dragged myself back to the house for something to eat, but all I wanted to do was go to the attic and collapse on the straw mattress. But I was ordered back to the barn to clean out the animal stalls next to the skinny, speechless POW.

The Schäfers and their foreman deemed shoveling manure beneath them and didn't find it necessary to oversee the task, meaning I didn't have to listen to their constant barking of orders to go faster, nor feel the back of his hand or the sting of his rope.

The loneliness was consuming, and I found myself wishing I had been sent to a work camp after all where at least I could talk with other girls before going to bed each night.

The prisoner and I both worked silently for weeks, scraping shovels full of manure into a wheelbarrow and spreading lime and clean straw into the stalls.

My heart grew heavier and my pace slowed with each passing day. I couldn't imagine nine more months of this.

"Take a break and sit on the stool over there," said the prisoner in broken German after weeks of silence. "I can do the cleaning today."

I stood frozen, scanning the barn to see if someone saw us. But the only voices were those of chirping sparrows as they scavenged grain and the flutter of barn swallows as they glided to mud nests plastered against wooden beams.

Should I be afraid? Should I run and tell someone? Should I put my head down and ignore him?

I can only imagine how great of a risk he took to speak to me. Why? Maybe he sensed my despair, or maybe he was as lonely as I was.

"My name is Anton," he whispered.

Looking around once more, I confided softly.

"I am Waltraud."

Thus began our friendship.

It didn't take long to realize we were more alike than not. Through different circumstances, we were both away from home, away from family, and forced into a situation both of us despised and neither of us could do anything about.

But I knew I had it better than him. At least I was well fed. Most of all, I knew I had an end in sight for this misery. There's no saying how long Anton would be kept a slave.

Despite its filth and the rancid stench of cow, horse, and pig manure, our afternoon routine was a respite.

Most afternoons, Anton and I whispered low among cattle and grunting pigs. We became attuned to the approaching foreman's presence who strode with heavy feet. And when he opened the barn door, the metal latch squealed, alerting a flock of wild pigeons to noisily bolt from their roost. Anton and I silenced our whispers when he arrived to check on us or call us out to help with some other chore.

I never had a big brother, but if I did, I imagined he'd be like Anton—kind, consoling, and sometimes cracking a joke at the expense of Herr Schäfer. I'd chuckle under my breath at his humor, making sure to keep quiet.

It was the only hint of joy.

At times, we reminisced about life back home and thought up elaborate schemes about how we might escape. But it was all a fool's dream. What would happen to either of us if we got caught speaking to one another, let alone escape and try to find a way home? We dared not find out. But I'm sure he would have taken the blame and brunt of any punishment in my defense.

Anton took pity on me and tried to ease my burden even though his was greater. I took pity on him, too, secretly hiding left-over food while everyone's head was down as they scarfed their dinner, or while cleaning after meals. The next morning, I'd sneak it to him—a slice of bread, some raw vegetables, and maybe even a piece of dried sausage.

We made up our own secret language of hand signals we used during meal times. A clearing of my throat and a scratch of my left ear meant a soft-boiled egg, his favorite. Before we left the table after dinner, we each held our right hand to our chest, as if complimenting the chef, but it was our way of saying, "Until next time."

One day Anton confided, "If I can't do the work, they'll send me back to the concentration camp. I know what awaits me there."

He didn't speak of his time at the concentration camp or what it was like there, as if it were too foul, too terrible to put into spoken word. But whenever the mention of it came up, he got an uncontrollable twitch in his right eye. It told more than words could ever say.

It became my mission to keep his strength up by

bringing him scraps of food. I became a master of deception and sleight of hand at meal times. A real Houdini.

After cleaning stalls, it was time for the second milking, followed by a light dinner. Twice a week, I attended the local chapter's BDM meetings held at the firehouse in town.

My new uniform consisted of a white blouse and black neckerchief with a brown leather braided knot, dark navy skirt, knee socks, and black shoes. Just like at home, we'd march through the streets, have physical fitness drills, or participate in service projects. By the time I got back to the farm, I was so exhausted I barely made it to the attic.

When harvest season rolled around, the work intensified even more. We worked the fields, shocking and bundling sheaves of wheat and stacking them upright to dry. Then came threshing time. The big, black machine bellowed and belched, separating seeds from the stalks and creating a cloud of dust, burning our eyes and lungs. The stalks spewed off a conveyor where Anton and I piled them onto wagons for use as bedding. The seeds fell into burlap bags.

The bags of grain weighed more than I did. But it didn't matter. I was ordered to drag them up a set of wooden stairs to empty into a trough at feeding time.

One particular day, I struggled to make it up the steps to the loft. I pulled and dragged the bag of grain up one step, then the next. Just one more pull and it would be to the top of the platform.

"Ok," I willed myself aloud. "One more step."

Leaning down, I lifted with all my might when it caught on a nail and slipped from my hand. In a panic, I reached to grab it, but the bag began sliding off the side of the steps, twisting and turning, my hand twisting and turning with it.

I sensed the menacing rage of the foreman if I dropped it, and the back of his bony hand across my face. The weight of the bag wrenched my thumb and wrist backward and the most excruciating pain jolted through my hand and up my arm.

I couldn't hold on.

The bag crashed to the ground, its side splitting open like a gutted animal, a mountain of grain spilling on the dirt floor below.

The screams kept coming. My screams. The pain was unbearable. The foreman came running with screams of his own.

"You stupid, useless girl!"

He heaped on more rage when he saw the pile of grain, his whip at the ready. Behind him ran Anton who sprinted up the stairs to my side.

"Get her out of here!" yelled the foreman as he reached for a shovel.

Anton whisked me down the steps where the foreman stood with red-faced fury and the shovel raised, ready to strike.

"Out!" he yelled once more and swung, missing me by a thread as Anton rushed me out of the barn.

Anton guided me across the yard toward the house as

I clenched my teeth, groaning and trying not to wail. When we were out of ear shot, he stopped to check my deformed hand.

"Your wrist," he said. "It's out of joint. I'll have to pop it back in place. It will hurt."

Could it hurt any worse than it already did?

"Do what you have to do," I said through gasps and tears.

Never had I felt so much pain. Anton steadied my arm and held it under his armpit.

"Look away," he said.

And I did. The world imploded around me as I breathed in short gasps. He felt for the bones in my wrist and applied some pressure.

"Think of blintzes and marmalade," he said as he adjusted his grip. "And pretty dresses and soft kittens, and —"

With a swift squeeze and a jerk, he yanked. Everything went black.

I couldn't use my misshapen hand for weeks. Would I ever knit again? Would I ever hold a pencil without pain or even be able to use a kitchen utensil? It was too soon to tell.

But there was no reprieve from the work. Everything was twice as hard, including milking the cows which took twice as long with only one hand. My despair deepened. I thought I was exhausted before, but I didn't know what exhaustion was then.

The tirades and abuses from the foreman multiplied, and every time he raised his hand, I fantasized about

Vati's own hands wrapping around his neck, lifting him from the ground until the life was squeezed out of him, never to scream again. I wished Vati were there to come to my defense like he did when Bruno's father showed up at our door.

But these bullies had no restraint.

Vati. I worried incessantly about him and how he was getting along. The occasional letter from Mutti shared little about him. The letter we received before I was sent away had even more black lines than the ones before. I feared I'd never see him again.

"You're losing your light, Waltraud," said Anton as we worked side by side.

"You're having to do more work because of me," I said. "Maybe the foreman is right. I'm useless."

"Don't let them break you. That's what they want."

It was too late. I no longer chuckled at Anton's jokes or tried to engage in conversations. He meant well and kept talking anyway. I tried to hold tight to Vati's words to be strong and brave, but felt neither.

When it came time to attend the BDM meetings, I couldn't bring myself to walk into town knowing I'd have to march among strangers or stay awake for another speech. When the notice was sent to Herr Schäfer reporting my absence, he rebuked me.

"You lazy girl!"

His screams and abuses didn't affect me anymore. I was dead inside.

"You've been ordered to pay a fine of five Reichsmarks," he said. "It will be deducted from your wages."

Wages? As if I were an employee and not a slave. There were no wages, only a pitiful stipend, not enough to buy a notebook for writing more stupid essays. I didn't care.

The next time I missed, the fine increased to ten marks. Then fifteen. Herr Schäfer grudgingly paid the fines and I was warned. One more absence from the meetings and I would be sent to a juvenile detention facility or labor camp.

Could it possibly be worse? I had no idea what a labor camp entailed, but fear raked over me at the thought, envisioning Anton's twitching eye. I willed myself to go to the meeting next time.

October arrived. I didn't think ahead to bring warmer socks or gloves. In my delusional mind, I thought I might have time to knit some before winter. But my knitting needles sat idle and the balls of yarn I brought along were the same size as the day I got off the train. Besides, my misshapen hand couldn't maneuver the needles anyway.

It was hard to tell when my throat started feeling sore and the chills began. Was it scarlet fever again? No, it was different. My appetite waned, but it didn't matter because I had a hard time swallowing.

Frau Schäfer insisted I eat in the corner with Anton for fear whatever was wrong with me was contagious and her two precious children would get it.

There we sat, both sipping broth. I because it was all I could swallow, Anton because they considered him less than human. I got sicker and sicker, and when I collapsed while walking to the barn, they summoned a doctor.

"Open your mouth," he said, holding my tongue down with a stick.

"Ah ha," he mumbled as he wrote something in a book.

He pressed on the sides of my neck with his fingers.

"Swollen lymph nodes," he stated decisively and wrote again.

He turned to Herr Schäfer. "May I speak with you in private?"

My mind raced as I tried to listen in on their conversation in the next room. Was I dying? For some reason, I was calm, and death wasn't frightening anymore. I strained to listen and caught fragments of the doctor's sentences.

"Infection... surgery... home..."

There was an agitated rebuttal by Herr Schäfer who blurted, "Who will do the work?"

Could it possibly be? Could whatever this was be my ticket home? I didn't want to get my hopes up, yet inside my soul begged God it was true. I didn't care whatever surgery I had to have or if I died on the operating table. All I wanted was to go home.

The doctor came back in the room. "You have a severe case of tonsillitis," he said. "We're sending you home for surgery. A tonsillectomy. You can take some aspirin in the meantime."

Tears flooded my eyes at the sight of the piece of paper ripped from his notebook, declaring his diagnosis. My passport out of hell.

"Don't be scared," he said. "It's a standard procedure."

He mistook my tears for fear or worry, but they flowed from pure relief. He handed me the paper with instructions to give to a doctor back home. I stared at it, unable to make out the scribbled writing through my tears.

I couldn't believe it.

I struggled to climb on the wagon the next day when it came time for Herr Schäfer to take me to the train station. I still felt miserable, and yet I felt lighter than I had in months.

Herr Schäfer put my suitcase in the back of the wagon on his own. A final gesture of decency from a man I despised.

I looked toward the barn, hoping for one last glimpse of Anton. He slipped out a side door with a pitchfork in hand and leaned against the door frame.

Was that a grin on his face?

The backdrop of the massive barn made him look small. How had I never noticed how beautiful it was with its half-timbered frame and thatched roof, the carved gables and perfectly painted trim? It was like a picture straight out of a children's storybook, but for me it was a grisly tale.

Herr Schäfer snapped the reins and the horse took a few steps before easing into a slow trot. My face was grimaced with heartache at the sight of Anton and the reality of his uncertain fate.

Would I have made it through without him?

Would he make it without me?

He lifted his right hand to his chest as a final goodbye. I lifted mine. But I knew there was no next time.

I'd never see him again.

CHAPTER 13
December 1941

I clutched my scarf tightly around my head as I hurried along. Locks of hair whipped in my eyes and I pulled the wool collar of my winter coat around my neck in a futile attempt to keep the bitter wind at bay.

I grumbled at the dark. "This is going to be another miserable winter, isn't it?"

The recovery from my tonsillectomy went well, and I was never so thankful to be sick in all my life. I tried to forget my time at Pflichjahr, vowing to do whatever I could to erase it from my memory. But thoughts of Anton kept it fresh in my mind as I imagined him getting thinner by the day.

I entered the gate and approached the kitchen door, stomping my worn boots on the stoop and cursing another frigid winter. It was only December, but we already knew there wouldn't be enough wood or coal again to make it through until spring. I suspected more trips to the woods with Werner once our supply ran low.

I opened the back door, removing my coat and boots, finding it strange no one was home.

I'd returned from another BDM meeting where they made us do marching routines around the block despite the cold. The speech afterward had something to do with appreciating what our men had to endure in the trenches and what they were going through on our behalf.

As if I were supposed to appreciate war.

My fingers were frozen to the bone and I rubbed my hands together by the wood stove. Off came my socks. I hung them to dry and held my fingers close to the metal door, spreading them wide and absorbing the warmth. A burning log shifted inside.

Muted voices came from Mutti's bedroom. Someone was home after all. Feeling started returning to my toes, and the tips of my fingers turned from a milky white to pink.

What were they doing in there so long?

I stepped aside, stooping to grab my slippers, already warm from sitting near the stove. I slipped them on, my feet encased in a hot envelope of soft wool. Ahh, a rare comfort.

That's when I saw the boots. Men's boots.

My senses heightened and my eyes canvassed the room for clues. Who was there? More importantly, why were they in Mutti's bedroom?

I tiptoed toward the bedroom, pressing my ear to the closed door, a faint light shining from underneath. The voices were low and it was hard to make out what they were saying.

The soft moans of a strange man entered my ears and swirled around in my head, ricocheting off the walls. I tensed.

Stories told by some girls in the BDM came to mind and got the best of me—of mothers whose husbands were away at war and who "bartered" with SS officers for extra rations. But as quickly as the vulgar thought entered my mind, it slipped away.

I shook my head in shame. Mutti would never stoop that low.

But what was going on?

I reached for the door handle and turned it in slow motion, counting silently in my mind. One. Two. Three.

I swung the door open.

I stood speechless in the doorway, my eyes wide and jaw loose, staring in utter astonishment. I stepped closer in disbelief, dropping to my knees next to the bed.

It was Vati.

Mutti sat on the edge, holding his hand and wiping his forehead with a warm washcloth.

She tilted her head. A twitch curled her lip and her eyes met mine, red with worry. Werner and Anneliesa sat quietly to the side with somber faces, not sure what to think or feel.

The room was heavy with the dank odor of a man who hadn't bathed in weeks combined with rubbing alcohol and something else medicinal.

"Vati?"

I was still shaken from my wretched thoughts, only to be confronted with the sight of Vati lying in Mutti's bed. His bed.

His face was ashen and his eyes hollow. His arm was wrapped in gauze, limp across his abdomen. It was indeed wretched, but wretched of another kind.

"My little Liebling," he said weakly.

It didn't even sound like his voice.

"Oh, Vati!"

Tears came quickly as I knelt by his side, stroking his haggard and stubbled face with my hand.

"Turns out my horse can't outrun bullets," he said half smiling.

His frame was draped in blankets. He had lost weight, but he looked whole, unlike other half-starved soldiers who were sent home with disfigured faces or stood in line for rations with one pant leg pinned to their thigh.

Whole on the outside, but there was no way of knowing what horrors he witnessed and the inner wounds medicine couldn't fix. But he was alive. It's all that mattered.

"He needs to rest," Mutti said as she got up, signaling for Werner and Anneliesa to exit.

"Come along," she called to me. "I'll tell you about it in the kitchen."

I didn't want to move from his side. It had been more than two years, and there were so many things to tell him, and so many questions. So much happened, too much to tell in a letter, too much to tell in a thousand years.

I was practically a woman at age fourteen. But inside, I

was a whimpering child who wanted to hold her father's chest close to hers and shut the world away.

Vati tried moving his arm and grimaced, moaning softly. He closed his eyes and let out a long sigh.

"Waltraud." Mutti quietly urged me from the doorway.

I touched his face one more time and stood, watching his chest rise and fall. I walked to the door, glancing back one more time before shutting him inside.

Safe for now.

I walked in the kitchen, glassy eyed and stunned, a complex mix of emotions inside me. Mutti sent Werner and Anneliesa upstairs. Good. I wanted Mutti's sole attention.

She sat slouched in a wooden chair, her head against the back. Her gaze traveled upward beyond the ceiling into another galaxy.

"Will he be ok?" I asked, afraid of the answer.

I sat, perching my elbows on the table. I placed my head in my hands. I desperately wanted Vati home, but not like this.

"He's been sent home to recuperate from his wounds," she said. "They removed most of the shrapnel from his shoulder and treated it for infection. They say he'll fully recover."

I let out a sigh. "Thank God. How did it happen?"

"He won't speak of it. Not yet." She kept staring, an expression I couldn't make out.

"But I thought they already took over France. What about all those victory speeches on the radio? Why would someone get shot if they've already won?"

Mutti kept staring without answering. There were no answers. I had so many questions, yet couldn't find the words to speak. All I wanted to do was go back inside the bedroom to sit with Vati and hold his hand, to study the new lines on his face and take in his labored breaths.

What does one do to take care of bullet wounds? I didn't know. In another time, we would have summoned Doctor Opitz to make a house call and examine Vati's condition, maybe even show us how to change his dressings. He would have healed him like he healed me and Anneliesa.

But he disappeared without a trace more than a year ago. Just like that, he and his entire family were gone. No one knew where. And no one dared press the matter or they would disappear, too.

"Three weeks," Mutti said as if speaking to herself.

"It will take a lot longer than that to recover, but at least he's home and can—."

"No," she interrupted, her gaze firm on the ceiling, her voice dull. "Three weeks. He has to report back in three weeks."

Something caught in my throat, a guttural noise escaping my lips.

"What do you mean, go back? What kind of butcher sends a wounded soldier back into battle?"

Mutti's head jerked, settling her eyes on me, "Shhh. He'll hear you."

"Who? Vati or Hitler?" I lowered my voice. "Mutti, it must be a mistake. What will one less soldier mean to them?"

"It's not for us to decide. It never has been. He already has his orders to return, but—but not to France."

I looked at her expectantly. Maybe there was hope. Maybe he would be sent to Berlin for administrative duties or some other city nearby.

"Where?" I pleaded.

Mutti lifted a shaking hand to cover her eyes, her face turning white. I recognized the expression now. It was fear, maybe even despair.

She took in a long breath.

"Russia."

I gasped again, my entire body cringing in repulsion. An inner rage steeped inside like boiling oil. I wanted to scream at the top of my lungs and weep at the same time. I wanted to burst through the bedroom door and beg Vati to stay.

To hide him in the closet.

To fake his own death.

To escape to the countryside.

Anything to avoid going back.

Going there.

Hitler promised he wouldn't invade Russia, but like all his promises, it didn't come true. He forged ahead with a surprise summer offensive six months earlier. It wasn't long after when more and more letters arrived to friends and neighbors expressing empty condolences over the death of a husband, a father, a son, a brother.

The Russians were known to be brutal, even savage. They'd massacre entire villages and burn them to the ground. They'd torture and kill enemy soldiers rather than take them prisoner. Their lust for vengeance and victory was unstoppable.

But Hitler didn't care.

So many promises. So many lies.

CHAPTER 14
January 1942

Within the week, Vati was well enough to eat at the table with the family. But the conversations were somber, consisting mostly of Vati reporting on how he was feeling and how sorry he was he couldn't cut down a tree for Christmas. I doubted the ranger would issue a permit for something so frivolous anyway, especially since the Reich was trying to banish Christmas every chance it got.

No one sold ornaments in the shops anymore, unless they had Nazi symbols on them, and most of the aluminum and glass was going toward the war effort. Our own ornaments sat tucked away in a box somewhere.

The Reich even came up with new lyrics to *Silent Night* hailing the Führer as the savior, not Jesus. And stars on top of Christmas trees were replaced with swastikas. No more celebrating the birth of a baby in Bethlehem.

The birth of a Jew, no less.

We reassured Vati it didn't matter whether we had a tree. And it didn't. Werner, now eleven, didn't feel the same way. He remembered Christmases past and visits from St. Nikolaus who brought candy and chocolates. But St. Nick had since been replaced with a pagan god named Odin.

I couldn't remember what chocolate tasted like.

At age five, Anneliesa had little recollection of what a real Christmas might be like. For her, it wasn't much different than any other day. She didn't remember the days of flickering candles and how they made the silver tinsel glitter, reflecting streams of light around the room like some fairy wonderland. She didn't remember the Christmas feasts of braised pork with red cabbage and luxurious tortes adorning the table, nor the best Christmas of all when Vati surprised us from behind the parlor door.

Those days were gone.

Unlike the early days of the war, we learned how to better manage our food rations, and Mutti and I got creative, stretching them out as long as we could. But the onset of another frigid winter meant we'd likely have to barter them for wood and coal again, if we could find any.

But we didn't share many of those facts with Vati. Our situation was easy compared to what he faced and especially so in light of what was still to come. Mutti abandoned our plan of conserving our rations and used them to purchase flour and some meat so Vati could build back his strength.

Opa and Oma Michaelis came to visit, but didn't stay long. Vati wasn't much for conversation. It mostly focused on the contents of letters from his brother, my Uncle Willi, who was also away at war.

When Oma mentioned the black lines crossing off parts of Uncle Willi's letters, Vati turned to Mutti with questioning eyes. When she nodded, his jaw clenched tightly and he stared at the floor the rest of the time, as though he were unaware company was in the room.

When Opa and Oma declared their intentions to leave, Vati snapped out of his trance long enough to walk them to the door. Before they left, there were long embraces and well wishes from Opa to stay safe.

Oma didn't want to let go, digging her head into Vati's chest. When she pulled away, she drew her hands to the sides of his face, holding him still and forcing him to look in her tear-filled eyes.

"You be a good boy," she said, as though Vati were a little child.

Vati stared hard and long, his eyes searching, peering as if trying to engrave her features into his stony blue eyes. Oma's thumb swiped softly across Vati's cheek, erasing a salty drop before it cascaded to the floor. He bent low to kiss her on the cheek, and they left.

News of Germany declaring war on the United States added to the heaviness in the air. Did Hitler think his Wehrmacht armed forces could conquer the world, even countries an ocean away?

He did. And just when I thought my disgust for him

couldn't grow more intense, a new root of bitterness took hold, clinging to the depths of my soul with its spidery tentacles.

I cursed him for what he was doing to Vati and countless other fathers. Vati wasn't himself. I longed for his laughter and quick wit. To see the way he playfully teased Mutti as she washed dishes or folded laundry, the way he used to touch her waist when he reached for a glass with a sideways glance and a smirk.

I yearned for the days when we'd go to the forest or the Sportplatz where he'd cheer me on, how he'd run up the bleachers two at a time to watch from the top for a better view.

His vigor was gone, and so was his spirit.

The calendar turned to 1942 and Vati slowly felt better, but it was impossible for him to improve enough to report for duty in another week.

Stories of battles in every direction were told over the radio, telling of tanks and trucks, bombs and Blitzkriegs, planes and paratroopers. And in the middle of the battlefield, I envisioned a high-strung horse stepping skittishly on its back heels, no match for the onslaught of machinery and fire power. It was spooked from the blasts of gunfire and canons, pounding at the ground with its hooves, its shrill neighing and thrashing head signaling its unwillingness to obey.

And in the saddle, Vati fumbled with the reins with one arm while the other dangled like a broken branch at his side. He dug in with his heels and screamed commands to no avail.

I had to put the thought out of my mind or I'd go crazy. I couldn't let my incessant worrying of what might be, rob me of what was right in front of me.

During the last week, Vati met with each of us alone. Anneliesa first, who practically considered him a strange visitor. She often asked me what Vati was like and I'd tell stories of how strong he was, how he made me laugh, and how he lavished us with affection.

That's not the man who came home, and Anneliesa must have wondered why I would concoct such imaginary stories about him.

Werner remembered, though, and his once boyish disposition was replaced with serious expressions of uncertainty. Vati encouraged him to do his chores, work hard in school, and to listen to Mutti's instructions above all else. From the looks of it, he took it to heart and vowed to do better.

When my turn came, Vati and I sat at the table, a steeping cup of rosehip tea in front of each of us. The water slowly turned a deep burgundy, sending its tangy aroma up in swirls of steam.

He asked me about my time at Pflichtjahr, and I only told him I was glad it was over. I didn't want to go into the horrible details and upset him. Instead, I talked about my plans to attend Berufsschule, a vocational trade school in Wolfenbüttel where I planned to pursue my education to become a Kindergarten teacher. Classes would begin soon, and an apprenticeship as a nanny for two small children in Braunschweig was already secured.

I didn't want to talk about life going on after Vati left,

but the topic brought a smile to his face and a light to his eyes, so I obliged.

"Waltraud," the mood shifted and the smile was gone.

"You're growing up and you'll want to make a life for yourself one day. But listen to me. You need to help your mother take care of the family."

I searched his eyes with confusion. Didn't Mutti tell him about my hard work, about the cooking and cleaning and caring for Anneliesa? I was already helping. Or was he somehow suggesting he no longer could?

"Of course, Vati. But maybe the war will end soon and we won't have to worry about it. Maybe you'll be sent back home and—"

Vati's stare returned, burning a hole into the table. He reached for his tea and held the thin handle, but the cup chattered against the dish underneath.

He let go.

Who was I kidding? The end? Each day was a new beginning of another horror story dragging on for ages.

"When will it be over, Vati?"

More staring.

"Hitler said it would be quick, yet he keeps going and going."

Silence.

I grew more upset with each quiet interval. Not upset at Vati, but at the insanity of it all.

"And now he thinks he can fight the Americans, too? It's like he can't be satisfied, like he thinks soldiers are expendable. If one dies, he sends another. A boy down the street was drafted. A boy! There's already half a million soldiers dead, and half the cities are bombed. And that madman is sending children to their graves!"

"Quiet!" Vati slammed the table with his fist.

The force sent tea sloshing over the rim of my cup, spilling it onto the tablecloth and staining it blood red. I sat stunned.

I didn't realize I was yelling until it rattled in my ears and his fist hit the table. But even so, Vati never raised his voice, no matter how heated I or anyone else might get.

Never.

He swept his hand through his hair and panted as though he'd run a race. He let out a sigh.

"I'm sorry," he said.

"No, I'm the one who's sorry. I shouldn't have said it. I was disrespectful. I need to keep things to myself."

"There are ears all around us." His hand nervously stroked an imaginary beard.

"Be careful, Waltraud. Stay quiet. I've seen soldiers sent to the front lines or simply disappearing all together for much less."

It was a rare glimpse into what Vati witnessed in the war. In the past few weeks, he couldn't bring himself to share about what he saw or what he did. Our only inklings were the night terrors. Indecipherable screams punctured the darkness, seeping through walls and writhing through the hallway to our bedroom.

"Yes, Vati. I'll be careful," I wish I never said what I said, and yet I meant every word.

There was more unbearable silence. I had to change the subject.

"I'll earn thirty-five Pfennigs an hour working as a nanny, and I promise I'll put it to good use. I'll do my best to help Mutti and the family."

"Good," he said, nodding his head slowly.

He closed his eyes and inhaled a big, long breath through his nose, his chest filling with air, then released it slowly through his lips as if blowing out candles in slow motion. He nodded again.

"You're a good girl."

"I'm almost fifteen, Vati." I forced a smile, trying to lighten the mood with a teasing remark.

He looked at me as if noticing for the first time how I'd grown, turning his head sideways with a contorted grin and furrowed brow. He parted his lips as if to say something, but nothing came out.

Did he notice only then how many years he'd missed, how many memories could have been made but weren't? Words finally matched his lips.

"Yes, you're—you're practically a young lady." He managed a forced smile. "I imagine the boys are after you."

I blushed, shaking my head.

"But you'll always be my little Liebling," he said with shimmering eyes.

"Always."

To hear those endearing words filled my soul and crushed it at the same time.

"I can't do it, Vati. I can't watch you leave again."

Our eyes met and he gave a wistful smile.

"Ah, but you can. You are Waltraud. Your very name

means strength."

He grasped my hand and pierced me with his blue eyes.

"You are unstoppable, and you will persevere."

"How?"

"The way it's always been done since the beginning of time. Love. Kindness. Faithfulness. Standing up for what you know is right in your heart. It's all in there, Waltraud."

He held his palm to my chest, then lifted my chin and softly patted my cheek. He grinned with sparkling eyes, willing me to believe.

"I want you to have this," he said, reaching in his pocket.

He took out a small ivory-colored cloth bag. A thin, red satin string cinched it shut. I was perplexed as he slid it across the table.

"Open it."

My hand reached for the bag and pried it open. Stretching my fingers inside, I touched what felt like a coin. I tipped it upside-down and a small silver medallion affixed to a delicate chain fell into my palm.

"Where did you find jewelry?"

"I bought it in France," he said. "I didn't dare send it through the mail."

"Oh, Vati, it's beautiful! I can't believe—" I flipped the shiny pendant over, noticing the engraving.

"You don't like it?"

"I, I—yes, thank you."

I traced my finger over the relief of the design, trying not to tense in his presence.

"When you wear it, you can think of me. And every time you put it on, you will pray, yes? Not only for me, but for all the soldiers."

"Yes, of course. I pray every day."

He managed a smile but his eyes were dewey and hollow.

"Here, let me put it on," he said, reaching for the necklace. He stood and came around the table behind me.

I handed it to him and he attempted to open the delicate clasp, but his arm still wasn't healed and the coordination between his fingers was less than ideal.

"I can do it, Vati," I said, noticing his growing frustration.

Defeated, he gave it back to me with a sigh. I held it out in front of me, one end of the chain in either hand, watching the medallion sway gently. I pinched the clasp, drew my hands behind my neck, and secured it in place.

"There, let me see." Vati turned me to face him and he sensed my unease. "It's not the finest of pearls, I know."

"I'm sure all the BDM girls will be jealous."

I fingered the smooth edges, lifting it from my chest. I examined the embossed swastika protruding from the surface. I clasped my hand around it, holding it close to my skin, conflicted and confused after our conversation only a few minutes earlier.

On the one hand, I was compelled to treasure it as a gift from the man I loved more than anyone in the world.

On the other, I wanted to rip it from my neck and throw it across the room into a thousand pieces because it symbolized the man I hated most.

I couldn't tell Vati how the sight of the crooked cross made my stomach turn. Even though I knew the pendant meant something else, I chose to wear it as a symbol of his love and as a reminder of the soldier he so unwillingly became.

Another week passed, and after many tearful sobs and long goodbyes, he was gone.

CHAPTER 15
February 1942

My hand trembled as I pressed the door buzzer. It was cold, and I was nervous. The steely bleat of a streetcar passed behind me as I stood on the sidewalk. I slipped my boiled wool mitten back on to stave off the chill. The door opened.

"Good afternoon, Fräulein Michaelis. We've been expecting you. Sieg Heil."

A well-dressed man welcomed me and I saluted.

"May I?" He pointed to my suitcase and I handed it to him.

"Are you Herr Voigt?" I asked.

He chuckled and told me he was their butler. He escorted me up three flights of stairs to an apartment above a furniture store where he opened a large, wooden door and invited me inside. He motioned to a green velvet chair.

"Please, have a seat. Allow me to take your coat."

"Thank you."

I slipped off my brown wool coat. The inner lining near the armpit was torn and I didn't find time to repair it. I folded the coat inward to conceal the rip and handed it to the man. He draped it over his arm.

"Should I remove my shoes?" I asked, looking at my scuffed boots.

"Not necessary. I'll let Frau Voigt know you're here," he said. "Your suitcase will be in your room."

I thanked the man and he left. I stepped across an Oriental rug spanning the width of the floorboards and sat, my senses overwhelmed at the sight of the lavish decor and scent of lavender sachets. An ornate light fixture towered above me, hanging from the high, paneled ceilings. Stately woodwork framed the doors, and thick damask draperies hung from the ceiling, bordering the windows and spilling onto the floor.

A large painting of a rosy-faced woman in a vibrant blue dress adorned with lace was surrounded by a thick, gilded frame and hung above the marble fireplace.

I peered around the room in awe, my mouth agape, my back straight, and hands held tightly on my lap as if ready to meet an heiress. I didn't see any sign of children except for two small portraits of a boy and girl sitting on an upright piano in the corner. Light spilled in through the windows, gleaming off the mahogany wardrobe and tables, making it feel like summer inside even though it was still February. The matching green velvet sofa was trimmed with carved wood and piled high with silk floral pillows.

I caught my reflection in a tall mirror across the room. My plain cotton dress made me feel like a peasant, and my hair pin had slipped down the side of my head. I reached to straighten it when a woman walked in the room.

"Fräulein Michaelis!" Her dramatic voice rang out.

Startled, I stood to attention. The hair pin sprang from my fingers, pinging off a glass vase. It fell to the Oriental rug, lost forever amid its busy pattern. A lock of hair fell across my face, resting on my cheek.

"I beg your pardon. Sieg Heil!" I said nervously, then blew the curl aside through the corner of my mouth.

I wasn't sure whether to salute, but since she was technically my employer, I thought it better safe than sorry. The woman was in her early thirties and looked more fashionable than seemed appropriate for a weekday afternoon.

"I'm pleased to meet you," I said extending my hand. "You must be Frau Voigt."

"The one and only." She smiled and shook my hand. "Have a seat."

I sat once again on the edge of the chair in as ladylike a position as I knew how.

"Wilhelmina," she called, turning to her side.

An elderly woman in a black apron with her hair wound tightly in a bun emerged through the doorway.

"Tea for me and our guest, please!" Frau Voigt turned to me. "Or do you prefer coffee? We have real coffee," she said with a lilt in her voice.

I was surprised but tried not to show it. Coffee

supplies were cut off and the closest thing most Germans had in two years was roasted chicory root. I was tempted to try it, but never had it before and thought it better to not take the risk, lest I not like it.

"Tea, please."

The woman nodded with a slight bow and turned to walk away. Frau Voigt spoke in rapid succession, as though she'd already had too much caffeine herself. I examined her features, a soft complexion and big blue eyes, her thick, dark blonde hair pinned away from her face and falling on her shoulders in soft curls, her cheeks rosy and plump. I drew my gaze to the portrait above the fireplace.

"Yes, dear. That's me. I thought it far too pretentious, but Karl, that's my husband, he insisted it be commissioned. You have no idea how many hours I sat in that God-awful dress looking over my shoulder with that pensive grin."

"It's lovely," I said.

It was.

"Ah, you're too kind. So, tell me about yourself."

I didn't have much to say. The pain of Vati returning to fight in the war only a few weeks earlier was still fresh on my mind. I nervously fidgeted with my necklace and shared about Mutti, Werner, and Anneliesa, and about my love of knitting and handiwork. I thought it might come in handy.

I only mentioned in passing about Vati being away at war. But I dared not speak of him in more detail or about his recent stint at home and his injuries for fear of bursting into tears in front of a complete stranger. All his talk about being strong would take some practice.

Wilhelmina returned with a beautiful porcelain tea pot and matching cups and saucers on a silver tray. She placed it on the coffee table.

"Do you care for sugar or honey?" Frau Voigt asked.

It had been ages since I had honey with my tea.

"Honey, please."

"It's wonderful to have so many of our brave men fighting so valiantly for the Fatherland," she said.

I simply mumbled, "Hmmm," neither agreeing nor disagreeing while stirring my tea with a tiny silver spoon.

Wonderful? Far from it. I lifted the tea to my lips, the sweet honey coating my tongue and soothing my throat that suddenly went dry.

"And Herr Voigt?" I asked, staring at the vibrant flowers bordering the edge of my tea cup. "He hasn't been drafted?"

"Who, Karl? Ha!" Her laughter was blind to the pang of sadness in my voice as I spoke of Vati.

"Karl's too old. He practically robbed the cradle when he married me."

She bent forward as if to tell a secret and spoke in low tones. "He's already in his fifties, dear. Ah, but he's a good man, and oh, does he love those children."

"That's nice to hear."

"Well, let's get on to business. I thought it best to get you situated before I introduced you to the children and talk through their routines, so I had Karl get them out of the house for a while. Shall I show you where you'll be staying?"

She led me through a doorway and down a corridor lined with artwork in every nook. As I followed behind, I reached out to touch the shimmering wallpaper, striped with varying shades of beige and cream.

"Here we are," she said as she unlatched the door and invited me inside.

My suitcase sat next to an ottoman at the foot of a large bed with a thick, white featherbed. Another oriental rug spread across oak wooden floors, and lace curtains were flanked by pastel floral draperies and a matching cornice. A bedroom set inlaid with intricate marquetry lined the walls including a headboard, footboard, dresser, and side table.

"It's beautiful," I said. "The furniture and decorations, I've never seen anything like it."

"Well, it should be. Karl and his brother own the furniture store downstairs. We get the pick of the lot. His older brother and his wife live on the second floor. Pays to be the shop owner."

I couldn't imagine who would buy such fine furnishings or hire an interior decorator during a war, but I knew there were those in the Reich who lived in comfort while the rest of us scraped by.

"And you? Do you stay home with the children?" I asked.

"Ha! Not if I can help it!"

Her forwardness left me dumbfounded.

"Don't get me wrong," she said. "I love my children, but I can't imagine being cooped up with them twenty-four hours a day. There's a reason we hired a nanny."

"Oh?"

"I need to devote my time to the theatre, dear. The opera, to be more precise. Soprano."

Without warning, she let out a high-pitch operatic trill. It bounced off the walls like a rubber ball and threatened to break the windows. The power in her voice caught me by utter surprise. I stood, stunned.

She laughed. "You better get used to it, Fräulein. I'm bound to break into song at any given moment."

I released my tension and smiled.

"Call me Waltraud, please."

"Ah, good. The children can call you Tante Waltraud."

I liked the idea of being called an aunt.

"You've not seen my name in playbooks? I'm quite well known in the music business."

"I'm sorry. I'm not familiar with the arts."

I was too embarrassed to tell her the only entertainment I took in were mandatory propaganda films shown during BDM meetings. The one time I stepped foot inside a real theatre was for a production of Cinderella as a child on a school field trip, a story about a girl who didn't fit in and wanted to escape the harsh realities of life. I had an affinity with the lowly servant girl.

I thought to bring up the production, how we even got a tour of the backstage and saw how the stage turned like a carousel with different scenes, but stopped short.

"Well, we'll have to get some culture in your life. Our beloved Führer is a big fan of the opera scene, you know.

It's thrived since he's been in charge. Did you know when he lived in Vienna as a young man, he used to attend performances nearly every day?"

I bristled at the thought of Hitler perched comfortably in an opulent opera house surrounded by lush velvet and gilded columns, being serenaded by arias and orchestras while millions of his soldiers cowered in trenches trying to drown out the blasts of grenades and machine guns.

"Oh, he loves Wagner. Can't get enough of it. Do you have a favorite Wagner piece? Oh, I suppose not. Anyway…"

She didn't notice I had long disengaged with her staccato'd remarks. But then again, she was the type of woman who carried on entire conversations without anyone else in the room.

She strode past the bed and opened a door.

"You can hang your clothes in this closet, and…" She opened another door. "…here is your bathroom."

Beyond the door sat a toilet, bathtub, and a sink surrounded by shiny white tiled floors and walls.

Was this real? My own private room? An indoor toilet? At home, I shared a room with Werner and we still used an outhouse.

"I hope it's to your liking. I wanted to replace the bedroom drapes before you came, but our supplier in Paris is having a terrible time getting goods. This damn war sure is messing up the textile industry."

Was Frau Voigt oblivious? That unaware? The entire world was engulfed in a blazing inferno and couldn't be doused, but her biggest concern was new curtains.

But I had to admit, I liked Frau Voigt in spite of her eccentric personality. It was refreshing to be in the presence of someone who didn't live with a continual frown or speak in morose tones all the time. And I liked the idea of shutting away the war and keeping it at bay behind a veil of pretty lace curtains.

"But I suppose there are worse things to worry about than redecorating a spare bedroom," she acknowledged. "But hopefully all this war business will be over soon and we can get back to normal, and your father can come home."

I nodded in wishful agreement, glad she acknowledged my plight.

"Speaking of which," she said as she walked toward the door to the hallway. "In case of an air raid, we use the basement. It's built like a fortress and we've got it stocked with everything we need. It's plenty comfortable down there. Mattresses, chairs, lanterns, canned goods, even a game table to keep the children occupied."

Talk of the bomb shelter wasn't exactly what I had in mind when I dreamed of shutting away the war, but I tucked away the information in hopes I wouldn't need it.

"Thank you for your kindness," I said.

"Why don't you unpack your things and meet me in the living room in a few minutes. We'll go over everything then."

Frau Voigt excused herself and shut the door behind her. I slid a drawer of the dresser and placed some items inside, then opened the closet door. The woodsy smell of cedar wafted from inside, reminding me of a peaceful forest. I hung the two nicest dresses I owned, other than the one I wore, in the closet along with my BDM uniform. I unlaced my boots and slipped on my loafers.

I examined the room in its fullness, taking in its fine features. I removed my knitting needles and yarn from the suitcase and set them aside. The bone in my wrist still protruded slightly after my injury at Pflichtjahr, but aside from the occasional ache, it healed well enough and didn't affect my handiwork.

I grabbed my toiletry bag, snapped the suitcase shut, and entered the bathroom to place my bar of lye soap on the sink. But a bar of soap was already there, finely milled and embossed with flowers and French writing. I picked it up and breathed in its aroma. It smelled like roses.

I turned on the sink and swirled the soap in my hands, its lather silky smooth, then patted them dry with a fancy embroidered towel. I lifted my fingers to my nose, closing my eyes in pleasure.

When I opened them, my reflection looked back at me from the mirror and I unleashed an involuntary smile, shaking my head in disbelief over my good fortune. To think less than a year ago I was at my lowest, a practical slave who did backbreaking labor and smelled of swine excrement. And now I stood inside a virtual palace, smelling of rose petals and being waited on like royalty.

I chuckled and placed a new hair pin in my hair, then walked through the bedroom toward the hallway. I grasped the brass door handle and stopped.

I forgot something.

Clutching my hands, I let out a laugh. I scampered

across the room, nearly tripping over the ottoman. I caught myself on the corner of the bed and flung myself around, my skirt twirling as I went. I steadied my legs and landed in front of the bathroom door. I swung it open and stepped inside.

I didn't dare leave without peeing in my very own toilet.

CHAPTER 16
Spring 1942

E va was five, an extremely bright girl who had a big imagination. She loved making up stories to tell me and her doll. They almost always included singing woodland creatures and a lost princess.

She had a gift for music like her mother, sometimes humming an intricate tune I didn't recognize. When I asked her what it was, she shrugged her shoulders, saying it was something she heard a bird once sing.

Peter was three, and his favorite word was *why* in response to most anything I said.

"Let's put on our shoes now."

"Why?"

"It's story time."

"Why?"

"You have to wait until two o'clock to have a biscuit."

"Why?"

In the morning, I prepared breakfast for the children,

perhaps some eggs or muesli. Wilhelmina arrived mid-morning to make lunch and then clean and do laundry until it was time to prepare dinner for the family. There was plenty of food and I didn't have to cook. What a relief!

We'd fill our mornings with lessons and stories, crafts, drawing, or reading a book. Eva was learning her letters and mouthed out many written words. In addition to animals, she loved learning about the different types of musical instruments from a book her mother bought her. Peter knew most of his colors, with red being his favorite.

Frau Voigt practiced singing scales by the piano after lunch, starting low and ending in a high pitch vibrato. I swore it could shatter glass if she held it a second longer. They were complex melodies thrust out in a language I didn't understand. Italian, I think. And half the time, I don't think she was singing any words at all, only belting out melodic gibberish.

The woman had a lung capacity three times greater than the average human, and I once jokingly suggested if the air raid sirens ever malfunctioned, the city should give her a call to do the job. Both she and Herr Voigt had a good belly laugh over that one. I was thankful they had senses of humor.

It felt good to laugh.

As soon as her mother started singing, though, Eva came to me with expectant eyes.

"Tante Waltraud, can we go to the park now?"

I'd enthusiastically agree it was a good idea. I couldn't hear myself think!

We'd stroll the ancient streets of Braunschweig until we arrived at the park with thick grass and a small play set for the children. They'd run off some energy as I watched while leaning against a tree or on a bench, simultaneously taking in the spring mating calls of birds, trying to listen for the tunes Eva sang once in a while.

The way they hid behind trees or played with a ball reminded me of Werner and myself when we were little. Carefree. Unaware anything at all was wrong with the world. Occasionally, I'd take them aside to teach them about different plants, birds, or small animals, just like Vati taught me when I was their age.

When the weather was bad, we'd go to the fourth floor attic where laundry was hung to dry and pretend to camp underneath draped sheets and blankets, sometimes roasting imaginary Weisswurst over an imaginary fire and telling stories of imaginary trolls who watched us from behind the chimney stacks.

In the evenings, I had a break from teaching and caring for the children. Herr Voigt played with them or simply let them sit on his lap while he listened to the radio before bedtime. They were closer to their father than their mother, reminding me of my own relationship with Vati and how, as a child, he sat us on his lap and read a book or told a story.

I watched them interact, quietly taking in their laughter or listening to Eva repeat the day's lessons, all while the click of my knitting needles kept time. Sometimes I'd knit a small dress for Eva's doll or a pair of slippers for Peter.

"You have such fine workmanship," said Herr Voigt

one evening. "You'd fetch twenty Reichsmarks for the sweater you made with the cable stitching."

I was a bit surprised he knew what a cable stitch was, and the idea of someone paying so much money for a homemade sweater sounded absurd. But his circle of friends was different than mine.

On Tuesdays, I'd go to classes all day in Wolfenbüttel. I'd be to the train station early in the morning and wouldn't get home until nearly dark. I still attended BDM meetings twice a week where I got to see Liesa, which is the only thing I looked forward to about them. Sunday was when I came home for visits. I didn't have much free time.

Mutti made good use of the extra money I brought home. And I was glad Werner was keeping his promise to help out more around the house. Other than the occasional air raid at night, it didn't feel like war, yet the constant worry over Vati and the rumblings of barbaric losses to the Red Army weighed heavily.

Shortly before my fifteenth birthday, Frau Voigt announced it was high time I visited the opera to get some of that culture she talked about.

"I've already got your ticket for this Saturday's performance. My present," she beamed.

Did she sense my panic? She already saw the three best dresses I owned. The thought of me sitting among the elite in a boring knee-length day dress with brown wooden buttons mortified me.

I could picture it—hundreds of women with painted lips wearing silk organza, hanging on the arms of tuxedoed men who wore bow ties and bowler hats. And there I'd be without a gown to wear to the ball and no fairy godmother to magically make one appear. An obvious outcast.

"It's very kind of you, Frau Voigt," I said. "But I don't have anything appropriate to wear."

"Nonsense, you must have seen the trunks in the attic."

There were, indeed, several trunks stacked in the attic, but I didn't know what was inside them.

"Do you know how many gowns I've owned over the years? I can't bear to get rid of them or donate them to charity. It's not like our soldiers will be wearing silk and satin on the battlefield. Wouldn't it be a hoot?"

The preposterous idea of it made me laugh. She led me to the top floor, then shifted one trunk aside and opened another, rummaging through a stack of clothing.

"No, definitely not appropriate," she said to herself as she flung a red silky dress to the side. "Ah, here's the one I was thinking of."

She pulled out a long gown and held it by its shoulders. The smell of moth balls hung in the air.

"We'll have to air it out with some sachets and give it a good pressing," she said.

She examined it and fluffed the skirt.

"I was several sizes smaller back then, so it should fit. Let's go try it on."

Frau Voigt dashed down the stairs excitedly and I followed her into my bedroom. She gathered the skirt around her arms, giddy at the idea of dressing me up, as if she were Eva's age and I was a doll being dressed in a new outfit. I slipped out of my dress and wrangled myself inside the layers of fabric as she helped pull it over my head.

"All right, turn around and I'll button you up," she said.

When she was finished she spun me around.

"Ravishing, dear. Simply ravishing!" She exuded pure joy. "Here, why don't you see."

She took my hand and guided me across the room. I surveyed myself in the mirror and my cheeks burned hot at the spectacle of me in a liquid satin gown.

"I got this one in Berlin before the war from a very good designer. It's still in fashion, though," she said as she puffed up the sleeves. "It could use a little altering at the waist, but you're so handy with a needle and thread I'm sure you can whip it up in no time."

I examined the stitching on the sleeve and could tell it was finely made. It was a pastel copper, like apricot jam. It wouldn't have been my first choice of color, but the way it reflected the afternoon rays of sunlight coming through the window made it shimmer, bringing a sudden change of heart.

The bodice clung to my frame and came to a V at my waist, releasing a parade of fabric beneath. The full skirt draped over my hips and swept to the floor.

Soft folds of fabric and a light overlay of gathered chiffon in the same color crisscrossed my flat chest, making it look much larger than it was. The sleeves puffed out at the shoulders, then conformed to my slender arms down to my wrists.

Maybe I'd be Cinderella after all with Frau Voigt as my fairy godmother.

The night of the opera arrived and Herr Voigt stayed home to watch the children while his wife performed and I enjoyed a rare night out.

In the preceding days, Frau Voigt chose more items to complement my dress. I slipped on white satin gloves and wore sparkly dangling earrings. A fancy broach inlaid with rhinestones was pinned below my shoulder, or perhaps they were real diamonds. I didn't dare ask.

A small silver clutch with a delicate chain hung from my wrist containing a white lace handkerchief to use in case the music moved me in such a way that it was necessary to dab my eyes. The final touch was a silver barrette with mother of pearl to hold back my shock of red hair set in curlers the night before.

I felt like a little girl playing dress-up, only this time it was real.

My escort arrived wearing a dapper tuxedo, an older cousin of Frau Voigt. Because I was a minor, an adult over the age of twenty-one had to accompany me. He was cordial and formal, extending his arm.

"You look lovely, Fräulein."

I blushed.

He led me to the front seat of his car. I had never been inside a car before, let alone in a long dress. How in the world was I supposed to fit in there? My chaperone gave a sideways look when I hiked up my skirt and plopped in the front seat. I'm sure it got wrinkled, but I figured I had no choice in the matter. I gathered the fabric and shoved it under my legs so it wouldn't get caught in the door when he closed it.

Upon our arrival, I fluffed out my skirt and took in the swarm of people in their best attire. I clung to my escort's arm, not letting go for a second for fear I'd lose him among the throng. In my beautiful dress, maybe I didn't look out of place.

Mammoth crystal chandeliers reflected off the white plaster walls and gilded columns. The air was filled with a pungent mix of women's perfume and men's cologne, a jarring fusion of floral and musk hanging like a curtain amid the colossal archways.

We found our seats in the balcony overlooking an expansive room filled with rows and rows of red velvet arching from one side to the other.

The orchestra began, a soft melding of horns and woodwind joined by a swell of cellos and violins. Fingers blurred against black and white keys on the grand piano, and the entire symphony increased in intensity to a feverish pitch, an ominous sense of suspense tingling in my chest.

The conductor's baton swung wildly, his hair flipping from side to side, strands clinging to beads of sweat on his brow. His hands suspended in the air, his entire body quivering as the tympani rolled, louder and louder.

With a flip of his wrists, silence.

I didn't realize I was holding my breath. Then, a release. The conductor hunched low and a single note emerged from the French horn section, holding long and steady. My shoulders relaxed and I leaned forward, wrapping my fingers around the brass railing. The curtain opened to reveal the intricate scene of a walled garden with cascading vines and archways.

Out strode Frau Voigt in a lavish gown trimmed in embroidered ribbon, gliding across the stage as if on wheels, her steps imperceptible.

I already considered her an attractive woman, but she was otherworldly in layers upon layers of fabric billowing around her. Her hair was coiled above her head in a perfect braid, her eyes rimmed in black, her cheeks pink, her lips bright red.

And there it was. A familiar voice.

Only this time it matched the room, lofting to the balcony and beyond, echoing in gentle waves off the high ceiling, swirling through the crowd who sat transfixed in awe.

As was I.

Instead of an ear-piercing shrill, her voice was soft and gentle, as if kissing the top of my forehead. With each movement, it transitioned between moments of both frailty and power. Vulnerable and dazzling at the same time.

Others joined her on stage, sometimes in an impassioned call and response, sometimes in haunting harmonies. It was an ocean, ebbing and flowing, sometimes crashing against the rocks, sometimes lapping against the shore, somehow holding me afloat in the vast unknown.

As I took it all in, the world almost felt right.

Almost.

I unclasped the silver clutch on my lap and removed the lace handkerchief, raising it to my cheek.

I knew the truth.

The world was not right.

CHAPTER 17
November 1942

Working for the Voigt family was a dream come true, but my conscience was constantly pricked by the guilt of living in such comfort while the world around me was falling apart.

I was especially guilt-ridden when thinking of Vati who was a world away in horrid conditions somewhere to the east. We only received two letters since he was redeployed to fight in Russia. It was unlike him to not write more often.

His first letter spoke mostly of the brutal winter weather and unspeakable cold when he arrived, how he was shivered to the bone and couldn't feel his toes. I imagined him trudging through waist-high snow and cracking through ice-covered streams, unable to shield his face from the driving wind.

Another harsh winter was in full swing and I feared for him with increasing anxiety. Did he have enough to eat and warm enough clothes? Were his boots worn? Did the barracks provide enough shelter? Or did he spend his time in fox holes surrounded by enemy fire?

He again urged us to stay strong and brave, and to pray more fervently for the setbacks to be temporary so he could come home.

> *...don't worry about me. I am getting along. Though others have fallen and the crack of artillery surrounds us, I still have a guardian angel watching over me. I miss you all with a longing my soul cannot endure. My heart dreams of the life we once knew. We'll be together again soon, if the Lord wills.*
>
> *With all my love,*
> *Gustav*

The second letter spoke of summer's heat, the bad roads, how poor the Russian people were in the countryside, and his constant longing for home.

> *...the enemy is strong and they have an unlimited supply of fresh, young men. Our group is growing fewer in numbers and more tired every day. There is little rest, but we must press on. Keep praying it will all be over soon so we can be together again. It's hard to know how things will end or if peace will come, but we need to stay strong. My love for you, dear ones, is never ending. Oh, to feel the warmth of your embrace and see the smiles on your faces.*
>
> *Send my greetings to all,*
> *Gustav*

I kept praying, but my prayers were like puffs of smoke ascending into the air and dispersing in the wind. I desperately wanted another letter, but the postman was empty-handed. The last three letters I mailed hadn't gotten a response. Did he even get them or the wool socks I included in a small parcel?

Meanwhile, the lists of names in the newspaper's obituary section spanned more pages than they had before, filling me with dread.

And there was a familiar name among them. Vati's brother, Uncle Willi. The news of his death shattered me, sending me into a tailspin of fear and panic over whether Vati would face the same fate. It was unbearable. Opa and Oma Michaelis were devastated, and Mutti was more worried than ever.

More and more nights were spent in the Voigt's basement as the frequency of air raids multiplied. Despite its relative comfort, each time we descended to the cellar, it became more and more like an underground tomb encasing me within its thick stone walls. There was no sense of time, and while waiting for the all clear, my chest tightened and my insides twisted as the walls closed in around me, certain we'd be buried alive.

Even Frau Voigt who was the eternal optimist expressed dismay on occasion at the bombed-out buildings in other parts of town. And the radio broadcasts told of bombings and their destruction in other cities. Düsseldorf. Bremen. Berlin. Hamburg. Hannover. Munich.

Every major city in Germany was getting hit, including

Braunschweig.

And small cities, too. One attack unleashed thousands of pounds of bombs on Frankfurt, but most of them missed their target and landed on a small town less than twenty-five kilometers away. Their poor aim became the brunt of many jokes, jokes no one laughed at.

If night raids weren't bad enough, bomber planes started coming during the daytime with hardly any warning. While attending classes in Wolfenbüttel, air raid sirens wailed. Screaming students came bolting into the hallway, knocking anything in their path to the floor, including me.

"Get to the bunker!" cried one young man.

"But it's the middle of the day," I yelled, wrangling myself upright and gathering my books.

Someone grabbed my arm and pulled me up, swinging me around.

"Just run!"

We ran into the street, rushing to the bunker a block away. No time to grab our coats. Adrenaline pumped through my body, making the crisp air feel warm as I sprinted down the street.

"Cover your head," someone yelled at me. "They'll see your red hair!"

I'd never heard anything so ridiculous, but I raised my textbook and covered my head, nonetheless.

The thunderous onslaught of bombers combined with the whir of propellors. The blue sky was filled with white, wispy ribbons trailing behind dozens of planes as they flew overhead. Their shadows slithered across the ground like giant winged ghosts, practically blocking out the sun.

Chest heaving, heart racing, throat raw from the cold air filling my lungs, I ran. I tripped. One of my books tumbled to the ground, its pages flapping in the wind. I scrambled back up, ignoring the tear in my dress and my bloody elbow.

Would I make it to the bunker in time? Or would a bomb descend down, down, down, blasting me into oblivion and splattering my flesh against the cobblestones?

I made it, and the planes flying overhead didn't drop their bombs on us. They were aiming for Braunschweig again, less than twenty-five kilometers away.

The danger was intensifying and everyone was on edge every hour of every day. Mutti was increasingly concerned living near the city and even more concerned with me living directly in it.

"We're moving to Ampleben," she announced one Sunday. "It's safer there. I want you to come, too."

Ampleben was a small village plopped in the countryside southeast of Braunschweig with only a couple hundred people. Somehow Mutti found work there in a bakery. But I dismissed Mutti's concerns and said I needed to stay to help earn money and finish my education.

Was I being selfish? Was I being persuaded by the lure of abundant food and the comfort of having my own room and indoor bathroom? Was it clouding my judgment and overshadowing reason?

I still had a year left to complete my schooling, and the

Voigt family already told me they would hire me permanently as a nanny to teach their children once my apprenticeship was complete.

I hated how the war threatened my future, threatened everyone's future, and I stood my ground. Mutti packed up the house in preparation for the move while I kept working.

On Sundays, I helped clean out closets and cupboards, but had a twinge of sadness as life was taking another twist.

"Why don't you and Werner go in the attic to make sure we don't have anything stored up there," Mutti instructed as we worked one Sunday. "I think I put a trunk of your father's clothes and old suits up there."

Werner and I climbed the ladder and felt a chill. A small ray of light shone on the attic floor. I knew the house was in disrepair since Vati left, but I didn't realize the roof had a hole in it. I'd have to inform Mutti. It would be someone else's problem now.

I turned on the single light bulb and knelt before the small, lonely trunk tucked beneath an eave. I unlatched the lid and opened it slowly, my eyes blurred by tears.

I tensed at the sight of Vati's things stuffed away in a drafty attic, out of sight and out of mind. I suspect Mutti was sad, even bitter, every time she opened the closet door in her bedroom to see Vati's suits hanging there, a constant reminder of the absurdity of it all and how he was gone. His unworn clothes mocked our once idyllic family, lifeless shells of deflated woven tweed that used to hold a man. Her man.

I, too, felt a deep longing for Vati's presence at the sight of his perfectly folded clothes. Yes, I understood why she put them away.

I snapped it shut.

"What's this thing?" Werner was scouring the rest of the attic for anything forgotten.

"Not sure," I said. I dragged the trunk near the opening leading downstairs.

I focused my eyes in the dim light and walked around the chimney to see what he found, right into a cobweb. I recoiled, picking dusty strands from my hair and face.

"Maybe it's a secret chamber!" said Werner.

"Ha! And what kind of secrets would be kept in our attic?" I ducked and walked toward him. "Here, let me—"

My heart stopped.

"Werner, get away!" I tried to stay calm, but my faltering voice betrayed the alarm rising within me.

"Quit yelling at me. I'm just trying to see what it is."

"Don't touch it! It's a bomb!"

Werner jerked backwards, hitting his head on a beam.

"Ow!" His scream sprang from the rafters.

"Quiet."

Werner rubbed his head and gaped at the bomb. "Is it ticking?" he said in a whisper.

"No, I don't think it's that kind."

It looked like a toy nestled among splintered wood and broken roof tiles. Small and cylindrical, about a meter long, it had drab green paint the color of dried tea leaves. Yet I knew its frightening power. There were many reports of children who were killed or lost hands from playing with undetonated grenades, bombs, or ammunition found in nearby fields. I didn't want us to be next.

We scurried on tiptoes toward the ladder. I grabbed the trunk handle, pulling it behind. Remnants of Vati couldn't be left in harm's way. We ran to tell Mutti.

She didn't believe us when we excitedly told about what we discovered in the attic. But I reminded her of another undetonated bomb in someone's backyard across town.

"There's a hole in the roof and everything!" cried Werner, frantic with fear.

She finally went to check for herself. She rushed back downstairs and ushered us out the front door. I don't think I've ever seen her so pale.

Mutti summoned the Feuerwehr. The entire fire department showed up and erected a barricade, evacuating everyone on the block. We waited across the street, terror-stricken, praying they could remove it without the entire house going up in a ball of flames.

They removed it without incident. Turned out to be an incendiary bomb, and it likely would have burned the entire block to the ground had it gone off. Our home and everything in it, our entire lives, would have been gone in a flash, and there'd be nothing for Vati to come home to.

Reality of the dangers hit home in a new way, and as the house was emptied and my family waited on the train platform for their final trip to a new home, I felt alone.

"Please, please come with us." Mutti pleaded. "I spoke with the postmaster in Ampleben last week. He has a job for you as a mail carrier."

"Mutti, I'm happy working as a nanny, and I'll still come by train on Sundays."

Her brow furrowed as she reached to grip my shoulder. She had new strands of silver in her hair and lines on her face, accentuated by the late afternoon glow of day turning to dusk. I knew she could force me to quit since I was still a minor, but I suspect she knew it was best to appeal to my reason. Or maybe she resolved I was growing up.

"Waltraud, it's too dangerous in Braunschweig now. Besides, your father is gone. I can't bear to lose you, too."

I pulled away.

"But Vati isn't lost. He's coming back," I insisted.

Mutti's words stung when she spoke of Vati in the past tense, as if he were already gone, already doomed to perish. I couldn't bring myself to lose hope in being together again. When, I didn't know, but I promised him I'd be brave and persevere, and I was doing it the best I knew how.

To be honest, I didn't know what being brave even looked like anymore. But I knew it didn't look like giving up. How dare she speak as if he were gone for good.

Mutti's doubt bothered me and I dug my heels in deeper, insisting I'd be fine and she didn't need to worry about me.

Mutti let me have that victory. They boarded the train and waved goodbye.

But deep down I knew she was right, not about Vati, of course, but about Braunschweig not being a safe place anymore. It was proven one day when I walked back to the Voigt's home from the train station.

The sirens blared, and I panicked. I didn't know where the nearest bunker was. I sprinted toward the furniture store, but the roar of approaching planes grew louder with each step.

I flung myself to the ground and lay flat like we were taught, my hands covering my head, my face plastered against the hard ground. I shook in utter terror, exposed and sprawled out on the sidewalk. I abandoned the training and curled in a ball, covering my head and leaning against a building, wailing with the sirens.

A legion of planes flew overhead and I looked up. Bombs rained from inside, falling without a sound like rocks off a cliff. I covered my head again. Explosions boomed on the outskirts of town, and shock waves traveled through the earth, creeping up my spine. I thought for sure it was the end.

But I survived. That time.

Yes, it was more dangerous than I was willing to admit, and every day was filled with constant dread of being blown to bits.

On one hand, giving up my apprenticeship meant giving up my schooling and the dream of being a teacher. But on the other, the echo of Vati's words rang true.

"You need to help take care of the family."

I knew what I had to do.

CHAPTER 18
Spring 1943

The breeze was cool against my face and my hair whipped in the wind. I rounded the corner at Elmstrasse, the main street in Ampleben, and headed toward the open road ahead.

The postmaster's old motorbike was much faster than using my bicycle for the mail route, but the engine made such a racket I swear it reached all the way to Munich. And it was unwieldy once it roared to life after pedaling it for what felt like forever.

I wondered whether the contraption was anything like the one Vati said he rode on occasion. If so, I understood why he preferred a horse on uneven terrain. Any small hole in the road practically launched me into the ditch.

I didn't mind delivering the mail once the weather got nicer, but some days made it less than enjoyable. Rain. Snow. Sleet. Cold. If only I could go back to my comfortable life as a nanny.

Maybe when the war was over I'd return to school, my apprenticeship, and the bustling streets of Braunschweig where there were endless things to do. But who knew how long it would be.

Until then, I was resigned to stay in Ampleben where the most exciting thing to do was go to the park to watch grass grow. I already thought Rautheim was small, but Ampleben made it seem like a bustling metropolis in comparison.

As Mutti suspected, the little town did feel safer than Braunschweig, but was not without its dangers. A delivery truck used to bring mail to the post office, but was routinely targeted by enemy planes. So, they started sending the mail by train to be picked up at the station in Kneitlingen a few kilometers away.

That's where I was headed.

A bug flew in my mouth and I almost lost control of the motorbike again as I coughed and spit.

"Aaagh!" I screamed to a lonely cow grazing beside the road. It looked up, unfazed.

I regained control, wrangling the bike back in a straight line. To think I could be drinking tea with honey and sitting on green velvet instead of eating bugs. Oh well.

There were still air raids, but bombs had not come to Ampleben. Yet. We heard of other villages being bombed, though. It was hard to comprehend how bombing a tiny town would make a difference in the war, but it didn't matter to the roaring lead birds overhead.

The bomb shelter was a wine cellar in the middle of

town. We'd already spent many a night there. It was damp and musty with a dirt floor, and after a while, it got hard to breathe. We nestled in between rows of bottles filled with wine and waited out the siren. It was only a block from our house, so we could get there quickly.

The Gasthaus served as the town's grocery store, post office, and restaurant. I worked there for part of the day, and it sat squarely above the wine cellar.

Herr Schulz was the shopkeeper and previous mail carrier who served as the postmaster. I'll never forget the day I met him. The bell to the shop door clanged when I opened it, and a last-minute shopper with a bag full of rations was leaving as I entered.

Out from behind the counter came an older man with a balding head surrounded by a ring of short, white hair with soft curls. His trousers were hemmed too short for his already stout legs, and he hobbled as he walked.

"Hallo, hallo! Come in!" he said.

"Are you Herr Schulz?"

"Yah, yah, you must be Fräulein Waltraud."

He was a jovial old man whose words bubbled playfully from his mouth.

"Why don't you lock the door behind you and turn around the sign." He pointed to the open/closed placard on the window. "Then we can talk uninterrupted."

"Thank you, Herr Schulz." I said as I flipped the sign.

When I turned to face him, the jovial expression was gone.

"Absolutely not! We will have none of that!"

I was taken aback. What did I do wrong? Of course, it

hit me. I didn't salute.

"I'm so sorry, Herr Schulz. Heil Hitler," I said half-heartedly, barely lifting my hand from my side.

I sighed inside. I hoped I wouldn't have to go through the routine of saluting every time I walked in the door.

"And we will definitely have none of that!" he chided. "No need for all this saluting nonsense."

His smile returned and relief flooded me. But I was surprised he spoke so openly about saluting in such a way. Some of the girls in my new BDM troop would report him for much less.

"Ah, my dear. What I mean is I will not have you calling me Herr Schulz."

"No? How do you prefer to be addressed, Herr—Uh, I mean…"

"You can call me Papa Schulz. Yah?"

He grabbed my hands in each of his and shook them approvingly with a hopeful grin.

"Your mother told me all about you and your family, and about your dear father away at war."

"Oh, I see."

Did he and most everyone in town look on us with pity? Maybe. But I knew we weren't alone. There were lots of pitiful families whose fathers, brothers, uncles, and sons no longer sat around the dinner table. Some might return, but others never would, forever lost to a pointless contest where, in the end, there were no winners. Now, our nation was mostly women, children, and the elderly trying to make it through another day.

He lifted my chin and held me at arms length by the

shoulders, looking me straight in the eyes.

"I don't ever want to suggest I could take his place, of course. But, until he returns, you can let me fill in. Yes? So, Papa Schulz it is?"

How could I say no? He was full of light and kindness, with the most infectious smile brimming beneath his white mustache. His cheeks were full and pink, and his eyes twinkled behind his spectacles. He exuded love.

My shoulders relaxed. "I would like that."

He showed me the Gasthaus with guest rooms upstairs and introduced me to Frau Schulz who cooked for those who passed through town, and she helped in the store at times. There was only one telephone in town, and it sat on top of a desk in Papa Schulz's office. It barely ever rang.

On the main floor was the grocery store and post office. Tall shelves were neatly arranged and sparsely spaced with canned goods, sugar, flour, and other essentials. Three cartons of eggs, a single loaf of bread, a large scale for weighing goods, and a cash register sat on the counter. Behind the counter were a few mail slots and an area for sorting mail.

"With my old knees, it takes me forever to deliver the mail. You'll get it done in half the time! And I won't have the whole town complaining about how their mail is always late," he said with a hint of laughter in his voice. "Ah, yes, they'll be happy about that!"

Our introduction was sweet and I soon fell into a routine. In the mornings, I helped Papa Schulz sell groceries and kept track of all the ration cards handed in by customers, organizing them by category and pasting them into a ledger in case the authorities needed to check them.

I was sworn in as a mail carrier, signing papers and taking an oath to not tamper with the letters or read anyone's mail. Since it was a small town, it didn't take long to get to know who most everyone was and where they lived.

I often parked my motorbike and walked some parts of my route, taking me past quaint little homes and old stone buildings with red clay roofs. The brick or cobblestone paths leading to people's doorsteps were lined with gardens that erupted in color each spring. The smell of lilacs and hyacinths made me linger a little longer, a brief diversion from life's worries. Except when I walked up to the Bürgermeister's door. He was the town mayor, and I dreaded delivering his mail.

He wasn't a bad man. Not at all.

It was because of the large, brown envelopes addressed to him, the ones with a black square around the outside. It meant they contained death notices, and it was his job to take the news to someone's home, to let them know a loved one had died in the war.

Every time I delivered one of those envelopes, I wondered whether it was Vati's name inside, whether I held his death notice in my quaking hands. Whether I held the end of hope.

I'd feel through the envelopes for clues or shake them to get a sense of their contents. Sometimes they bulged with papers and other times they were light with something jingling inside. But they never revealed their secrets.

Within a few days, everyone in town knew. I kept a rough tally in my head of fathers and young men who I knew were away at war, and each time I delivered a black-rimmed envelope and the news got out, I crossed another one off the list.

The list was getting shorter.

We received only one letter from Vati since we arrived, which was a huge relief to know he would know where to find us when the war was over. He wanted to know all about our new home and the town, and asked us to write.

He also asked us to send photographs. Was he forgetting what we looked like? Or did he want to tuck the photographs in his coat pocket to pull them out when he was especially lonely and homesick?

His children were growing up without him. Anneliesa was already seven years old and full of personality, but she had so few memories of Vati. Werner was twelve and still a misfit, especially since I lived at home again and was around to do more chores.

And I turned sixteen.

Other than asking for pictures, the letter contained more of the same. Talk of the weather, bad food, his lack of sleep, his longing for home, and the unrelenting pressure from the Red Army.

So far, he stayed out of harm's way. It's all that mattered to me. He could have written in cryptic symbols or hieroglyphics for all I cared, as long as I knew he was still alive.

There was only bad news about the Eastern Front, but victory was always right around the corner according to Hitler. Such a joke. He was blind to the bombed-out cities and the soldiers whose blood soaked the land he wanted to conquer. Even if Germany did win, what would be left?

Vati's letters as much as said so without having to say so. It was easy to read between the lines, even the thick black ones.

Even though I preferred my job as a nanny, I liked delivering letters. It made me feel like I was helping in some small way, helping soldiers like Vati stay in touch with their families.

And despite how temperamental it was, I also liked riding the NSU motorbike. Werner sure was jealous, and some of the BDM girls and Hitler Youth boys were, too. Or maybe they didn't like me, the new girl in town. All I knew was I didn't fit in.

As I arrived at the railway station, I cut the engine and coasted the rest of the way—anything to conserve fuel. I rocked the bike back on its kick stand and headed toward the little red brick building alongside the tracks.

It was usually a ghost town when I got there after lunchtime to pick up the mail, except for the train station attendant who sold tickets and watched over things. It was even more quiet than usual when I walked to the building, though. The stillness put me on edge.

I placed my hand against the door.

I listened.

Nothing.

I pushed it open. Its hinges groaned. My mind was playing tricks on me.

"Hello!" I shouted.

Silence.

"Hello! I'm here."

I stepped across the tile floor. Nothing was out of place. The railway map hung on the wall like always and a big picture of Adolph Hitler stared at me, giving me the creeps. I swear his eyes were following me and his tiny mustache twitched.

I headed toward the back of the train station to fetch the full sack of letters.

"Hello!" I yelled once again. Maybe he was out back. I turned the corner by the ticket counter. "I'm here to pick up the—"

I screamed, but no one heard me. Not even him.

Who knows how long he'd been there, his lifeless body sprawled out on the floor. A crimson puddle crept from beneath his chest, catching the light. His eyes were open and dull, staring coldly into space. Bile rose from my stomach at the sight of blood and I felt faint. But I couldn't pass out. Not now.

I ran, heading for the door. Just as quickly, I turned to face him. I don't know why or what I was thinking, but I jumped over his lifeless body, avoiding the pool of blood. I grabbed the full sack of mail and sprinted to the motorbike, pedaling until it came to life.

I burst through the Gasthaus door in hysterics.

"Papa Schulz! Come quick!"

Two women were getting some rations and were

startled at my sudden entrance. They stepped back, one letting out a shriek.

"God in heaven!" said one of the ladies.

"What is it child?" asked Papa Schultz. "You look like you've seen a ghost."

We stepped behind the counter. The two ladies eyed me suspiciously as we hid ourselves away inside the office out of ear's reach.

"The train station," I whimpered. "Something happened. The attendant. He's dead!"

His white caterpillar eyebrows raised high above his glasses.

"You stay here and help these ladies. I'll get the police chief."

I broke down crying, visions of the man's dull eyes haunting me.

"Now, now. It's all right. We'll take care of it. Be strong."

There were those words again.

I composed myself as best I could. Papa Schulz took off his apron and hung it on a hook, then headed out the door.

Questions hung thick in the air when I walked out of the office, and the two women exchanged whispers after Papa Schulz left so abruptly.

"Is something the matter?" one of them asked as she approached me with a list of items in her hand.

It was Frau Huber. She was a large woman, older, with gray hair pulled so tightly in a bun it stretched her forehead and pulled at her eyebrows, giving her a persistent look of surprise. She was the town gossip, sticking her nose in where it didn't belong, and anxious to get the latest nugget of information. Of all people to be in the shop.

I stared at the list in her hand, but couldn't focus.

"Is everything all right, child?" she asked again, holding out her sheet of paper, unwavering in her insistence to get what she came for.

"I'm sorry, I'll get your things."

I grasped the list from her hand and turned away, scanning the shelves for her items.

"Did something happen? You can tell me, dear." Insincerity dripped from her lips.

"No. Nothing," I said.

I wasn't about to give Frau Huber the satisfaction of being the first to hear. I could already see her scampering down the street to spill the juicy details to her neighbors, adding more embellishments with each telling.

I reached to grab a box of sugar. My hand shook. I withdrew and focused again on the list.

Margarine.

Eggs.

Milk.

"I'd like a small can of herring, too, please," she called behind me.

"I'm sorry, we're all out."

"Out of herring?"

What did she think I meant? But I kept my composure.

"Yes. Hopefully we'll get more supplies next week on

the train." My voice caught in my throat. The train. The man. They flashed in my mind.

The other woman approached the counter and spoke kindly, "Fräulein, you're clearly upset."

I turned to face them, tears welling in my eyes. The woman reached out and touched my arm across the counter.

"I'll come back later. I hope everything is okay."

The door chime rang and she left. Frau Huber stood firm, still wanting her rations. I filled her order in silence, finishing with her final item, a ration of skim milk.

"Oh, I want whole milk, please," she said.

I froze. Only pregnant women and those with breastfeeding infants were allowed to receive whole milk. Everyone else got skim, and I was sure the wrinkly old Frau Huber knew it. Was she trying to take advantage of me because of my emotional state, or maybe she thought I was none the wiser.

I spun around.

"Oh, and when are you expecting?"

"Excuse me?" she said, her eyes ablaze.

"The baby," I said. "You must be pretty far along."

I couldn't resist the dig. She obviously didn't have any problem living off rations.

"I beg your pardon! What kind of manners are they teaching children these days? I have a mind to report you."

"Report me? You can't report me for following the rules. Only pregnant women get whole milk, and I'm sure you know it. Unless you're the next immaculate conception, maybe I should do the reporting."

I shouldn't have said it, but it wouldn't be the first time my mouth got me in trouble. And I had no doubt I'd be the tantalizing topic of conversation at her next afternoon tea.

She stiffened and clenched her jaw.

"Well, I— I—. Just complete my order," she said through gritted teeth.

And I did.

I had never been so cross with a customer before, and I'd hear about it from Papa Schulz soon enough.

When it came time to pay, it took forever for her to reach inside her satchel for her coin purse. She painstakingly counted out her change. Meanwhile, I stood stone-faced, pinching my lips lest I scream.

Breathe, I kept telling myself. She finally slid exact change across the counter and turned to leave.

"Excuse me," I called after her. She stopped in her tracks. "Aren't you forgetting something?"

I knew what she was trying to do.

"Am I?" She feigned forgetfulness.

"You didn't give me your ration stamps."

"Oh, silly me," she replied with a phony chuckle.

Once again, she took her sweet time examining the sheet of rations and doling out the correct ones. I tucked them inside the ledger underneath the counter.

"The war will be over soon," she said out of nowhere as she grasped the door latch on her way out. "It's taking its toll on all of us, dear."

Was she trying to be gracious? Was this her idea of an

apology? I wasn't sure and I didn't know what to say or whether I should say it. So I said nothing. The door shut behind her and I was glad to see her go. Yes, the war was taking its toll.

"Apparently it's turned you into a big, fat liar," I yelled at the empty room. I don't think she heard, which is for the best.

I ran and turned the sign on the door over. Closed. I couldn't handle another customer walking in and dealing with them, especially if they were anything like Frau Huber. I turned the lock and leaned back against the door, closing my eyes.

The tears came leaking out, spilling down my cheeks. The dead man's stare was etched in my mind. His eyes used to greet me every time I walked into the train station. And now they were lifeless on the floor.

I traced the timeline in my mind. The train with the mail arrived around noon each day and I picked it up at half past. He was killed sometime in between.

What if I showed up ten minutes earlier?

Would I have encountered the killer?

Who did it?

Why?

Was there an enemy in our midst, or did someone on the supply train shoot him and hop back on board to terrorize the next town down the line?

So many questions swam in my head.

When Papa Schulz returned, he had few answers. No one knew why the station attendant was killed or by whom, but I was to be extra cautious when picking up the mail in the future, and the police chief would check in and patrol the area more frequently.

Turns out, the carefree country life wasn't the safe haven Mutti hoped it would be.

CHAPTER 19
Summer 1943

We lived on the corner of Elmstrasse and Murrgasse Street in a beautiful two-story house with a half-hip gabled roof. Vati would have approved. I was sure of it.

The owners lived in one half and we lived in the other. They were an older couple who kept to themselves mostly, except for the occasional exchange while hanging laundry out to dry or paying rent. Our side of the house was large enough to have my own bedroom, which was a big relief. But it was hard to go back to having to walk outside to the outhouse. Oh to have an indoor bathroom again, let alone my own.

Mutti was less on edge than she was in Rautheim. Even so, I rarely saw her smile. I rarely saw any emotion. Except for one morning when I woke up before the sunrise.

A giant yawn came from deep inside as my feet

shuffled into the kitchen. I rubbed my eyes and Mutti came into view. Clutched between her fingers was one of Vati's letters. She kept them in an old wooden box with ornate carving, the one she hid away in a closet in her bedroom.

The box sat open on the table with a stack of letters nearby, looking like they'd been read for the hundredth time. Did she put herself through this tortuous ritual before break of dawn every morning while everyone else was still asleep, reading old letters and notes from Vati in the morning's stillness?

At the sight of me, she sniffled and sat up straighter, snatching up the letters and placing them back inside the box.

"Mutti?"

"You're up early." She closed the lid and fastened the latch. "Are Werner and Anneliesa up, too?"

"No. I couldn't sleep and thought I'd drink some tea."

"There's hot water on the stove. Help yourself."

I made a cup of tea and sat next to her in awkward silence. I stared at the box.

"Is everything all right?"

She brushed her skirt. Moments passed.

"Just wishing we would get another letter," she said.

I wished the same. In fact, every time I sorted the mail, I'd look for any coming from soldiers, hoping against hope there would be another one from Vati. There wasn't.

"Can I read them?"

Mutti's eyes softened and I swear she winced at my

request. She reached for the box and opened the lid.

The folds in the paper were starting to rip in several places, confirming my suspicion she read them often. The dates went all the way back to his time before the war began when he was conscripted for training in Braunschweig. I counted the years in my head.

It couldn't be. Six?

The math didn't add up. Had it really been that long? It was an eternity all the same.

All I wanted was for things to be the way they were when I was a child, when I was oblivious to the evils lurking around every corner, when our family was whole and happy, before power-thirsty men sent Vati and millions of others to do their bidding. But there was no way to recapture those years. No way to go back.

Some were eager to fight for Hitler, even willing to lay down their lives for him. But Vati wasn't among them. He refused to join the Nazi Party and endured his share of ridicule and rebuke for it. No. He wasn't one of them. But it didn't stop them from forcing him to fight for their cause. Whatever their cause was.

Mutti and I sat beside each other at the table silently reading through his words, clinging to each one. I imagined his voice speaking the words to my soul. But it was getting harder to remember what his voice sounded like. Was that why Mutti wanted to read his letters over and over again? Was she forgetting, too?

She slid her hand across the table and placed it on top of mine. Our sad eyes met. She shook her head slowly but said nothing. It was unusual for her to show this side.

"It has to be over soon," I said, a crack in my voice. "Then Vati can come home."

"I want to believe. I really do," she said. "But the rumors—"

"Rumors?"

I'd heard about the bombing in Hamburg that killed thousands, and about the dozens of German submarines lost at sea, their soldiers entombed in watery graves. I knew Germany was losing, no matter what the radio said. But then again, everyone loses in war. But did Mutti hear something else? And from who?

"The Russians are pushing back the Eastern Front." I could tell she was debating whether to say more. She finally said it. "They're not taking prisoners, only—executions."

Mutti took a big breath and let it out swiftly, relieved to have actually said the words out loud.

She brushed her skirt, full of crumbs that weren't there.

Maybe she did show emotion, but reserved it for the early morning hours when no one else was watching.

"I've heard the rumors, too," I confessed. "I don't want to believe them. I can't bring myself to think of it, to think if—"

I shook my head. Unlike Mutti, I couldn't say the words. I couldn't bring myself to voice out loud the thoughts consuming my every waking hour.

What if he didn't come back?

"We can't live in a world of what if. That's what he always said, right?" Mutti said plainly. "We just need to keep working and waiting."

Her wistful state was gone in a flash and she gathered the letters once more, placing them inside the box.

"And praying," she said. She closed the lid with a snap, grabbing the box and walking to her bedroom. Shuffling noises came from the closet.

It was curious how Mutti mentioned prayer. She didn't pray, as far as I was aware. And we hardly went to church anymore, except for Easter. The village church, Dorfkirche, was less than a five minute walk, but the thought of waking up early every Sunday after a week full of work, BDM meetings, service projects, and air raids felt impossible. It was the only day I slept in.

Besides, any thoughts of God were mostly filled with questions. Why does he allow wars? How come there's not enough food? When would he bring Vati home? I should have paid better attention in my confirmation classes. Maybe there were some answers to all my questions and I missed them.

"I'm leaving for work," Mutti said as she walked back in the room. It was barely light outside, but Mutti's job at the bakery started early.

I called after her. "I'll be late tonight. I'm meeting Trudi after work."

"I wish you wouldn't spend so much time with her. But as long as you get your chores done. Just don't get into any trouble."

She stepped out the door.

Gertrude and I became fast friends—Trudi for short. She and her mother and father lived down the lane from us. Her only sibling was a sister who was fourteen years older and already married, so she was practically an only child.

Trudi's father came from the Ukraine. Her mother was from Poland and peculiar. Odd, really. She fretted about anything and everything and even made Trudi feel uncomfortable most of the time. Poor girl.

Her family was well-to-do before the war, but money was tight for everyone, and her mother had a hard time handling it all. They weren't citizens either, which made her mother even more nervous. Who knows what Hitler's cronies would do if they knew aliens were in their midst. I'm sure they knew, though. They knew everything.

Perhaps it's why Mutti cautioned me about spending time with Trudi. She didn't like me associating with foreigners. Even though she wasn't fond of Hitler, she wasn't too keen on outsiders either.

Trudi had jet black hair and dark eyes, an exotic combination of her mother and father. And since she wasn't German, she was prohibited from joining the BDM. She didn't have to go by train to Braunschweig twice a month to watch a propaganda film either, or write a report each time. Believe me, I envied her. But I couldn't fault her for it.

Others did though. It was all the more reason for girls in the BDM and some townspeople to look down on her and her family, saying they weren't patriotic enough, weren't German enough. At meetings, girls would talk about Trudi, saying they needed to keep an eye on her because she wasn't "one of us."

They knew about our friendship. Maybe I needed to watch my back, too. I wouldn't put it past them to plan something horrible.

Trudi and her family kept quiet, not venturing out after dark, not making waves in any way, hoping they wouldn't be reported for some made-up accusation.

When Trudi and I went somewhere in public, she kept her eyes low, rarely making eye contact with others. She wasn't a timid girl. Just smart. She was another person altogether when she wasn't under watchful eyes.

I was glad to have someone my age outside the BDM to talk to, especially someone I knew wouldn't report me for God knows what. We were careful to only talk about certain things in private.

Trudi stopped by the house after I got home from work, and when I opened the door, she let out a gleeful squeal. That was the real Trudi.

"Oh Waltraud, you look wonderful!"

"It's not too much?" I asked. "I put my hair in curlers last night and tried to keep a scarf on while delivering the mail, but the wind sure took its toll. I looked like Medusa!"

Trudi gave a hearty laugh.

"It's not funny!" I said. "I did a lot of work to get it to calm down and look halfway decent."

"It's perfect," she said. "And the hair pin is a nice touch. Helps pull it away from your face. Oh, and the dress! I think the photos are going to turn out perfect!"

Trudi's father was a photographer on the side and owned a nice camera. When I told her about how Vati wanted photos, she said she'd take them and her father would develop them.

But I felt a bit odd all dressed up on a late Tuesday afternoon in my best dress, the cream-colored one with the small flowers and paisley print.

Trudi and I walked toward a row of hedges. She thought it would make a nice backdrop. It sure was a fuss, but I didn't want to send Vati an old picture. I wanted him to have a new one showing how grown his little Liebling had become.

"How do you know how to work the camera?" I asked as she removed it from its leather case slung across her shoulder.

"I've watched my papa do it countless times, and he taught me all about the aperture and proper lighting. Today's a perfect day for it. Just a little overcast. Not too bright, not too dark. Don't you worry."

Trudi exuded confidence when we were together. It's another thing I loved about her, and it helped put my mind at ease. I sat on the stool we brought along and waited as she placed the camera on a tripod and adjusted the settings.

A young man appeared across the street, a little older than I. There weren't many men his age around anymore. When he saw me sitting in the open, he stopped. Curious, I suppose. His broad shoulders came to rest against a lamp post and he crossed his arms. Our eyes met and I felt self-conscious. What did he want?

"Okay, I think we're ready," said Trudi. "Now, cross your legs. No, the other way. Now rest your arm on your knee. No, the other one."

I clumsily did as she instructed, still distracted by the young man.

"And place your other hand on your forearm."

I tried to position my arms, adjusting myself on the stool when it tilted to one side. I looked like a contortionist at a circus, stiff and disjointed, trying to counterbalance my weight so I wouldn't tumble off the stool. It was too late. I untwisted my arms and legs in time to catch myself as my butt slid to the pavement.

I was mortified.

"I'm sooo photogenic," I said sarcastically with my legs splayed out in front of me. Thankfully, my dress didn't fly over my head.

The man across the street stared, his entire body pulsing to the beat of his own chuckling.

Trudi burst out laughing at my awkwardness. My cheeks turned crimson, but I laughed, too.

"Don't stand there," I urged. "Help me!"

Trudi stepped from behind the camera and came to my rescue. I brushed off my dress and sat on the stool again. She methodically placed my arms and hands in position and straightened my dress so it softly cascaded to one side. A wisp of hair managed to fall across my forehead and she tucked it behind my ear.

"Ok, now sit up straight," she said. "Square your shoulders. Turn toward me. There, perfect! Don't move!"

I wasn't about to for fear I'd land on my backside again. She ran back to the camera and peered through the viewfinder.

"Just a little more adjustment and I'll be set."

She adjusted the camera some more, and the young man watched, taking in every moment. I shook my head in horrified embarrassment. His wide smile confirmed how entertaining of a spectacle I was.

"Are you almost ready?" I asked. "It's hot out here."

"Really? Feels a bit chilly to me," responded Trudi, oblivious to her surroundings. She didn't notice the man amid all her fidgeting.

"Okay, okay, it's all set. Now, look straight at me."

I was relieved to have a reason to look away from the young man, yet I didn't really want to. My eyes stayed fixed on the camera, reminding myself why I was going to all the trouble. I thought of Vati and the letters in the box, and imagined his image reflecting back at me from the lens instead of my own. The flutter of nerves was gone and I waited for Trudi to snap the photo.

The shutter clicked. Then again, for safe measure.

"That should do it," she said. "I just know they'll turn out."

I uncrossed my legs and stood on shaky ground. The young man left his perch from the lamp post and strode across the street toward us with a wry smile.

"I didn't know I'd get to witness a photo shoot today," he said. "Which fashion magazine will it be featured in? Modenschau?"

I blushed. Trudi knelt on the ground, placing the camera back in its case. She glanced at him with downcast eyes and kept about her business.

"I'm Hans." He extended his hand.

"Waltraud. Pleased to meet you. This is my friend, Trudi."

Trudi gave a nod and I extended my hand. But instead of shaking it, he lifted it to his lips, planting a kiss on top. Electricity shot through my body.

"The pleasure's all mine," he said.

I withdrew my hand, overwhelmed by his forwardness and unsure what to do or say. His soft brown eyes were enveloped in dark, long lashes, and the corner of his mouth was raised ever so slightly as though withholding a secret.

My lord, I thought. *He's even more gorgeous up close.*

Trudi kept fussing with the camera.

"I haven't seen you in town before," he said. "Are you new?"

"Kind of." I composed myself enough to speak. "Can't say I've seen you either as I've driven around town."

"Driving? I'm impressed!"

The look of surprise on his face brought great pleasure, and I had a sudden rush of confidence.

"Maybe," I said teasingly, relishing in the possibility I might impress a boy, that one would be interested in me at all.

But my ruse was quickly exposed.

"Not real driving. She delivers mail on the motorbike," Trudi said matter-of-factly. "She's been everywhere."

"Is that so?" he said coyly.

"Yes," I confessed, feeling a little miffed at Trudi for so quickly exposing the truth. "I work at the grocery store in the morning and deliver the mail in the afternoon. Are you new?"

"Me? No, I grew up here. My father is the blacksmith. Just home for a few weeks on leave from the army."

"I see."

It explained why he looked so out of place. Maybe Vati would be granted leave, too.

"It's nice you get a break. How long can you stay?"

"Only a few weeks. Not much time, so I plan on making the most of it." He extended his arm as an invitation. "Starting with you. May I walk you home?"

"Me? I, uh, I have to help Trudi."

"I can handle it." She lowered her gaze again and fidgeted with the camera case some more. "You're all dressed up. It's a shame to let it go to waste."

"I couldn't agree more," Hans said, his eyes fixed on me, barely acknowledging Trudi. He extended his arm once more and I placed my hand in the crux of his elbow.

"I'll see you tomorrow, Trudi."

Again, only a nod. The real Trudi shrank back into her shell and the timid one was on full display.

Hans and I walked toward home, my shoes clicking with each step. He did most of the talking, but it was all a blur. We arrived at the garden gate.

"Now, that wasn't so bad, was it?"

"Yes, I mean no. I... I..."

I stammered uncontrollably. What was wrong with me? Why was I talking like an idiot?

Hans raised his finger and touched my lips.

"Shhh," he said. "I'll come by Friday evening for a

walk. Six o'clock?"

"Sounds wonderful."

He lifted my hand once more and caressed it with a gentle kiss. My knees went weak.

"It's an official date then."

He reached for the gate and swung it open with an exaggerated gesture, motioning for me to walk through, then closed it behind me.

"Good night, Waltraud. I'll see you Friday."

He placed his hands in his pockets and jumped off the curb, striding with a spring in his step toward the center of town.

CHAPTER 20
Summer 1943

Friday couldn't come soon enough. There wasn't much to do in Ampleben, but a romantic walk sounded perfect to me. In the days in between, he stopped by the store each morning to visit and chat. He waited patiently in between customers, gazing at me with those big, brown eyes.

Six o'clock on Friday finally arrived. Werner was reading a book and Anneliesa played with her doll while Mutti stood by the wash basin scrubbing a pan.

I told Mutti all about Hans after he walked me home. She was suspicious of the sudden news a boy would come calling.

"He's not a boy, Mutti. He's eighteen."

"All the more reason to be careful," she said. "If he's been away at war for any amount of time, he's bound to want more than taking a walk. Believe me."

"Mutti!" I was embarrassed at her insinuation. "We're

only going to walk around town. In broad daylight, no less!"

A knock came at the door and I rushed to open it. There stood Hans as gorgeous as ever.

"Good evening, Waltraud," he smiled. "You look pretty."

"Thank you." I blushed.

I spent extra time on my hair, placing and repositioning my hair pins a thousand times, and I tried on three blouses before deciding on the light blue one with white buttons.

"Please come in. My mother wants to meet you."

Hans stepped inside and approached Mutti. Werner stared and Anneliesa smiled with gleaming eyes, excited for the beginning of a fairy tale when a prince comes to call.

"Good to meet you. I'm Hans," he said with a slight bow toward Mutti. "Thank you for allowing me to spend time with your lovely daughter."

Mutti's eyes scanned him skeptically for an awkwardly long time.

"You'll have her home before dark." It was a statement, not a question.

"Of course," he said.

I introduced Werner, then Anneliesa who delightedly gushed over Hans and made an embarrassing reference to Hansel and Gretel. Hans and I chuckled over her innocent remarks.

"We'll be sure to steer clear of any witches on our walk," he said.

Anneliesa let out a girlish laugh. She was almost as smitten as I was.

Hans and I walked out the gate and down the street, around corners and past the pond. He spoke of growing up in the small town, and had an affinity for his family's roots in Ampleben and the generations before him. Still, he had a yearning to escape for bigger adventures after the war.

"It can be exciting at times, but the war isn't exactly my kind of adventure," he said.

He didn't speak much of his time away at war. Part of me wanted the gory details, hoping I'd get a better grasp of what Vati was facing. Another part of me wanted to avoid the subject altogether, not wanting to face reality or spoil the mood. So, I didn't prod for more details and he didn't tell. Maybe as time went on he would share more.

He wanted to know about my nomadic life, being born in Beienrode, moving to Süpplingen, then to Rautheim, my year in Braunschweig, and now in his hometown.

"Who knows," I mused. "Maybe our family will make a life here when the war is over and my father comes home."

We strolled through town, eventually coming to stop by the church cemetery. It was a sizable plot of land, and there weren't nearly enough headstones to fill it, leaving a large open area of grass that looked like a park.

We laid on our backs, staring at the lofty clouds floating by. Hans reached over and grasped my hand, wrapping his slender fingers around mine.

Everything felt right. No planes. No bombs. No air

raid sirens. Just the mournful coo of a dove echoing from the church belfry and the faint tap of a horse's hooves clicking against the cobblestones in the distance.

The evening light cast long, dark shadows across the lawn, and the sky became a watercolor canvas streaked with blue.

"I better get you home or your mother will have my head," said Hans.

We reluctantly returned. At the gate, he took my hand and kissed it as he had before, then held it to his chest. Our eyes met and I swear he'd hear my heartbeat.

He leaned forward and rested his cheek against mine. I took in his musky scent and the brush of his warm breath on my neck.

He whispered soft and low. "May I see you again Sunday afternoon?"

"Mmm," was all I muttered.

His hand slid behind my neck, drawing me closer.

"I'm very fond of you," he said softly in my ear.

"And I'm fond of you," I said.

The click of a door latch caused us to promptly withdraw. Mutti stood in the doorway waiting impatiently with a glaring stare. Why did she have to ruin everything?

"I'll come calling on Sunday," he said with a crooked smile.

I nodded, then turned and hurried up the walk to slip past Mutti through the door. It shut behind us.

"That boy is up to no good," she said. "I can sense it."

"He's very nice, Mutti. He isn't forcing me to do anything."

"He doesn't have to. He's trying to seduce you with his sweet talk. I saw you through the window."

"Mutti! I can't believe you're spying on me."

I was fuming. And embarrassed she saw us embracing. How dare she think I'd succumb so easily. Of course, I wanted his kiss to move from my cheek to my lips, and had Mutti not interrupted, I'm sure it would have happened. I could taste it. But why did she expect the worst?

"I'm trying to protect you," she said

"Protect me from what? The only thing in life that makes me happy right now?"

I knew I shouldn't snap back at her. But it was true. Thoughts of Hans made me feel something. Something wonderful. When I was with him, I forgot the world around me.

"You've barely known him a week. Things are moving too fast. The last thing we need around here is another mouth to feed."

The accusation stung. "You think I'd sleep with him? I barely know him, and you obviously don't know me."

I stormed out of the kitchen to my room, slamming the door behind me. Mutti called after me, but I didn't make out her muffled words. I expected her to come bursting in, but there was silence.

I walked to the window and pulled back the curtains. The colors of the sunset were faded, and the remaining light cast strange shadows on the streets below. I felt unsettled. Hopefully there wouldn't be another air raid. I groped in the darkness for my nightgown and slipped it on.

I wanted to spend every waking hour with Hans before he returned for duty, for him to claim me as his girl so I'd be there waiting for him when he came back.

As I lay awake, I planned it all in my head. When he left, we'd write to each other. Absence would make our hearts grow fonder. At last, when the war was over, we'd be together. Maybe even get married and have a family.

And Vati would walk me down the aisle.

Of course, it was silly to think so far into the future after only one date. But it felt good to conjure up ideas of what life could be like outside the reality of war, and worry, and weariness.

I fell asleep dreaming of a life with Hans, believing our summer whirlwind of a romance might just be the beginning of something wonderful.

CHAPTER 21
Summer 1943

Hans and I set out for a countryside picnic north of
town on the main road and up the sloping hill
toward the forest. Crickets chirped in farmers' fields
stretching on either side, and the road was lined with
apple trees.

"This one's ours," I pointed out as we walked by one
of the trees.

Families paid the government to harvest fruit from an
apple tree along the road. I stopped and held a branch in
my hand. Tiny apples were forming on the one assigned
to us. It was a good sign we'd have enough to can jars of
applesauce or hang apple slices in the attic to dry,
assuming no one stole the apples, of course. The thought
of applesauce on top of potato pancakes made my
stomach growl.

We did everything possible to preserve food during the
summer. Fruit and vegetables harvested from our own

backyards didn't count against our rations, so our entire yard was a garden. We even tucked sorrel and other greens in the front yard among the flowers, and replaced a couple roses with gooseberry bushes to make gooseberry jam. We canned everything from pumpkins and beans to carrots and beets. On occasion, we still got rabbits from Opa Rose and we canned the meat from those, too, but he said he wasn't feeling up to it lately. I didn't blame him. Everyone was tired of the war.

But on that Sunday afternoon, I had a skip in my step. Hans and I walked toward the woods under blue skies with pillowy clouds while the scent of summer alfalfa wafted in the air. I held his hand as we walked and talked about the days ahead.

A transport truck rumbled by with spits and sputters, and the driver lifted his hand to greet us. Something else caught my ear.

"Did you hear that?" I asked.

"Probably the truck motor. Sounds like she doesn't have much life left in her."

But instead of growing fainter as the truck drove away, the murmuring grew louder.

"Planes!" Hans yelled.

He grabbed my hand and pulled me forward.

"But there's no siren!"

"Just run for the woods! We're sitting ducks in the open!"

I dropped my parcel of food and we sprinted toward the forest's edge. Two planes came out of nowhere, soaring high above the tree line. The staccato of gunfire blasted through the air and Hans took command, pulling me after him into the ditch.

"Get down!"

We crouched in the ditch, my entire body trembling.

"Are they bombers? Are they going to bomb the town?" I asked, thinking he must know.

I burst into tears, thinking of Mutti, Werner, and Anneliesa helplessly sitting at home with no warning to get to the bomb shelter.

"No, they're after each other. A dog fight. Quick, they're past now. We've got to get to the forest!"

Once again, he grabbed my hand, pulling me after him, our legs pounding beneath us, bolting to the trees. The planes grew louder once again.

"They're coming back!" I screamed.

"Quick, behind the tree!"

We reached the forest's edge and took shelter behind a massive oak. He leaned his back against the tree, his chest heaving and his shell-shocked eyes staring into the canopy of leaves.

I buried my head into his chest, relief sweeping over me. He held me close, then released, dropping to his knees and peering around the edge of the tree. I stood behind him, my fingers gripping its channeled bark.

"They're pretty high, so there's little chance we'll get hit," he said. Was there a hint of excitement in his voice? "But you can never be too sure."

The two planes—one a Luftwaffe, the other an American fighter plane—maneuvered left, then right. They ascended higher, trailing after each other. Guns blasted and engines roared. The American plane was in front and banked quickly to one side, turning sharply. By some aeronautical miracle, it was now in pursuit instead of being pursued.

"Isn't it amazing?" said Hans.

The planes were acrobats, soaring through the sky in an awkward dance, back and forth. The Luftwaffe pilot flew vertical, defying gravity. The enemy chased from behind, climbing higher and higher. The American fired.

White streaks tore through the sky, hitting the German plane. It spiraled out of control. Chunks of metal and thick black smoke trailed behind as it disappeared beyond the tree line. Moments later, an explosion in the distance.

Meanwhile, the American pilot tried to pull out of his vertical ascent, but it was too late. The plane reached its limits, stalling and tumbling backward through the sky, disappearing behind a cloud. It emerged, spinning like an injured bird.

It kept falling nose first, farther, farther down. The engine wouldn't start. The pilot jumped from the cockpit and a parachute started to unfurl like an umbrella. But it was too late. He was too close to the ground, and it barely opened before he hit the earth. He was as lifeless as a twisted rag doll. I covered my eyes.

The plane crashed into the field and a massive explosion shook the earth. The fireball sent a gust of hot air toward us, a windy furnace forcing every leaf in the forest to cling for dear life. We ducked behind the tree to let it pass by. The smell of burnt metal and fuel filled the air. Then, silence but for the crackling of the blazing fire.

"We've got to help that poor man!" I cried.

I sprung up to go to him, but Hans grabbed my arm.

"There's nothing you can do, Waltraud. He's dead."

Tears spilled out and I fell into his arms. He held me for a long time and stroked my hair. I pulled away, but he drew me closer, turning me around and resting my back against the tree. His eyes were intense and glassy, and he pressed his body closer against mine.

"You were so brave," he said. He leaned in and kissed me. "Very brave indeed."

He kissed me again and I recoiled, scraping the back of my head against the tree.

"What are you doing?" How could he possibly feel romantic when a crumpled dead man lay a hundred meters away and a scorching inferno raged? Even so, an unsettling chill crawled beneath my skin, telling me it wasn't romance on his mind.

He kept pressing and reached for the top button of my blouse, no hint of the gentle caresses he'd lavished on me at the garden gate. The button went flying, bouncing off a nearby log. I tried to push back, but he was too strong.

"Get off me, Hans," I insisted, hoping he didn't sense the alarm ringing inside me. "The tree is hurting my back."

"Fine. Have it your way," he said, spinning me around and taking me to the mossy forest floor, pinning me to the ground.

"Better?"

"I'm not joking. Get off me!" The terror of seeing the

dog fight was replaced with another kind of acrid fear.

"But I'm only here a couple more weeks. Is it wrong for a man to want to have a little fun while he's home?"

He had a sickening grin. His hands held down my shoulders and I struggled to break free.

"Fun? We just saw a man die!"

"I know. Wasn't it remarkable?"

"What is wrong with you?"

My eyes locked with his. He thought it was a playful game. He was amused with himself. Panic rose inside me, sweeping over me in waves.

Was that a chuckle?

Another explosion came from the burning plane and Hans jerked in alarm. I had my chance. I thrust my knee into his groin with all my might and shoved him off me.

A deep guttural groan escaped from his lips. He released his grip and doubled up, pulling his legs to his chest. I leapt to my feet and ran for the road heading back toward town. It wasn't long before he was in pursuit.

"Waltraud, wait! I'm sorry! I don't know what came over me!"

But I kept running, passing the burning plane in the field, a crater formed beneath. The heat reached the road, blowing hot against my skin. Another truck approached from town with two men in the back. They jumped out and ran toward the American pilot who lay in a heap and untangled his lifeless form from the strings of the parachute. It was too late.

Hans stopped running after me at the sight of the other men, and it was safe to slow my stride.

What just happened? Is this what war did to people, or was the Hans I thought I knew only a ploy, an act? I was bewildered and betrayed, reflecting deeply on how the burst of bullets and explosions transformed him into someone I didn't know. Someone I could never trust.

I didn't look back as I walked in a huff the rest of the way home. I approached the garden gate, opened it, and walked through.

Alone.

I felt foolish over the laughable, girlish dream of building a life with him. The dream was fleeting, lost forever among the silent timber.

CHAPTER 22
February 1944

Was it me, or were all the winters during the war unbearable?

They were.

I swear they weren't so brutal when I was a child, or maybe my attitude changed. The winter of 1943–1944 wasn't exceptionally cold, but the snow fell unrelentingly, making delivering the mail nearly impossible on the motorbike.

It didn't matter, though. In addition to diminishing food rations, it was nearly impossible to get fuel, so I pedaled the motorbike most days, or simply trudged through the pillowy drifts on foot.

I got over Hans, although the incident in the woods unnerved me for some time. I couldn't admit Mutti was right about him, but she was nevertheless glad to see it end.

So was Trudi. She told me she didn't trust him the

minute she laid eyes on him.

"Why didn't you say something?" I asked.

"You were so infatuated with him it wouldn't have mattered."

I shook my head, embarrassed by my poor perception and inability to be a better judge of character.

"What gave it away?"

"What kind of man knows about the Modenschau fashion magazine?" said Trudi. "I'll tell you who. A man who likes looking at pictures of girls. That's who."

I suppose she was right. Trudi was right about a lot of things.

I avoided Hans every chance I got during his remaining time on leave, but it didn't take long for him to forget me and find someone else. That same week, Klara, a pretty girl with honey blonde hair from my BDM group, talked about Hans, claiming him as her new boyfriend and spilling all the sordid details.

I thought to warn her, but from the sounds of it, she wasn't an unwilling participant in his idea of "fun." She deserved the likes of him. Besides, anything to distract her and the other girls from Trudi and her family was okay in my book.

After Hans left, he and Klara sent each other postcards. When I held the first one addressed to her in my hand, I contemplated my oath to the postmaster to never read anyone's mail. I certainly never opened any letters, but I reasoned notes written in plain sight on the back of a postcard were fair game.

Their love notes to each other all but confirmed my

suspicion Klara was more than willing to give Hans exactly what he wanted.

The postcards upset me at first. The notes written on them made me feel like I was played for a fool. And the fact he sent postcards with pictures of snowcapped mountains, glassy lakes, and quaint villages nestled among the slopes and valleys of Austria where he was stationed gave the sense he was somehow away on holiday instead of at war. It wasn't jealousy. Just a deep sense of unfairness.

Eventually, I found the correspondence amusing, though, except for when they gushed about their marvelous Führer. I was tempted to find a black marker of my own and cross off parts of their notes like they did to Vati's letters.

But I dared not.

Whenever Klara brought up the subject of Hans and their future together, I played along. I had a sense things wouldn't work out between them. Klara always signed her postcards with love, but Hans only signed them with fond regards.

Besides, there was other, more important mail to deliver. Another letter arrived from Vati as winter took hold. He received my photo and said he looked at it often, and found it hard to believe I was so grown up.

I liked the idea of Vati glancing at my photo on occasion to remind himself of one more reason to do whatever it took to make it home alive. Maybe he even kept it in his coat pocket close to his heart, and pulled it out once in a while.

It was a much better thought than images of him dodging artillery fire or helping a bloody fallen comrade.

His letters always included a lament about the weather and how miserable it was there, wherever he was. From the way Vati described it, I wondered why Hitler would ever want to conquer such a forlorn place. Vati said the rain and snow turned the roads into mud, making them impassible for all the military equipment. Even tanks got stuck.

Food was scarce and his rations consisted mostly of Zwieback bread. He hardly stayed in one place for long, making it hard for supplies to keep up. Hitler couldn't even feed his own soldiers, so Vati and his fellow troops got food from the land or abandoned farmsteads.

Vati wasn't one to take what wasn't his, yet he wrote it so nonchalantly it made me shudder. He was more homesick than ever. And more hopeless.

Most concerning, he no longer served as a courier. He was put in charge of a group of men whose leader was lost in battle. This news sent me and Mutti reeling, knowing it brought him closer to the front lines and even more in harm's way. And the news back home said Hitler was diverting troops to the west to rally against the Allied fighters there, leaving many soldiers on the Eastern Front to fend off the Red Army with fewer and fewer men and resources.

Hitler's strategy was failing, and because of it, I handed over more and more envelopes with the black square to the Bürgermeister. I swear he visited a family every week to break the news about another loved one lost at war. I could count on one hand the number of soldiers I knew of who hadn't perished.

I stood above the mail-sorting table in the shop, staring at yet another black-rimmed envelope. I calculated the odds in my head and traced the black outline with my finger.

Whose name was inside? Whose life would be forever changed at the news another soldier died in the war? Would it be the son of the farmer outside town? The brother of a girl I knew in the BDM? Hans?

Or would it be Vati?

I gripped it in both hands, gazing intently and wishing my stare could penetrate its rough fibers. But did I want to know? The envelope was skinnier than most which usually bulged with several personal effects. But this one felt lighter, as though nothing were left of the man whose name was inside. I pressed through the thick paper sheath, but there was only something small and hard inside.

Papa Schulz approached. "Ah, another one. The letter no one wants to send and no one wants to read."

A deep dread overtook me.

"It's him," I whimpered. "I know it is."

"Now, now, you don't know that."

He patted me on the shoulder and held his hand there, squeezing reassuringly. Something inside me held a deep connection to the contents inside the envelope. Something I couldn't explain.

I placed the sorted mail inside the bag and draped its long strap across my shoulder. There wasn't any fuel for the motorbike again, and any unpaved streets turned to an icy muck. I headed out on foot.

With unsteady steps, I approached the Bürgermeister's home. Patches of ice covered the walkway and a small drift formed near the entry. The cold wind blew snow off the roof, pelting my face and making it feel like a squall despite blue skies.

I approached the door and hesitated, my mitten suspended in the air. I rapped the metal clapper against the timbered door.

"Come in," shouted a voice from the other side.

I entered to find him sitting behind his desk reading through a newspaper. We each gave a cursory salute.

"Your mail," I said, placing a small bundle of letters on his desk.

"Ah, thank you," he said and leaned forward in his chair, reaching to grab them. He sorted through the letters and reached for his letter opener, only to realize I still stood there waiting.

"And another death notice."

With quaking hands, I pulled the envelope out of my mail bag. His shoulders slumped.

"Another one. My God, when will this be over?"

"I have a bad feeling about this one," I said, biting my bottom lip for fear I'd break down in front of him.

"I'm sure you do with each one of these. It's the worst part of my job," he said. "And yours."

He knew about Vati being in the war and how each delivery of a black-rimmed envelope made me anxious. He stood and reached to take it from my hand. I didn't realize my grip wouldn't let go, and when I did, he placed it on his desk with reverence.

"Yes, indeed," he sighed. "The absolute worst."

I should have turned to go, but I stood frozen, unable to move, unable to walk away from what I knew in my bones was the end of hope.

"Are you going to open it?" I asked, my voice faltering.

"Not yet." His eyes met mine. "I assure you, it's a duty I don't take lightly. I prefer to be alone. Just me and Him."

He pointed to the sky.

"I see," I said. "I'm sorry to keep you."

"It will be all right. I'll take care of it."

He guided me to the door and it shut softly behind me with a click. I walked the path toward the street, envisioning him behind his desk as he opened the envelope, certain the notice inside contained Vati's name.

Three days passed, and with each one, more relief swept over me. My frightful premonition hadn't come true after all, and my constant worrying was for nothing. But whose family was torn apart this time?

I went into work and helped with groceries all morning. I sat at the counter tallying ration cards in the ledger book when the Bürgermeister stopped in to speak with Papa Schulz. I found it funny whenever the two of them were together because they looked a lot alike.

They headed into a side room and emerged ten minutes later. Exchanging farewells, Papa Schulz escorted the Bürgermeister to the door. He was about to slip out when our eyes met. There was a look of unmistakable pity on his face.

Then, he was gone.

My eyes darted to Papa Schulz, searching his, hoping it was my imagination or my heart playing tricks on me again. I half expected him to smile and repeat some silly story he heard. But there was no smile. Only the same pity-filled expression I saw on the Bürgermeister's face before he slipped out the door.

Every muscle tensed as he approached. I stood, the stool crashing backward. I steadied myself against the counter, holding on for fear I'd sink into the depths of panic rising within me.

"No," I uttered weakly. "No."

I couldn't breathe. I stared at Papa Schulz pleadingly as he walked toward me, every footstep in slow motion and echoing off the floorboards.

It wasn't happening.

It couldn't be happening.

I desperately hoped it wasn't true.

"Your mother needs you at home, Waltraud."

It was all he needed to say. I knew.

"Nooooo!"

It was a long, visceral wail, louder than the wail of sirens we became so accustomed to. My heart crumbled into so many pieces I thought it would stop beating. Papa Schulz reached to hold me and said something, but I couldn't hear him through the rush of thunder in my head.

I ripped myself away and bolted past him, crashing through the door to the biting wind, nearly knocking over a woman approaching the store. I sprinted toward home, barely able to see through the sea of tears, stumbling along the way and crashing onto the icy cobblestone street. I clawed my way back up and ran to the door of our home.

A door Vati would never walk through.

I burst through. Mutti sat alone at the kitchen table. Her eyes were swollen and red, a stark contrast to her colorless, expressionless face. Vati's dog tags dangled from her fingers, and a tear-stained letter sat before her on the table.

The last letter.

Then it hit me. In some twisted and haunting way, I delivered my own father's death notice.

An uncontrollable howl rose from deep inside and ricocheted off the plastered walls. I dropped to my knees, collapsing into a rumpled ball, my head in my hands, tears pooling on the floor.

Waves of deep, choking sobs kept coming, wrenching my soul, filling every crevice of my being with despair. Mutti's hand stroked my hair as she knelt beside me.

"It can't be true. It can't be true." I whimpered.

I leaned into her. It was our first hug in years, and it didn't carry the warmth or comfort I imagined it would. She tried to be gentle and speak reassuringly, but all hope evacuated my soul. And hers, too.

Life would never be the same.

We would never be whole.

I would never see Vati again.

Never.

Vati was dead.

I never allowed myself to envision what life would be like without him. I only dreamed of him returning and forever calling me his little Liebling, even until I was old and gray. I only dreamt of him coming home. Now, it would never happen.

Mutti was a widow, and I was half an orphan.

I couldn't cry any more tears, so I pulled myself upright and sat at the table.

"Do Werner and Anneliesa know?" I asked.

"They're still in school. I'll tell them when they get home."

"What are we going to do?"

"I suppose we'll do what we've been doing for years," said Mutti. "We'll get by somehow."

Her cold answer pricked my already tender wound. I wanted to respond, but my thoughts were too tangled. I numbly reached for the letter.

Dear Frau Michaelis,

I have the sad duty to share with you that your husband, Sergeant Gustav Michaelis, bearer of the East Service Medal and the War Merit Cross Second Class with Swords, on January 11, 1944, by heavy defensive fighting southwest of Gomel in Belarus, while performing his soldierly duty true to his oath of allegiance to the Fatherland, has died.

More tears came along with a deep sense of scorn. My deepest fear came true. Hitler wouldn't be satisfied until he fertilized the enemy's land with the nation's blood. Vati's blood.

> *As group leader he served the company as a dutiful and brave soldier. During an enemy attack against the forest encampment, he was fatally struck by a rifle bullet in the head. His wound was so severe, death came instantly.*

It sounded so simple. So inexplicable. My mind raced with thoughts of the chaotic scene surrounding him as he breathed his last breath. Was it true he didn't suffer? His death was instant? Or was it another lie told by one of Hitler's minions to make Vati's death more bearable? As if it ever could be bearable.

If it was a single gunshot, was it from combat? Or was it from a Red Army firing squad I heard so much about? Was he lined up in front of a trench and executed?

> *I express to you along with his comrades my deepest sympathy. The company will always have honorable memories of him. As a consolation during the heavy sorrow that has befallen you, know with certainty your husband, as part of the great society, gave his life for the greatness and preservation of our people and country.*

Greatness and preservation? Of what? Most of Germany was turned to rubble and its people were either beaten down or lost to bombs or battles. There was nothing great left to preserve. It was so senseless, so unfair. And for what? For who?

For Hitler.

I hated him, and I hated what he was doing and what he did to bring everyone to their knees. The war was as good as lost.

But he wouldn't give in. He wouldn't give up.

I wrapped my fingers around my necklace. Its pendant hung heavy from my neck, pulling me to the depths. I touched its revolting engraving and wanted to rip it from its chain and bury it in the deepest pit. The crooked cross betrayed everyone, including my father.

But I couldn't discard the last thing he ever gave me. The conflicting feelings melded with my grief as I clutched it in my palm and closed my eyes. I tucked it back under my blouse.

The letter concluded with some procedural information about unpaid earnings and a pension, along with heartless condolences. I set it down and glanced at the dog tags again, running my thumb across his name and a number etched into the metal.

I knew and bore his name.

Hitler only saw the number.

My head ached from crying, and my mind was tormented with questions that would never have answers.

Mutti sat like a numb statue, waiting for me to finish reading.

"We can't even give him a funeral?" I squeaked.

She shook her head and held out her hand. She wanted the letter back. When I handed it to her, she glanced at its crudely typed words once more, then solemnly folded it and stood to go to her bedroom. The door closed softly behind her.

Inside, the closet door opened and a small, latched box scraped long and slow across a wooden shelf. Moments later, the lid snapped shut.

Mournful cries crept through the keyhole, and I sat in the kitchen.

Alone.

CHAPTER 23
October 1944

N o light could dispel the dark shadow. It consumed me for months. Even if I could chase the darkness away, there was no light to take its place. My deep sorrow was intensified by the growing anxieties of increasing air raids, fewer rations, and the news of more lost battles and more lost soldiers.

America, Britain, and Canada stormed the beaches of Normandy at the height of summer and liberated northern France. Germany's forces and air power were easily overcome. By then, rumors and foreign news were breaking through, and someone said Allied planes outnumbered the Luftwaffe thirty to one.

Everyone knew it was only a matter of time before enemy forces advanced through Germany. We were caged animals pacing from one side to the other, distressed with questions of who would reach us first—the Americans or the Russians. We hoped beyond hope it wouldn't be the

Russians who pillaged villages and raped women and girls in their vengeful conquests.

Thoughts of Vati filled every waking hour. The faint hope I once clung to was replaced with haunting visions of Vati in his last moments.

I still wondered where his body was and whether someone buried him, or at least covered him with a blanket for some veil of reverence, maybe even fashioned a cross out of sticks and twine to mark his grave, if he even had one.

Was his body left sprawled in the countryside, rotting as fodder for carrion and wolves? Was my photo tucked in his breast pocket when he died? I wished it were so, hoping in some small way a part of me was close to his heart when it pulsed for the very last time.

Those dark thoughts came often, along with others, mostly guilt and regret over what should have been. I should have written more letters. I should have prayed harder. I should have pleaded more desperately for him to escape to the country or devise some plan to not fight, to not go back, to run away.

But who was I kidding? Deserters were hunted down, shot, and strung up on telephone poles like pigs with a sign reading "traitor"—a lesson to show others what happened if you dared defy the Führer's orders. And if aided by family, they were shot, too.

No matter which scenario I spun in my head, whether Vati fought or fled, Hitler got his way and, in the end, Vati was dead.

Months passed, and I avoided talking with others as

much as possible knowing they would ask me how I was doing. But working in the store and delivering the mail inevitably put me in their paths. The thought of making small talk with customers was impossible. I couldn't stand their pitiful glances so I pretended to cope.

At home, I'd hide myself away in my room after chores. Trudi tried to get me to do things to take my mind off my troubles, but I wasn't good company. Everything reminded me of Vati and resulted in tears welling in my eyes—the sight of a horse out to pasture or the smell of cedar trees, like the smell that used to permeate his suit coat after he pulled it out of the closet.

One day, his voice called to me and I spun around, only to discover it wasn't a person at all, but a loose metal sign swinging by a single nail. It swayed in the wind and scraped against a wooden post in a ghostly tone calling, "Liebling, Liebling."

Having now lost both his sons to the war, Opa Michaelis took to the bottle, drowning his sorrows in schnapps and homemade wine. The few visits we had were clouded by his drunkenness and berating comments about how Hitler was a traitor to his people and how the blood of his sons and all of Germany was on his hands.

We feared for him, hoping his tirades stayed behind closed doors and he wouldn't go spouting off in public. The Brown Shirts and SS were becoming increasingly desperate, trying to squelch any hint of dissent. If they knew what Opa was saying, I have no doubt he'd be sent to prison.

For BDM meetings, we still marched through the

streets, now in worn shoes and threadbare stockings. No one could afford new shoes, let alone find anyone selling them unless it was through the black market. Anyone who had new clothes or enough to eat was automatically under suspicion.

But the zeal of most teenage boys and girls remained fixed. They were convinced even small sacrifices for the Führer were honorable and Germany would reign victorious in the end. For me, the war was already lost.

And so was I.

After Vati was killed, money became even scarcer. Contrary to the promise Mutti would receive any unpaid earnings and a widow's pension, nothing arrived. When she went to the army office to inquire about it, they had her fill out some paperwork, but nothing came of it.

Another of Hitler's lies.

I still took a train to Braunschweig twice each month to watch a film and write a report. I looked forward to those train rides, not because of the films, but because of Liesa. We'd get to see each other, even if only for an hour or two. I still considered her my best friend from childhood and it was good to remember happier times with her. I cried on her shoulder, and it brought comfort.

The BDM troops from Braunschweig and surrounding towns often met together to conduct service projects. Our projects used to consist of collecting items for the poor or needy, but nearly everyone was poor and needy by then, and we were hard pressed to find anyone willing or able to donate what little they had left.

Besides, there were more pressing service projects to

perform, mostly cleaning up after bombings.

One night, a bomb struck a barn near the center of Ampleben. After we emerged from the bomb shelter, everyone in town formed a bucket brigade to put out the flames and keep them from spreading to neighboring structures. Four cows were trapped inside, and the bloodcurdling shrieks and bellows of helpless cattle being burned alive mixed with the roar of the fire.

The ancient rafters and cedar shake roof blazed hot and it was difficult to get near enough to make much of a difference with our useless buckets of water. We might as well have been spitting at a volcano.

The barn was turned to ashes, and my local BDM troop and the Hitler Youth boys were instructed to bring shovels for cleanup the following Saturday morning. Even Werner was required to come. Thankfully, someone dragged away the carcasses of the burnt animals by then, but there were still smoldering embers underneath some of the piles of debris spilling out onto the road.

We knocked down what remained of the fieldstone foundation with the help of the farmer and someone's tractor, then shoveled the barn's remains into piles and onto wagons until dark. By the time we got home, we were covered in soot and filth, and my hands were raw from gripping the shovel's handle. Every muscle ached. A hot bath never felt so good.

When we heard Braunschweig was bombed again during the early morning hours of October 15th, I knew our BDM troop would be summoned to help. Since the city wasn't far, the bombers flew over our village, causing our own air raid sirens to go off.

On that mid-October night, we found our places in the wine cellar in town. An endless swarm of lead hornets passed overhead. When we emerged hours later, the sky was glowing to the west and a luminous and eerie light emanated from the earth. If we hadn't known better, we might have thought it was the sunrise peeking from behind the horizon.

Four days later, our troop assembled at the train station. Aboard the train were other young people from neighboring towns, and the plan was to meet with even more youth in Braunschweig. We'd work during the day and stay in a bunker at night. I wasn't sure how many days I'd be gone.

Since the bombing, reports reached our small town telling of hundreds of deaths, the mass destruction, and how entire blocks were completely gone. Were my friends in Rautheim okay? What about Liesa? It was less than ten kilometers from the city, after all.

And what about the Voigt family living above the furniture store in Braunschweig? The fortified basement where I spent so many nights alongside them likely withstood the bombing, but what about the firestorm we heard about that swept through neighborhoods like a tinder box? How much damage occurred to the beautiful city center with its ancient timber-framed homes and shops?

I often strode those narrow streets with Eva and Peter on our way to the park. Were those quaint neighborhoods gone, too? The reports must have been overblown. Surely, it couldn't be as bad as they said.

Our train approached the city and everyone stretched their necks to see out the windows. The charred odor of something burning hit our nostrils long before we saw anything. The city came into view in the distance, its skyline oddly different than before and clouded under a shroud of smoke and dust. The train slowed to a crawl and stopped long before we reached the train station.

"Achtung!" called out one of the leaders. "We're getting off here and walking the rest of the way."

Groans echoed through the cabin, much to her displeasure.

"But why can't we get off at the train station?" someone asked.

"No questions!" she barked. "Just exit the train and get into formation."

The train stopped on the edge of town. The air was thick with a ghostly haze as we stepped into an open field. We marched in unison, carrying our rucksacks, and soon discovered why we couldn't make it to the station. Twisted metal sprung up where the tracks had been.

Buildings came into view, or what were buildings at one time. A stately church spire once towered above the city. Now, it looked like a stump in the desert.

Marching became impossible as we followed the leaders, stepping over stones and scaling piles of concrete, bricks, and iron beams. Pillars of smoke ascended from gaps in between the rubble, flanked by smoldering heaps where buildings once stood. The thick air was carried by the wind, weaving through an obstacle course of windowless openings, burning my lungs. A layer of ash blanketed everything, and our shoes and ankles were soon gray with its soft, chalky dust. Everything was gray.

It was hard to take it all in. I wanted to turn around and return to the countryside to escape the horror of it. I walked those same streets before. I was sure of it. But they were unrecognizable now, lined with the skeletal remains of burned out structures and streetcars.

A disheveled elderly woman wearing a bright red headscarf stood out from the ashen landscape. She hobbled and weaved aimlessly through the streets carrying a small suitcase.

We hopped from one piece of rubble to another and passed a demolished home where an old man was lifting debris and tossing it aside as though trying to reach something underneath. Or someone.

I looked away. The destruction was so great. How would our small band of teenagers make a dent amid all these splintered ruins?

The mechanical clatter of bulldozers melded with the clamor of workers trying to clear the streets. We left our overnight bags at a bunker and walked past the debris into a clearing. Large trees dotted the landscape, their incinerated leaves fluttering like brown confetti. It smelled like a campfire.

Was it the park? I was so disoriented I couldn't tell. I might as well have been in another country because everything was foreign.

Liesa appeared beside me.

"Liesa!" I embraced her in relief, weeping silently into her shoulder. "I'm so glad you're okay."

"Isn't it awful?" she said as she pulled away with a pitiful sigh.

"I've never seen so much destruction. You must have been so frightened."

Liesa told of the terrifying night in the bomb shelter and how the ground shook in waves as thousands of bombs fell nearby.

"When we came out, the entire city was on fire in the distance," she said. "It burned for three days."

"What in the world can we even do?" I asked. "It will take an army."

"We'll probably clean and stack bricks again like we did after the last bombing," said Liesa. "About the only good thing is we won't have to worry about more air raids for now. I don't think there's anything left to destroy."

We were called to attention and lined up in formation. I stuck close to Liesa toward the back of the line in hopes we'd work alongside each other. Our column surprisingly marched away from the desolate scene behind us, under low arching branches and alongside once manicured hedges burned to a crisp. A shortcut, I surmised.

Our group rounded a corner and was ordered to stop when a thick, putrid smell wafted over us. My stomach turned. Someone ahead fell out of formation and vomited onto the ash-covered lawn. The leader squawked for her to get back in line.

I thought I'd surely be next. I covered my mouth and nose, wishing I had a handkerchief to stifle the stench.

But it permeated everything and everywhere. I peered above the group. A low ridge of earth spanned about fifty meters wide, blocking our view beyond.

"Grab a shovel," yelled one of the leaders, pointing toward the mound of dirt. "The faster you shovel, the faster we'll get out of this godforsaken place! Begin!"

The odor was overwhelming. Liesa and I each grabbed a shovel and scaled the mound of dirt. Gasps of horror rippled through our group as we reached the summit.

"My God!" shrieked Liesa.

My nausea turned to full-scale retching and I emptied the entire contents of my stomach at the sight of what appeared on the other side. A row of hundreds of snarled bodies lined the bottom of a trench.

It finally struck me. We weren't in the park. We were on the edge of the cemetery. Beyond the trench, rows of etched tombstones rose from the earth.

Some bodies were unrecognizable as human from their charred remains, with blackened sticks for arms or legs. Others were unscathed but for their bulging, distended bellies and the legions of buzzing flies swarming around them.

Children no older than Anneliesa were tangled together with stiff arms jutting out at awkward angles. The bare legs of mothers and the elderly protruded from beneath skirts and flannel nightgowns, stacked like cordwood, some barefoot, some still wearing shoes.

I turned and fell to my knees, clinging to the handle lest I fall into the trench with the decomposing corpses. I heaved again, unable to control my gag reflexes. Others down the line did the same while the rest feverishly shoveled. Another stream of bile spilled out, burning the back of my throat.

"Shovel faster," someone screamed.

I was on my knees again, doubled over.

"You! Get up!" She pointed at me and berated me for my weakness. "Get back in line!"

"Waltraud, you've got to pull yourself together," urged Liesa as she reached for my arm and helped me up.

She was crying but somehow kept working without vomiting. I couldn't see how.

"You're going to get in trouble."

I filled my shovel, turning to throw it on top of the people below. The thud of dirt on the dead bodies felt like a punch to the stomach, and another wave of nausea came.

Why? Why did I look? I shouldn't have, but I did. The silty loam trickled down the face of a teenage girl about my age and covered a braid of her light brown hair. Her mouth was slightly open and some of the dirt fell inside.

I threw up again.

"Please, Waltraud," begged Liesa. "Just get through this and we can get out of here."

"Dear God, why can't they use the bulldozers for this?" I groaned miserably under my breath, not expecting an answer.

"They're probably being used to clear the streets."

How she found reason in the midst of this repugnance was beyond me.

Hours passed. Inch by grueling inch, the cold, dead

bodies sprawled in the October air were entombed beneath the crumbled earth. I dared not look again until I was certain I couldn't see their faces anymore.

We finished, eventually moving on from the cemetery to help with other cleanup over the next two days. Liesa and I said our goodbyes, and our troop headed back to the train tracks utterly drained and numb.

I felt hollow inside and wanted to close my eyes. But visions of the spiritless children and others in the trench filled my thoughts. Unlike the chatter filling the train ride on the way there, the return trip brought complete silence. I stared out the window with eyes as lifeless as those we buried.

This was the total war Hitler bargained for. His antiaircraft arsenal encircling the city was no match for thousands upon thousands of Sprengbombe—incendiary bombs—that fell and set the streets ablaze. Neither was his precious Luftwaffe any match for the Royal Air Force and other Allied air powers. The Allies wanted to break our spirit and our morale.

Well, it worked. At least for me. I swore I couldn't take anymore.

When I arrived home filthy with dirt, soot, and sweat, I was sure the foul smell of decomposition lingered in my hair and clothes. When I told Mutti about our assignment, she was appalled a band of teenagers was forced to serve as undertakers.

"Thank goodness Werner didn't have to go," she said.

They weren't the soothing words I hoped for. The only comfort she offered was to say I should take a hot bath.

Tears spilled into the warm water as I scrubbed and soaked. I didn't think I'd ever be clean again. But I eventually dried off and slipped into my nightgown, skipping dinner and going straight to bed.

But sleep didn't come. I wanted to take solace in someone's arms, to be held until the ache inside was swept away. Mutti was incapable, especially since Vati died, and the chasm between us grew wider with each passing day.

What I longed for most was Vati's embrace and how he could convince me of anything, maybe even convince me everything would somehow turn out all right. But nothing would ever be right again. I turned to my side and stared blindly into the darkness, tears soaking my pillow.

Not only had I lost Vati, I lost a part of myself with him. And even more slipped away with each shovelful of dirt heaped upon rotting flesh.

CHAPTER 24
March 1945

S tarry, moonlit nights brought a sense of dread, and sunny days that once cheered a weary soul put everyone on edge. We prayed for cloudy skies, snow, rain, sleet, and wind. A monsoon would be better than clear skies.

That's when the bombers came.

Nearly every BDM meeting involved being dispatched to clean up debris from bombings in nearby cities. After a bombing in Magdeburg, we were summoned to help clean bricks from a bombed out church. I imagined its steeple once pointing toward the heavens. Now, it lay scattered on the earth, interwoven with shards of stained glass that once bore the images of saints. Every muscle ached at the end of the day, but at least I didn't have to dig any graves.

Our family spent most nights in the bomb shelter, unable to sleep beneath the muffled air raid sirens, rustling children, and pungent body odor encased within the cold, stone walls.

Many nights, the sirens wailed, but I stayed in bed staring at the blackness. Mutti begged me to go with her and the others to the bomb shelter, but the thought of dragging myself out of bed and trudging to the bunker with heavy feet felt impossible. I stayed in my bed, listening through rattling windows to the rise and fall of sirens and the distant thud of bombs.

There were many false alarms and I took my chances. Berlin was being bombed daily and I imagined there was little left of it. Our small town was in their flight path, too.

On nights when there were no sirens, visions of ghostly, dead bodies haunted my dreams, begging me to save them from the trench of corpses. They had empty sockets for eyes, and skin draped off the bones of their outstretched arms like tattered rags. The sleepless nights filled with nightmares and wailing sirens left me utterly exhausted.

I started skipping BDM meetings again and paid more fines. I was warned. If I didn't attend, I'd be sent to solitary confinement with only bread and water, or a concentration camp to the north. Even Trudi urged me to go, afraid I'd be sent away and never return.

But I was so tired. So numb.

Rumors ran rampant of occupying American and British forces taking over parts of the country, but we had yet to see them with our own eyes. Someone said they crossed the Rhine River and were advancing our way.

"But, of course," they said quickly with a nervous smile. "It's a momentary setback. The Führer has everything under control."

Anyone who suggested Germany wasn't winning was considered a defeatist, punishable by death. I knew of an old man in town who spouted off at the beer hall, saying we were going to lose like we did in World War One. Someone from the Gestapo showed up at his doorstep. No one knows what happened to him.

If all you listened to were the radio announcers, you'd think Germany had already won. They insisted Hitler was in control and the Third Reich would reign victorious.

But deep down, I don't think anyone believed it. Hitler rarely gave speeches on the radio anymore, which was more than fine with me. He was probably hiding in a fortress somewhere to save his own skin.

On a particularly clear night with sirens blaring, I dragged myself out of bed and headed to the bomb shelter. When the droning sirens waned, we emerged to see the sky lit up by a huge fire in a nearby field. An English plane had crashed and sat ablaze. The Bürgermeister and a couple others went to investigate but didn't find any survivors.

While on my mail route a couple days later, I passed a barn down the street from the Gasthaus. A glint of something shiny sat outside the barn door, catching my attention.

Empty dinner plates.

A picnic in a barn? I considered looking inside to see who was there, but decided to keep going. Maybe Klara was there with a new boyfriend. I didn't need to see that.

When I returned from my route, Frau Schulz was saying her goodbyes to some unfamiliar SS officers who were paying for a midday meal. They always stayed beyond their welcome and lingered in the shop for no reason at all.

Since Ampleben was so small, we rarely saw superior officers in town. Instead, it was mostly Brown Shirts who were eager to report the most insignificant infraction. But we knew who to avoid and which townspeople couldn't be trusted.

"Well, gentlemen, I'm sorry we didn't have any meat to serve with your Spätzle. Not much to come by these days," said Frau Schulz.

The men's faces remained stern with an air of frustration as she handed them their change from the cash register.

"Sieg Heil," she said, gesturing toward the door with a less than subtle hint. "Waltraud, come help me clean up the table."

I saluted and gave a suspicious glance to the two men as I passed by. Frau Schulz and I strode toward the adjacent room where meals were served, leaving the two SS men to stand alone in hopes they'd be on their way.

"Who are those men? I've never seen them before." I said quietly.

"Typical SS," she whispered, looking over her shoulder. "They're investigating the English plane that crashed outside town a couple days ago. Takes forever to get rid of them."

"What do they want?"

"Someone from town found empty parachutes nearby and reported it. They're looking for the pilots. I don't know why people don't mind their own business."

"I thought there weren't any survivors," I said with a hush.

"That's what I told them." Her voice returned to normal volume, "If they did survive, they're deep into the Elm Forest by now. Probably died from their injuries there."

The door chime rang, indicating their departure. The tension filling the air lifted and the lines across Frau Schulz's brow eased.

"Finally," she sighed.

"Good riddance," I said as I walked toward the table to clear the dishes.

I stared at the empty plates.

"What is it?" she asked.

I picked up the dish, examining the delicate pattern of multicolor roses and the faded gold edging encircling the outer rim.

"Aren't they lovely? These were handed down to me from my mother. She got them in Bavaria. Some people stick their good dishes in a cabinet never to be seen. But I figure it's best to put them to good use before they're all destroyed by a bomb."

She chuckled and took the plate from my hand, noticing my quizzical look.

"Is everything all right?" she asked.

"The pattern. It's the same one I saw on some dishes

in front of the barn down the street."

Frau Schulz's face went pale, and shattered China broke the silence.

"Oh, what have I done?"

She bent low, scrambling to gather the broken pieces. I'd never seen her so frazzled.

"I'm so sorry!" I didn't know what to say other than to apologize. What for, I wasn't sure.

"I'll get a whisk broom."

I returned and helped her sweep the fragments of colorful porcelain.

"What's the matter?" I asked.

Frau Schulz remained awkwardly silent as we swept every last shard.

"Are the dishes by the barn yours?" I asked. "I can go get them."

"No!" she shrieked.

I stiffened, wondering why she became so upset over a broken dish, even if it had been from her mother. She glanced over her shoulder toward the open door to the shop and hurried toward it.

Peering through the door she sighed as she closed it shut.

"They're gone. Thank God. You never know with those sneaky bastards."

I'd never heard Frau Schulz swear before.

"What's going on?"

"Waltraud, I can trust you, can't I?" She was winded for no reason.

"Of course."

"What I'm about to say can never leave this room. Do you understand? You must keep it a secret." Her face became gravely serious. "Our very lives depend on it."

"I promise," I said.

I meant it. I didn't know what she was about to say, but sensed the gravity of the situation. We sat at the table and she grasped both of my hands in hers.

"Those dishes by the barn. They're mine," she said. "We're hiding those English airmen in the loft. Three of them survived. I bring them food."

My eyes grew wide.

"So they're not dead?"

Frau Schulz shook her head.

"But what if the SS keep looking around town and see those dishes? They'll find the men in the barn and—"

We locked eyes.

"And they'll recognize the dishes like I did... And come back."

I jumped up, grabbed my mail bag, and bolted through the door to the street.

"Waltraud, no!"

"I'll be careful!" The door slapped shut behind me.

I looked up and down the street for the officers. They were nowhere in sight. I bolted for the barn. Rounding the corner, it came into view and I headed for the door. The plates were still there, gleaming in the sunlight.

Thank God.

With one last glance to make sure no one watched, I knelt to pick them up, placed them in my mail bag, and headed back to the Gasthaus.

They appeared out of nowhere. Frau Schulz was right. They were sneaky. The two SS officers strode toward me with suspicion, their shiny black boots clicking against the cobblestones like a metronome.

"Well, well, well… What are you up to?" one asked gruffly as he grasped me by the shoulders. "Where are you running to? Weren't you at the Gasthaus?"

"Yes," I said, hoping the plates wouldn't clink as they scraped against each other in my bag, or chatter in chorus with my shaking legs.

"I, I…had another delivery and I—"

"Well?" he screamed.

"I'm only doing my mail route, sir," I said shakily.

"Herr Kurtz," the other man said. "We don't need to waste our time interrogating a useless Fräulein. Let's go."

The gruff man gave me a piercing gaze up and down my body.

"Get out of our way."

He shoved me aside and they kept walking. I slid behind a hedge and watched through budding branches as they passed by the barn.

They stopped.

They approached the door and looked around, then stepped inside. I thought for sure my heart would burst out of my chest, fearing the worst. Should I return and distract them? No, it would only cause further suspicion. But what if they checked the loft?

Just as quickly as the thought entered my mind, they came out and went on their way.

By the time I returned to the Gasthaus, Frau Schulz

was beside herself with fear and worry.

"Oh, Waltraud, thank God you're back. Did they see you?"

"Yes, well, no. They didn't see me by the barn. They looked inside, but kept going."

I removed the plates from my bag and held them in my hand.

"Here. You better tell those soldiers to be more careful."

A wave of relief fell over Frau Schulz as she collapsed in a chair, placing her head in her hands.

"What have we gotten ourselves into?"

"Who else knows?" I asked, placing the plates on the table.

"Besides you? The Bürgermeister, Papa Schulz, and the farmer who owns the barn," she said. "They were the ones who got the airmen out of the parachutes and helped them hide."

There was a long silence and my mind raced.

"I can help," I said.

"No, no. We don't need to drag a teenager into this mess. It's too risky."

"Don't you see? No one will suspect the mail carrier walking the streets, but if they see you or Papa Schulz heading to the barn every day with packages of food, they'll be suspicious. I already walk past the barn on my route. I can hide the food in my mail bag and no one will know or think anything of it."

"I don't know," she said. "It's treason. You know what they do to traitors."

I did know. But I didn't care. I felt something deep inside, something other than the hopelessness and despair I'd wallowed in for so long, and I didn't care about the consequences. Not since standing up to Bruno as a young girl on the playground had I felt such determination.

Vati's words were lodged in my mind, "Stand up for what you know is right in your heart."

I was compelled to do something. Anything.

"Let the girl help," a voice came from across the room.

We spun around. Papa Schulz stood in the doorway. He closed the door behind him and walked toward us.

"She's right. No one will suspect her," he said.

I had a hint of uneasy exhilaration. I'd forgotten what it was like to stand up for something, to have a purpose. Was it courage or foolishness? Probably both. What if we got caught? It would mean certain death.

Would Vati approve or would he think I was aiding the enemy?

This I knew. I felt alive for the first time in a very long while, and in my heart I sensed a distant voice saying, "That's my girl."

CHAPTER 25
April 1945

There were no signs of life inside the barn other than the chirping of sparrows and the smell of horse manure. I stared at the stillness of the hayloft as I brushed the few remaining crumbs off the empty plates.

The slap of something falling against wood startled me, spinning me on my heels. I gasped. An orange cat with a white-tipped tail sat crouched by a horse pen with a mouse in its jaw, glaring at me with its brilliant green eyes as though I might snatch away its prey. A fallen pitchfork lay nearby. I let out a sigh of relief. Still, not even a rustle came from the loft.

They were good at hiding.

I placed the dishes inside my mail bag and closed the door behind me as I walked into the daylight. No one in sight, I turned up the street.

I suggested the soldiers probably didn't care if they ate off nice China, but Frau Schulz gave a sideways glance of disapproval at the thought. It was heartwarming. She didn't have a lot of food to spare, but always managed to provide something. For Easter, she included three soft-boiled eggs with pencil drawings of flowers and a cross on the shell.

Easter. Another one came and went without an Osterfeuer. The huge bonfire was set ablaze in a field on the night of Holy Saturday, and it was as big as a house. But such a large fire would be easily seen by the nighttime bombers and draw too much attention to our small town.

When I was a child, we watched the Osterfeuer as a family, feeling its intense warmth and believing in its symbolic power to shine light into the darkness. Oh, to feel its light and warmth again. Not only feel, but believe.

Thoughts of Easter often brought to mind the gypsies who used to carry large sacks and chase porcupines running from the fire. They were such a colorful and odd bunch, catching, killing, and roasting the porcupines, spines and all. Oh, yes, and eating them, too.

I let out a small laugh, followed as quickly by a sigh.

There were no more Osterfeuers and no more gypsies. They disappeared just like the Jews.

Three weeks passed since the SS officers were in town. Having found no signs of the downed pilots and no one willing to talk, they gave up. By this time in the war, as Allied troops drew near, German officers had bigger concerns on their minds.

They were wounded animals, prowling around with hunched shoulders and a defeated look of desperation and doom. It was only a matter of time, and I'm sure they knew it. Everyone did. But we were extra cautious when they were around. Wounded animals are the most unpredictable and dangerous.

Meanwhile, the British pilots remained hidden in the barn. I was sure their skin had turned as white as buttermilk from lack of sunlight. How long could they possibly stay in the hayloft?

However long it took, I supposed.

Despite my comings and goings, I never saw them. They were like reclusive hermits or imaginary trolls from folklore. Food magically disappeared each day without a hint of their presence.

At home, not much changed. Werner was still the same and Anneliesa, almost nine, was old enough to help with some chores. I hadn't noticed my demeanor changed for the better since finding out about the pilots, but Mutti did. When she asked me about it, I only expressed my anticipation and hope the war would soon be over.

"Don't be too eager to welcome the enemy," she said. "You never know what they'll do, especially if it's the Russians. They've surrounded Berlin, you know. We might be next."

I knew she was right but brushed it off with forced optimism.

I continued to walk my mail route. I didn't use the motorbike anymore because every refinery in Germany was a target for bombers, and there wasn't any fuel.

So when the scent of petrol hit my nostrils, it shook me from my daydreams. Metal scraping against metal melded with the roar and whine of engines approaching the outskirts of town.

Two children rushed from behind, passing by as they sprinted toward the town square. My ears became attuned to the rhythm of shutters clapping open and shut on every street as white bed linens came billowing out over flowerless window boxes. There was an electricity in the air.

"Waltraud, come quick!"

Trudi appeared on the edge of the road ahead and the two children nearly collided with her.

"They're coming!"

Instantly, I knew what she meant and rushed to meet her.

"Please tell me it isn't the Russians." As if she could change the answer.

I didn't know what to feel—fear or jubilation, horror or hope.

"It's the Americans!"

Her expression wasn't one of joy, but of pure relief, and we both burst into tears and hugged each other.

"Is this it?" I said with anticipation and fear as we hurried along. "Could it really be over?"

"Oh, God, I hope so!" she said.

We rushed toward the town square, stopping at the store to drop off my mail bag. Should we hide inside or see what was happening? We decided to go.

Please let this be the end. I found myself silently begging God as we ran. I didn't know what would happen, but I prayed they'd have mercy on us.

Trudi and I tucked ourselves behind the corner of the

butcher shop. A small crowd gathered while most retreated to their cellars or peered nervously through curtained windows. A smattering of women held white kerchiefs in their hands, and children watched from behind telephone poles and stone fences. Werner was among them.

"Werner," I yelled, motioning for him to come to me.

He glanced down the street and dashed toward me and Trudi. I'd never seen him run so fast.

Breathless, he exclaimed, "The Bürgermeister! He's at the edge of town waving a white flag!"

We craned our necks toward the end of Elmstrasse, the flag cloaked in a cloud of dust. A truck emerged, its brakes squealing as it came to a stop. The soldiers said something to the Bürgermeister who said something back. He began leading the way, still waving his flag—an old bedsheet tied to a rake handle.

A tank and a small caravan of trucks carrying American soldiers brandishing rifles followed him toward the center of town where women with dour faces feverishly waved white kerchiefs. Some soldiers smiled while others nervously scanned the small crowd with darting eyes, looking at rooftops and windows in search of snipers.

But there was no resistance.

For as monotonous and boring as small town life was, it offered one benefit—there were no German soldiers stationed in town to put up a fight or "defend" us. I only hoped there weren't any fanatical Hitler Youth who would get any stupid ideas.

The townspeople, a mix of elderly bitter-faced men, widows, and children, stood stoic, downtrodden, and defeated, uncertain of what they should do. What is the proper protocol for surrender? They didn't teach us how to surrender in school, and the radio certainly never told us.

"Are those black men?" asked Werner, pulling on my sleeve and pointing to some dark-skinned soldiers riding in the back of a truck.

We'd never seen a black man in real life before, only in propaganda films and cartoons showing Americans using them as cannonballs. Others depicted them as subhuman. But among their troops, they were soldiers like everyone else.

Smiling soldiers yelled something foreign and ran to a group of children. One ran to us, too, and we shrank back in fear. He approached Werner and extended his hand.

"No!" I panicked and drew Werner close.

Was he going to take Werner prisoner, mistaking him for an overzealous Hitler Youth? How could he know Werner wasn't very zealous about anything?

For as irritating as my little brother was, I did love him desperately and had a maternal instinct to protect him. I held him tight.

The soldier held something in his hand. Werner slipped from my grip and rushed toward him, taking what he offered.

"Chocolate!" Werner screamed, grabbing it from his hand.

The soldier looked at Trudi and me.

"Chocolate?" he said in a strange accent as he tipped his hat.

A gleaming smile erupted across his face as he held out two small chocolate bars wrapped in paper and foil. We cautiously accepted without saying a word.

"Hey Jerry!" A surly soldier appeared behind him, motioning for him to keep moving.

They exchanged some words in English and the nice soldier returned to his troop. The other one stopped in front of me and stared intently, his eyes turning to slits. It was like Trudi and Werner weren't even there.

He approached within inches, a sweaty sneer across his rough, dusty face. His jaw chewed grotesquely on a piece of chewing gum, something else I'd never seen before.

"Hello Fräulein." His sinister tone mixed with saliva and made my blood run cold.

He reached out his finger and methodically traced my stiffened jaw, then held his fingertips beneath my chin. I froze in sheer panic.

What did he want? Maybe the Americans weren't any better than the Russians after all. Maybe they raped and pillaged villages, too. Maybe I'd be his first victim.

His hand moved down my neck to the top of my dress toward my breasts.

"Nazi," he growled.

Tears welled in my eyes, the cords in my neck tensing at his touch. I was certain he'd kill me, or worse. With a sudden jerk of his hand, I felt a twinge of pain. In his fingers, hung Vati's necklace.

"No!" I screamed and lunged toward him, but Trudi and Werner held me back.

"Are you crazy?" scolded Trudi.

A noxious laugh emerged from his lips as I watched him walk back to his fellow soldiers. The necklace and pendant dangled from his outstretched hand like a trophy as he strutted toward his buddies. He slid it in his breast pocket.

Why was I so careless? So stupid? What did I think they'd do if they saw my necklace bearing a swastika? Salute?

My heart sank and I fell to my knees, wailing, knowing I'd never see it again.

My tears had nothing to do with the symbolism of the crooked cross I came to detest. It could have been a lump of coal hanging from my neck for all I cared. No, I'd lost another part of Vati and his memory.

The culmination of six years of war had come to this, and it brought a stinging revelation I'd lost so much more than Vati.

I lost my childhood.

My innocence.

My country.

My spirit.

Trudi and Werner pulled me up and tried to console me, but tears flowed as troops roamed the town.

Why should the Allied troops care about our tears? It's not like they should take pity on us. They didn't start this war. Hitler did. Germany and its people were reaping what we sowed. What he sowed.

Soldiers dispersed into small groups, walking each street and knocking on doors, confiscating everyone's hunting rifles and firearms. They placed them in the back of a truck, later to be dumped in a local pond. There was no need to search our house, as Vati didn't own any guns. He was a pacifist until he was forced to fight in the war.

Placards started going up all over town, instructing us in German about the new curfews, how no one was allowed on the streets after dark, and no one could leave town without authorization. Officers headed for the old fortress on the edge of town to claim it as their headquarters.

Cheering erupted down the street and a throng of soldiers came sprawling into the town square, ushering three disheveled men with overgrown beards and wearing leather jackets with shearling collars.

Hip, hip, hoorays and shouts of joy and excitement trickled through the troops as the three men were ushered toward a truck carrying the main officers. So many soldiers were cheering and patting them on the back, they almost knocked them over.

"The pilots," I murmured under my breath.

My grief waned at the sight of the bedraggled men. Their smiles were brilliant and they looked well. Very well, other than being in desperate need of a bath and shave. They made it, and my heart felt a little lighter.

Trudi noticed the sudden shift in my mood upon seeing them.

"Do you know who those men are?"

"Yeah, who are they?" Werner echoed.

"I—I've never seen them before in my life," I answered truthfully.

Tears flowed, melding two emotions into one.

Something lost. Something found.

CHAPTER 26
Fall 1945

For the most part, the Americans showed mercy on us. Perhaps it was because of the mercy our town extended to the rescued pilots, hiding them from the Nazis and keeping them safe and fed for weeks. We were certain it didn't hurt our situation. We were likely one of their easier conquests.

Still, we didn't trust the troops, especially at first.

That's why Werner and I dug a shallow grave in the backyard the day they arrived. Shovel in hand, I heaped the dirt on top. Werner knelt to pat the freshly turned earth, then stood and pressed it with the heel of his boot.

He especially mourned the loss, sighing with discontent. But after the unsettling incident with the mean soldier, we didn't want to take any chances.

"Such a shame," he moaned as he walked through the back door.

Dejected, he plopped on the daybed.

"It's not worth risking our lives over," I said.

Mutti and Anneliesa agreed wholeheartedly.

The chocolate we entombed in the back of the garden next to a row of spring onions was poisoned. At least, we convinced ourselves it was so. Better to bury it, we reasoned.

Eventually, however, we accepted candy from the troops after not hearing of anyone succumbing to strychnine.

There was another grave—the American paratrooper who died when he jumped from his plane during the dogfight I witnessed. At the time, our townspeople buried him on the edge of the church cemetery with a simple cross as its marker.

Despite his decayed body, the soldiers dug him up. They treated the task and their dead countryman with such reverence and dignity, vowing to return his remains to his family in the United States for a proper burial with honors.

I envied the family, whoever they were. They were getting their soldier back, albeit in a wooden box. I still silently hoped Vati's remains would be returned someday for a proper burial. But deep down I knew it would never happen.

By now, his body had become a part of the forest floor where he was killed, intertwined with fallen leaves and ferns. Maybe he was resting beneath a majestic fir or among a stand of birch trees whose paper bark fluttered in the breeze.

Perhaps he was happier there, among woodland

songbirds, rustling leaves, and dappled shadows than in a cemetery tucked beneath a cold piece of stone with his name on it.

I had to believe it was so.

The American troops were relatively kind and considered themselves liberators, not conquerors. It was an answered prayer. And there was another.

Hitler was dead.

And with him, his power. It was only then I truly believed the nightmare of war was over. Until he breathed his last, the fear remained. I'd never have to salute again.

Ironically, the habit of saying "Heil Hitler" when greeting others took some time to break after so many years. People would come into the shop and instinctively say it with raised arm, only to sheepishly withdraw their hand and smile nervously.

Vati would have found it humorous, too. I could almost imagine his chuckle and merciless chiding.

Almost.

I reached for my necklace as I always did when thoughts of him came to mind.

Gone.

My fingers lingered, pressing softly against my protruding collar bone, feeling the ridge of skin against bone. How much weight had I lost?

We got new ration cards, allowing even less food than we had during the war. It's not that we didn't have money to buy bread and butter. There wasn't enough bread and butter to go around. Hitler was better at producing factories than food. Now, Germany had neither, and the entire country was starving.

I thought I knew what hunger was before. I had no idea.

The Reichsmark became worthless and people started bartering for whatever they could. A set of silverware for a loaf of bread. A piece of jewelry for a pound of sugar. The black market thrived.

For years, I longed for the war to end, with expectant thoughts of life returning to the way things were before. It wasn't to be.

Thankfully, as summer and fall came around, we could dig potatoes and beets, and harvest beans and other vegetables from the garden. We ate some and canned the rest for winter. Bigger cities didn't have such luxuries.

Even though food was scarce, the air was lighter, and the brooding fear of air raids and ducking into bomb shelters disappeared. The constant anxiety of looking over your shoulder for fear of someone turning you in to the authorities for the most minor offense was waning. It was hard to remember what it was like to not be in a constant state of fear and suspicion.

Despite the hunger, it almost felt like hope.

After a few days of chaos when the troops arrived and the war officially ended, I resumed delivering mail. But I hoped the days of sifting through rubble were over since the BDM and Hitler Youth groups disbanded. But we were assembled anyway and issued passes to go to a nearby city again to stack bricks. Even Trudi came along.

Poor Trudi. She wasn't too keen on doing hard work, but at least it took her mind off her mother who was sent to an insane asylum. The strain of war and losing everything made her go crazy. Trudi told me through tears about how her mother started screaming and lashing out with a wooden spoon, hitting anything in her path. The furniture. Trudi's father. Their cow.

She even knocked down an entire shelf filled with jars of preserved food in the pantry. She walked over the broken glass with only her stockings, leaving a bloody trail through the house. Her father came home to find her sitting in a chair staring blankly at the bloody floor as though she didn't know how it got there.

It was the final straw, and he had her committed. He visited her each week and said she was improving. She was begging to come home, though.

"Not yet," said Trudi, repeating her father's words.

While stacking bricks, Trudi and I shared our deepest longings over things we once only dared to dream. There was still so much uncertainty, and it was hard to imagine how the Allied troops would begin to set things straight. But things would get better someday. They had to.

"Maybe one of those soldiers will take a liking to me," she said as she examined a broken brick, then tossed it on a wagon.

I laughed. "They might take a liking to you, but it doesn't mean they'll want to marry you."

"Oh, I don't know. I guess I don't care!" she said. A dusty smile spanned her lips. "One of them asked me to go to the dance hall with him."

I stopped in my tracks. "What do you mean? Since when is there dancing?"

"The war's over. Haven't you heard?"

"Of course, I know the war is over, silly."

I resumed scraping a piece of mortar off a brick with a wire brush.

"No, I'm talking about the dance hall," she laughed. "I thought for sure you'd know about it before I did. An Arthur Murray dance studio opened right next to it in Shöppenstedt. We should go."

I pretended I wasn't interested, but wanted to know more. I was as surprised about the dance hall as I was about a soldier inviting Trudi. By now, our town had been handed over from the Americans and was declared a British occupied zone. Either way, soldiers weren't supposed to fraternize with the Germans. But Trudi's natural good looks caught the eye of many a young man since the war was over.

"I don't know if it's a good idea," I said.

"Oh, come on! They even offer lessons. I could use a distraction."

I contemplated her proposition. Shöppenstedt was a little bigger town only five kilometers away from Ampleben, and the idea of dancing sounded like a thrill. How long had it been since I did anything resembling fun?

Mutti, on the other hand, wasn't thrilled when I returned home and declared I'd be going to the dance hall with Trudi on Saturday. She scoffed at the idea.

"Why would you waste your money on such foolishness when we're practically starving to death?"

"It's not like our money can buy anything, Mutti," I

said. "Don't you think I'd rather walk to the store and buy a hunk of sausage if I could?"

I couldn't. And she knew it.

Her greater unspoken fear? I'd be friendly with the soldiers. Or worse, I'd trade "something else" for food and end up pregnant like some other girls.

Since I turned eighteen, Mutti wanted me to find a good German boy to marry someday. The problem was there were no good German boys. At least in my mind. The only ones I knew were former Hitler Youth, and most others were either in POW camps or killed in the war.

The war. Why did I have to think of it? Why did I have to interrupt my pleasant thoughts of a night out on the town with images of Vati lying dead on the battlefield?

I pushed the haunting thoughts away. Yes, I needed the distraction from reality as much as Trudi did.

I knew going to the dance hall was frivolous, even wasteful. Nevertheless, with Trudi by my side, we walked the railroad tracks to Schöppenstedt.

We strode the main street toward the center of town in search of the dance hall, but we didn't need directions. The muffled music ricocheted off the walls from several blocks away, growing louder with each step.

A young man came tumbling out as we approached, a pretty girl under his arm. She giggled as they ran across the street. Both were drunk.

I looked at Trudi, hesitant. She grabbed my arm and pulled me inside where cigarette smoke hung thick in the air.

When had she become so brave and I the timid one? The real Trudi was growing more bold and adventurous every day.

The music. It was unlike anything I'd ever heard before on German radio. No patriotic tunes. No depressing folk songs. Instead, every note felt like spring. Fresh. New. Alive.

Syncopated rhythms blended with playful melodies. Horns and wind instruments kept in perfect cadence with the percussive beat of drums and bass, pulsating through my body.

The consuming weariness I'd felt for so long lilted to the high ceiling with each beat, and I found it impossible to not tap my toes.

Trudi felt it, too, and we grinned from ear to ear as we stood to the side of the room, watching. Those on the dance floor looked free, spinning and gliding effortlessly, their feet in perfect step. I closed my eyes, taking in the upbeat melodies.

Who knows how long I stood there lost in the music. Trudi tapped me on the shoulder and I opened my eyes. But she wasn't there. Instead, a young man stood with hand extended.

"Tanzen?" he said. I couldn't help but smile at the soldier's poor pronunciation of the word "dance" in German.

"No, thank you," I said. "I don't know any of these dance steps."

He didn't understand a word I said and kept standing

there holding out his hand, pleading with his eyes and a wide smile. Beyond him on the dance floor, Trudi was smiling and laughing, dancing in the arms of another soldier. Well, if you could call it dancing. But he paid no mind to her awkward steps and flailing arms, and neither did she.

I held out my hand and he whisked me to the dance floor. He tried to lead me, but I had no idea what I was doing. Even so, the cares of this world melted away. We inched our way toward Trudi and her newfound dance partner. A curl had let loose onto her forehead from all the bouncing, and her head tilted back, laughing in glee. I'd never seen her so giddy and carefree.

"Thanks for leaving me stranded," I shouted sarcastically as we nearly crashed into one another.

"Looks like you managed just fine," she shot back with a glint in her eye as she looked at the young man I was dancing with.

The song came to a close and the two men bowed graciously. Trudi and I headed back to our previous positions along the wall.

"I'm pretty sure they're regretting that decision right about now," I said jokingly.

"What? It wasn't so bad."

"Oh, it was bad," I said, laughing. "Really bad. I think we stepped on their toes more than the floor!"

It was hard to hear our own breathless laughter above the crowd and music.

"Well, maybe we should take those dance lessons after all," she said.

"Maybe," I said, fully intent on doing so.

I closed my eyes again, taking in the music and feeling a rush of emotion, a feeling so alien, so incredibly foreign it caught me off guard. I thought it would never grace my weary soul again.

It was joy.

CHAPTER 27
Fall 1946

My finger traced the gold embossed letters on the blue ruffled ribbon.

First Place.

At the time, the dance hall was such a wonderful diversion from post-war anxieties. Weeks of lessons prepared Trudi and me for the dance contest at the Arthur Murray Studio—the waltz, fox trot, and even the tango.

It was a big event and it drew a sizable audience. Even parents came to watch, except for Mutti, of course. She still scoffed at the idea. I thought the end of the war would help change her disposition, but she retreated inside herself, keeping me and the entire world at arm's length.

Papa Schulz took us to the dance competition in his enclosed buggy and cheered us on from a bench off to the side. As I waited for my turn to dance, I caught glimpses of him tapping his foot and slapping his knee. His bushy eyebrows pulsed to the beat of the drums while his head bobbed back and forth. He had terrible rhythm, but he sure was having a good time.

My dance partner and I beat out twenty other students —a vast improvement over my fumbled attempt with the soldier who almost lost his toes.

I sighed and placed the ribbon back inside a tin box that once held dried biscuits and put the top back on.

That was a world away.

I looked around the room. Plaster had fallen off the walls in the corners and the whole place was confined and stuffy. The apartment was small and in disrepair. I wished for a room of my own like before, but slept on an old, dusty sofa in the living room instead.

The window groaned and creaked as I lifted the sash, and I put a stick in place to keep it up. It was strange to not see a garden outside my window. Instead, there was a barren sidewalk and a dusty cobblestone street.

"Hello Waltraud!" came a voice from outside the window. "Coming? We can't miss the wagon."

"I'll be there in a minute," I said.

I grabbed my headscarf and entered the kitchen, walking past Mutti and Opa Rose on the way toward the side door.

"Come right home after work," Mutti said as she slid a cup of chamomile tea in front of Opa.

He stared expressionless at the rising steam.

"And no hanging around with those Russians."

I rolled my eyes and snatched a piece of bread from

the table.

"They're not Russians, Mutti. They're Ukrainian."

"No difference. Just come right home."

I didn't answer and shut the door behind me.

I resented the move to Beienrode, and felt guilty for feeling so, and I couldn't push either sentiment from my mind. Opa Rose's cancer came on quickly, and he needed someone to care for him. It was hard to see him so weak.

He was a hard worker, caring for animals and sharpening tools for local farmers. And who could forget the cunning way he raised rabbits in his basement without the Nazis ever having a clue.

He always had a mischievous and endearing expression on his face, but it was replaced with a persistent grimace of pain and a pasty, yellow hue to his complexion. It hurt to see him that way, waiting to die.

I knew coming to the tiny apartment at Number Twelve Steinumestrasse in Beienrode with Mutti and Anneliesa, now ten years old, was the right thing to do. Werner, who turned fifteen, stayed in nearby Süpplingen with a cousin since the apartment was so cramped. He had an apprenticeship and was training as a baker, coming to visit on the weekends.

I had since given up on the idea of returning to school and becoming a teacher. I found out the Voigt family lost everything in the bombing, including their furniture store. And the opera house was severely damaged, meaning her future as an opera singer was up in the air. They couldn't afford a nanny anymore.

I struggled to know what I would do with my life, and

doubted Beienrode held many prospects for a bright future. It wasn't a bad little town, no bigger than Ampleben. It's where I was born and spent the first few years of my life, but I missed my friends.

And I missed my job as a mail carrier. It was far better than working in the sugar beet fields outside town. It was backbreaking work and the pay wasn't as good. The only perk was the sugar they gave us to take home once in a while after it was processed at the factory in Süpplingen —practically worth its weight in gold.

I greeted my friend, Olga, outside the door. "Good morning."

"Good morning," she said. "Isn't the sunshine beautiful?"

"I suppose so."

There were, in fact, blue skies overhead. I hadn't noticed the sunshine after several days of overcast September skies and the occasional rain shower, making it hard to work the muddy fields. But Olga herself was sunshine, able to find something good in almost any situation. She had a perennial sparkle in her crisp, blue eyes.

Olga Tomtschik lived a few doors up the street in a two-room apartment with her mother and youngest brother, Johann, at Number Five Steinumestrasse. She had three older sisters who were already married and lived elsewhere in town—Lydia, Emma, and Martha.

And another brother named Emil stayed in a room at the Rittergut, a large estate on the edge of town owned by descendants of an ancient baron. It was a beautiful manor with several adjoined buildings surrounded by thick, stone walls. A practical fortress. Spanning an entire block, it towered over everything else and looked out of place for such a small village. Most of the land in the area —the fields Olga and I worked in—were part of the estate.

It's where Opa worked with the animals before he got sick. Three dozen cows and a herd of sheep were kept in the barn, emerging in the morning to scurry down the road with ear-popping bleats and clamoring hooves to graze in nearby fields. No one needed an alarm clock.

The grounds of the Rittergut weren't like a farm at all, though. More like a park with waterfalls, fountains, a greenhouse, and majestic trees. Even the cemetery was beautiful, a place of rest for barons and princes from centuries before. Opa got Mutti a job there as a gardener and groundskeeper.

It was strange to see the estate teeming with British soldiers who took it over as their headquarters. Olga's brother, Emil, worked for them in exchange for room and board because he spoke several Slavic languages— Russian, Ukrainian, and some Polish. And German, of course. He translated for Russian prisoners of war who were kept there.

Olga and her large family were the "Russians" Mutti spoke of. Like millions of other refugees and displaced persons during the war, they were trying to make a new life in a new world. They journeyed by wagon and foot across fifteen-hundred kilometers over the course of a year, traveling through Poland and Czechoslovakia, then

Germany, trying to stay one step ahead of the Russians who were pillaging villages and murdering anything and anyone in their path.

It was a death march, Olga told me, especially during the winter with only the shelter of a few blankets and their covered wagon.

"My sister's baby boy froze to death," Olga said one day while working in the fields. "There was no way to wash or dry his diapers, and she couldn't keep his tiny body warm, no matter how close she held him. We buried him somewhere in Poland."

Her stories were heartbreaking, yet she spoke of her homeland with such warmth and endearment.

But to return to Ukraine could mean certain death, or worse. Siberia. She already had an aunt and uncle who were sent to the gulags there. Olga and her family were ethnic Germans and owned land in the Ukraine, but the communists confiscated it and turned it into a collective farm years earlier, basically making Olga's family into slaves.

As far as Mutti was concerned, however, Russians and Ukrainians were all the same, and she didn't trust them. Even though Olga and her family were ethnic Germans, they weren't true Germans in Mutti's mind.

She also resented so many of "their kind" flooding into the country during the last months of the war, taking what little food, jobs, and housing were left to go around. It's one reason we lived in such a small apartment—there was a limit on how many rooms you were allowed based on the number of people living there. Many who owned homes griped about having to lease out rooms to others whose own homes were bombed, or worse, lease them to refugees like Olga.

After a short walk, Olga and I arrived outside the courtyard of the Rittergut and climbed on the horse-drawn wagon. It took us and the rest of the work crew to the fields where the days were long, but conversations with Olga helped pass the time. Spending all day working side by side, we grew to be good friends.

At the end of the day, we walked back to Beienrode alongside a wagon filled to the brim with sugar beets. Olga and I collapsed on a bench outside the Rittergut.

"Thank goodness we only have a few more days left of picking beets," I grunted. "I'm beat."

"Well, you should have eaten more than a piece of bread this morning," Olga said in a motherly tone. She rested her head against the stone wall.

"True," I said, leaning back and closing my eyes.

I knew better than to complain about my growling stomach in front of Olga. Her family endured unspeakable hunger and famine in Ukraine in the early 1930s. It didn't seem possible for millions of people to starve to death in the Bread Basket of the World, as it was called, but the Russians controlled all the food and land, leaving the Ukrainian people with nothing.

She had many horror stories of surviving the genocide, and how Emil almost died of starvation as a child. Their hardships made anything I endured pale in comparison.

Fear of the Russians still remained. Their occupation

zone was less than fifteen kilometers to the east, and we were nervous about their close proximity. But the British assured us they had a firm grip on our town and their zone.

Olga spoke about the Russians and how they tortured and killed dissenters. I'd known oppression and heard of brutalities, but such level of disregard for human life was unfathomable to me.

I thought even the Nazis couldn't possibly have been so ruthless as to starve human beings and try to eliminate an entire nation of people. But stories spread about atrocities in Nazi prisons and concentration camps, about the starvation of prisoners and killing of Jews.

At the time, I brushed them aside as embellished propaganda. After all, for years the Nazi government told lies about how terrible the Americans and British were. The Nazis made them out to be monsters, but it wasn't true. I figured the tables had turned and the occupiers were now issuing their own propaganda and sensational lies about the Germans.

It was too unbelievable. Too inconceivable. Human beings couldn't possibly do such things. Not Germans. But Olga's first-hand account of cruelty and barbarism inflicted by human hands made me second guess my own senses. If the Russians did such things, could the Nazi's? I didn't know what to believe.

"Are you asleep?" Olga asked, interrupting my thoughts.

I smiled, my eyes still closed. "With a stone wall for a pillow? Not likely."

"You must be thinking about something. What is it?"

"Oh, nothing."

I opened my eyes, staring into the distance.

"Maybe the flax harvest will be easier than picking beets," I said.

I didn't want to bring up the rumors and dampen Olga's spirits.

"I'm sure it will be," she said. "The fields are so beautiful when they turn gold."

Her optimism made the world a brighter place. "You think everything is beautiful," I joked, lifting my head.

"No. Not true," she said. "I don't think either of us are too beautiful right now."

We laughed at the sight of each other. Dirt and sweat mixed on our faces, leaving a filthy grime. Our hands were calloused and dirty, our shoes were caked in mud, and our skirts had a permanent ring of brown on their hems. She removed her head scarf and wiped her face, then shook it out into a dusty plume.

I, too, removed my kerchief, revealing my red hair beneath—the only relatively clean thing left on my body. Wiping my face of the grime, I shook the filthy rag.

"Ah, yes, quite beautiful. When's the next beauty contest?" I joked and we laughed some more.

"I'm sure you'd win." A man's voice rang in, cutting off our giggling.

Olga's brother, Emil, stood behind her with a coy smile.

"How long have you been standing there?" she scolded, snapping him with her kerchief. "You know not to sneak up on me like that."

"Long enough," he said.

Our eyes met, and I was sure he'd see the blush in my cheeks underneath all the dirt. His sandy blonde hair was tousled playfully above his ears and framed his chiseled features, softened by dimples when he smiled. He had the same piercing blue eyes as Olga, the color of the sky. But the sparkle was replaced with something mysterious.

"I better get home," I said, rising to my feet. "My mother is waiting for me."

"Will I see you after dinner?" Olga asked. "I'm going for a walk."

"Gee, sounds thrilling," I quipped.

"I'll come along, too," said Emil. "I mean, if you don't mind."

"We'll see." I looked at Olga and smiled.

Emil was suddenly beside me. "I'll walk you home."

"I'm pretty sure I can find my way." I glanced at Olga with a bemused look. "I only live a block away."

"I don't mind."

I walked a little slower than usual with Emil by my side. I had known him for a couple months on account of my friendship with Olga. I didn't dare fall for him, though. Mutti would surely lose her mind.

"I hope you'll join me for that walk later," he said.

"I thought it was Olga's idea."

"Yes, I suppose she'll be along, too," he said with a smile.

While Emil and his family spoke flawless German, a hint of Ukrainian accent lingered on his lips. My entire world was limited to about fifty kilometers. His nearly spanned a continent, and it intrigued me.

"It would be nice to see you tonight," he said. "I won't be able to see you tomorrow."

"Oh? Why not?"

"I'm going to Helmstedt. For some business dealings."

"Don't you get nervous? Helmstedt is on the border of the Russian Zone."

He shook his head. "I stay on our side."

"What kind of business dealings?"

My question was met with an evasive grin.

"Does the British army pay you anything besides room and board?" I asked.

"Not really. Sometimes they give me some British coins," he said. "I can't buy anything with them, but I figure the silver is at least worth something. And their army rations are better. Here."

He reached into his pocket, pulling out a piece of candy wrapped in wax paper. His hand grasped mine as he slipped it into my palm and wrapped my fingers around the small token. Our eyes met.

"Oh, thank you."

I accepted the sweet gesture with a smile. My cheeks felt hot again.

"They let me keep my horse in the stables, too. She has it pretty good there. Better than the prisoners in the Rittergut."

He let out a chuckle.

"A horse?"

"Yes, Nina. A mare."

"Such a nice name."

"She finally fattened up a bit after the long journey," he said. "Was skin and bones when we got here. Came with us all the way from the Ukraine and helped pull the wagon. We've been through a lot together."

He took pride in his horse. The thought of Emil caring for a mare brought a sense of warmth, a welcome familiarity. A memory of Vati on his horse, Minna, the one he cared for and loved, sprung to mind. Even the names of their horses were similar.

"My father was good with horses," I said.

"Oh? Well, he's welcome to ride mine."

"He was killed in the war."

"How stupid of me. I knew that. I'm sorry," he said, flustered.

"It's okay."

It wasn't okay, but I didn't know what else to say.

"I didn't know my father," he said. "He was robbed and murdered after selling grain at the market when I was a few months old."

"I didn't know. I'm sorry, too."

"It's okay," he said, echoing my response.

I suspected it wasn't okay for him either.

"You didn't answer when I asked what you do in Helmstedt," I said.

"You're right. I didn't."

He smiled again and looked me squarely in the face. I knew not to press him on it.

"Well, be careful," I said.

"Why? Are you worried about me?" he said teasingly.

"Should I be?"

"I know my way around," he said. "And I'll be careful. Especially if I know I have someone to come home to."

The blue eyes veiled under dark eyelashes transformed into gleaming gemstones, penetrating to my soul.

"Waltraud!" My mother's voice startled me.

I broke my gaze and walked the remaining few steps toward the door, shooting a look of scorn at Mutti.

"I told you to come right home," Mutti said. "Helmut is here. You shouldn't keep him waiting."

She was speaking to me, but her eyes bore through Emil with a glare of disdain.

"Good evening, Frau Michaelis," said Emil.

Mutti didn't respond.

"Get inside," she said to me coldly, ushering me in with the dish towel in her hand.

I gave Emil one last apologetic glance and ducked in the door. It slammed behind me.

"Hello, Waltraud." Helmut, a handsome young man from town, turned and stood. "I've been waiting for you."

Anneliesa sat beside Helmut drawing on a piece of paper. Opa Rose sat nearby in an upholstered chair with a blanket. His expression told it all; he was bothered to have to make small talk with the young man.

"What are you doing here?" I asked.

"I was hoping we'd go for a walk, or maybe to the beer hall again," he said.

Walks and beer halls were the only entertainment in Beienrode, and I had little desire to do either with Helmut. He'd been courting me for weeks, and Mutti was urging him on. The few dates we had were a bore, but I did get a couple nice meals out of it.

"I already have plans," I said.

Helmut caught Mutti's eye, as though there were a secret pact between the two.

Mutti glared at me. "What plans?"

"I'm visiting with Olga."

Mutti grabbed my arm and pulled me into the living room, closing the door behind us.

"I told you not to hang out with those people," she half whispered in a huff.

"I'm not a child, Mutti. I'm nineteen years old and can decide who I want to spend my time with."

"They're no good," she clapped back. "Helmut has been waiting for an hour. He's a good man. You owe it to him to give him a chance."

"A good man? You forget he was an SS officer."

"That's all over now," said Mutti. "It's time to put the past behind us. Besides, if he were so bad, he'd be in a POW camp right now. Now, get out there and talk to him."

Without warning, she flung open the door and shoved me into the kitchen. I stood before Helmut, my face still red with anger over my exchange with Mutti.

He looked innocent enough in his trousers and wrinkled shirt, a far cry from the crisp, tailored uniform he must have worn as a Nazi officer. He was tall and thin, a few years older than I.

"Shall we?" Helmut stood, extending his arm as an invitation.

"I'm tired, Helmut. I've hardly eaten anything all day. And I'm filthy."

Mutti dashed in front of me and placed a plate on the table.

"I'll fry up a couple eggs for you. Go wash and change," she said eagerly.

I didn't have it in me to fight Mutti. I was tired from working all day. I relented and retreated to the living room to change and wash up in the wash basin, then returned to the kitchen.

Helmut let out a beaming smile. So did Mutti.

While I ate my eggs and a piece of bread, Helmut kept talking to Opa about rebuilding Germany and some other blatherings. Opa nodded, neither agreeing nor disagreeing. At one time he even closed his eyes and I thought he might have fallen asleep, but Helmut kept talking.

We stepped outside the door and walked toward the Rittergut where Olga and Emil were seated on a bench. Disappointment and confusion clouded their faces and I turned away, fixing my eyes instead on the cobblestones, ashamed I didn't have it in me to stand up to Mutti's insistence.

Helmut talked nonstop, unaware of anyone or anything else around him, including Olga and Emil. He reached to hold my hand and I pulled away, lacing my fingers behind my back.

I looked back to see Olga stand and walk in the opposite direction. Emil stayed seated, gazing at me intently with his blue eyes, urging me to return. He stood and followed after his sister.

Everything in me wanted to turn and run after them, but maybe Mutti was right. Maybe I needed to give Helmut a chance.

CHAPTER 28
Spring 1947

The distant silhouette of storks dancing in the field across the water was captivating, and their ancient raucous call pierced through the stillness of the early evening. It was magical.

It was nice to see them returning to nest on the wagon wheels perched on the roof of the Rittergut. They were placed there for that very reason. The storks stopped migrating during the war with all the bombings—at least I never saw them—and I feared they wouldn't return.

But nature proved more powerful than war.

The sun was setting to the west, casting magnificent hues of crimson and gold. I breathed deep, taking in the smell of spring, the water gurgling over a log, and the light breeze touching my cheeks.

He and I spent many a night sitting together on the banks of the Schunter River, talking about our past life and dreams of the one to come. The walks I once considered mundane became life to me, even during the chill of winter. They often brought us to the river's edge where we'd watch in awestruck wonder. We'd grown closer and I came to appreciate our conversations, his wry sense of humor, the way he teased me about my hair, and his zeal for life. I was glad I didn't give up on him.

"It's amazing how the sky reflects off the water, isn't it?" He broke the silence. "Almost like stained glass."

"Yes, so peaceful," I said.

The colors of the sky blurred any memories of air raids, the endless nights spent hiding in bunkers, and the Christmas tree bombs that painted the sky in a much different way. A horrible way. The glory of the sunset was such a stark contrast to the haunting thoughts of my past. Try as I could to forget, they lingered.

I shuddered.

"Are you cold?"

He removed his jacket and moved in closer, draping it over my shoulders. It had a sweet, earthy scent. His scent. His nearness sent a flutter through my stomach.

The sunset's reflection danced in his eyes, a kaleidoscope of colors more magnificent than the sky itself. Those eyes. They told of a longing for something. Something more than I could ever offer him.

I reached for his hand, the one I rejected so many times before out of fear. Fear of falling for him. Fear of what the future might bring. Fear of who he used to be, could be, might be.

"I'm sorry I've been so stand-offish for so long," I said.

"I understand," he said. "It's who I am. My past. I can't change it."

"I know."

We sat silent again for a long time, holding hands. My head came to rest on his shoulder. It felt so right.

He reached to caress my cheek, turning me toward him.

"What is it?" I asked.

"Will you be mine, Waltraud? You must know how I feel."

There was a sweet tenderness in his voice, a vulnerable pleading mixed with uncertainty. He leaned in, gently stroking my hair. His cheek touched mine as he mumbled in my ear.

"You look beautiful tonight."

He pulled away and gazed into my eyes, but I closed them shut, trying to quell the intensity coursing through my entire being. His lips came to rest on mine, softly enveloping them, warm and delicate, then released slowly. A soft, involuntary moan rose from within me.

Oh, how I wanted to know what his lips felt like against mine, and it was more delicious than I imagined. His kisses fell softly as his hand caressed my shoulder.

Was I making a mistake? Was I wrong? No. Everything was right. I couldn't deny how my love had grown over the last few months, even though I didn't show it at first. I knew it was my destiny. I made my decision.

"I love you," I said.

He melted into me with relief. We held each other close, and I lost myself in his warmth. I'd never known this kind of nearness, this kind of love.

It was nearly midnight when I tip-toed through the back door and snuck toward the living room.

"Where have you been?" Mutti's voice was low and menacing.

I gasped and turned.

"Why are you lurking in the dark, Mutti? You about scared me to death."

"I asked where you were." She turned on the light.

I didn't answer.

"Helmut was here again asking for you. He waited for two hours," she said.

"Well, I'm sure you and Opa had a grand time listening to him talk the whole time."

"Don't use that tone with me."

"I'm going to bed." I headed toward the living room.

"I told him to come tomorrow. That you'd go out with him after work."

I stopped dead in my tracks.

"Excuse me?" I couldn't believe my ears.

"Helmut will be here tomorrow to take you to—"

"I heard you," I blurted. "Why don't you hear me? I'm not going out with him."

"But you haven't given him a ch—"

"Mutti, I don't have feelings for the man and I can't manufacture them. I can't stand his incessant chattering. I swear my ears go numb half the time."

"He just likes to make conversation."

"Really? Maybe you'd like to hear him talk about Nazis and the good old days after he's had too much to drink."

My voice was raised, and I was sure I'd awaken Anneliesa and Opa. The air was heavy with tension.

"Your feelings for him can grow," Mutti pleaded.

"Mutti, I can never have feelings for him. Never."

I took a breath.

"I have feelings for someone else."

Her eyes narrowed.

"Not that Russian," she snarled.

I shook my head in frustration. "His name is Emil."

"That's who you were with tonight?" she said coldly.

"Yes. And tomorrow night. And the next."

"He's a good-for-nothing foreigner! He should go back to where he came from!"

Her anger bordered on hysterics, and it took everything in me to not get into a screaming match, but there was no reasoning with her.

"I'm done talking about this," I said.

I turned to exit the room, retreating like I often did when arguing with her, when the door from Opa's bedroom creaked.

Mutti and I stood silent. Opa emerged from the darkness, frail and weak. The shrunken form of who he used to be shuffled in the room like an ancient sage.

"I'm sorry I woke you, Opa," I said, flustered.

"I don't sleep much these days," he said.

He hardly ever spoke anymore, and the labored breath and rasp in his voice over the few words he just said revealed how much effort it took.

"Do you want some tea?" asked Mutti.

He waved her off as though she were a fly hovering by

his head. He sat at the table, the awkward silence lasting an eternity.

"You love the boy?" asked Opa.

"Yes."

"Just feelings," said Mutti. "Feelings can cloud a person's judgement."

"You should know," said Opa, looking sideways at Mutti. "You've forgotten what it's like to fall in love."

Mutti's demeanor softened, appearing to grow wistful of another time, then switched back to defiance in an instant.

"She can't go around sleeping with foreigners," she snapped.

"What? Who said I was sleeping with him?"

"I don't want you to make the same mistake we—" She pinched her lips. A heavy silence filled the room.

"What do you mean, mistake?"

Opa leaned back in his chair, a strange smirk on his face.

"I thought you were good at math, Waltraud," he said with a half-hearted chuckle. It morphed into a deep, violent cough that shook the floorboards. But he came out of it with the same cheeky grin. It was the first hint of anything other than misery I'd seen on his wrinkled face for a long, long time.

Math? Of course.

I never made the connection before. I had no reason to, but the glaring fact loomed thick in the air. I rattled my brain, trying to recall dates in my head. Mutti's and Vati's wedding was November 12, 1926. I was born in May, six months later.

"So, I was a mistake?"

My heated temper was replaced with this new, somber realization. Was I ever wanted? Was this why Mutti and I had a constant undercurrent of resentment and irritation toward one another?

"No, I didn't mean it that way. We were going to get married anyway. It's not what you think," she said. "I thought you figured it out after all these years."

"I never put two and two together, I guess. Never had a reason to."

"I don't want to fight," she said. "But you have to trust me on this."

"You're wrong about him, Mutti."

"I'm not."

The stare down with Mutti was palpable. I walked toward Opa and leaned to kiss him on the cheek.

"Good night, Opa."

I closed myself away in the living room and listened through the door. Opa's voice crept beneath the doorway. It was impossible for him to whisper.

"What is it you don't like about the boy?" he asked.

"He's not our kind."

"Ah, sounds familiar."

"What do you mean?" Mutti asked.

Opa spoke in pained rhythms.

"You and Gustav. His family was well-to-do. Spoke high German. Cultured people. Us? Not so much. We weren't their kind either."

"That's different," said Mutti.

"Ahh. Is it? His parents didn't want you to marry him. Remember?"

She didn't respond.

"Funny," Opa said. "Funny how some things repeat from one generation to the next."

There was a long silence. I tried to imagine the scene unfolding behind the door. Was Mutti taking his words to heart? Or was she giving him the silent treatment in protest?

Chair legs screeched across wooden planks and Opa let out a groan.

"Here, let me help you back to bed," Mutti's voice broke in, followed by shuffling feet.

"Love always wins," he said. "You can't fight love."

His bedroom door shut.

CHAPTER 29
June 5, 1948

O lga was practically giddy as she arranged everyone in a line.

"Here, you stand in the middle," she said as she doted on me and handed me the hand-tied bouquet, a mix of roses, wildflowers, and sprigs of cascading willow branches.

Olga and I grew closer over the last year and I considered her more than a friend. She was like the big sister I never had. But it was more. Olga's outlook on life defied the depressing realities around us. I couldn't help but be drawn to her.

Then it dawned on me. She was my sister now. Well, at least my sister-in-law.

After getting us in position, Olga took her place as the maid of honor. The photographer took an awkwardly long time to captured the moment as the summer sun baked the tops of our heads. The shutter clicked. Some smiled. Some were caught off guard. I was happy and sad at the same time.

Someone was missing from the photo.

Mutti refused to attend the wedding and forbade Werner or Anneliesa from doing so either. As our wedding party walked to the chapel, all three stood alongside the road watching, a public denunciation of our union.

I stopped in front of them, hoping they'd join the wedding party. But Mutti stared stone-faced with clenched jaw while Werner looked down at his shoes. Anneliesa had clearly been crying, her eyes red with sadness. But they brightened at the sight of my long white dress. When she reached out to touch the lace, Mutti grabbed her arm and pulled it away.

Emil squeezed my hand and we walked away without saying a word. He handed me the handkerchief from his breast pocket, but I waved it away. I was dying inside, but refused to cry.

Not on my wedding day.

The ancient stone chapel was the oldest building in Beienrode, built in the 1400s, and stood across from the Rittergut. It was tiny, so tiny we ducked our heads when we walked through the arched doorway. It was more like a church for gnomes than people. Pastor Lutz, a Baptist minister from Neindorf, conducted the ceremony. He pastored a small church there consisting mostly of exiled Ukrainians.

I looked out at the few rows of pews, hoping I'd see Werner or Anneliesa. Maybe they would defy her. Or maybe Mutti herself would sneak in the back on that early June morning. People lined the walls, but the only faces looking back were those of Emil's family.

My family now.

He and I wanted to get married much sooner, and I begged Mutti to grant permission. The government still considered anyone under age twenty-one a minor, and she refused to sign the papers. So, two weeks after my twenty-first birthday, there we stood.

How did Mutti and I grow so far apart? We were never close, but I loved her. And I thought she loved me, too, in her own way.

Opa Rose would have been here, I thought. But he died nine months earlier. The cancer took its hideous time before he passed, and Mutti's heart hardened even more.

And what about Vati? Would he have come? He would. And he would have convinced Mutti, too. He would have reasoned with her in his diplomatic way and persuaded her. He could have convinced her of anything. I was sure of it. And then he would have walked me down the aisle as I always dreamed he would.

But he was gone. Instead, one of Emil's cousins, a practical stranger, did the honors.

After the ceremony, everyone was so happy and laughing, eager for the reception to start. Emil grasped my hand like a school boy and rushed me down the street toward the banquet hall. His entire family followed.

I laughed as we ran, but the pain of Mutti's rejection clouded the day despite the bright sunshine. But there was also a fresh sense of optimism, a hope life would get better. I grasped my long veil and wrapped it around my arm as we scurried down the street.

Emil was handsome in his new suit. He insisted on looking his best for the wedding, but didn't have the money. A week earlier, he told me he sold Nina, his horse, to buy a new suit for the wedding. I cried over the loss of his faithful companion who carried him through his darkest days. My sadness melded with disbelief over someone who would sacrifice so much for love. So much for me.

We ate a humble meal and greeted members of his family. Women brought exquisite fruit tortes and lavishly decorated cakes, lining them up on a table alongside the wall, a silent competition for who could make the best dessert.

Emil's mother sat at our table along with Olga and a few others. His mother rarely smiled, and her long, drawn face made her look decades older than she really was. I suppose she had every reason. Emil told me she had twelve children in total. Only six remained.

As the reception drew to a close, many of the older people and children went home. Our small wedding party lingered and walked to the pub, and beer and schnapps started flowing.

Had Emil's mother been there, it would have been met with great displeasure. She was a strict Baptist and drinking was of the devil. But in the years after the war, alcohol was how many Germans chose to wipe away the memories of oppression, bombings, hunger, and unspeakable evil, if only for a little while.

Emil's friends ushered him across the room as I sat chatting with Olga. When he returned, he had a big grin on his face.

"How does it feel to be the official Frau Tomtschik?" he said as he plopped next to me, his bow tie askew around his neck.

I smiled. His eyes were slightly glazed and his cheeks rosy. He leaned to kiss me, his breath thick with the spice of alcohol. I made a funny face and turned away, raising my hands to ward him off.

"What, no kiss for the groom?" he joked, then turned to his friends. "She's already rejecting me!" he called out with mock despair, holding a raised glass in his hand, his words slightly slurred.

Everyone laughed, and I shrank in my chair, embarrassed by his chiding. I didn't like it when he drank, but I'm sure if there was ever a cause for celebration, this was it.

"Why don't you join us?" Emil's friend, Arthur, shoved a glass of beer in front of me.

"Oh, nothing for my Fraulei—I mean, Frau," said Emil with a laugh, heading Arthur off at the pass.

He grabbed the beer and took a sip.

"I'll have to get used to saying that," he said. "Meine Frau!"

I didn't drink. Never had. I didn't like the taste, but I had even more reasons now. Emil rejoined his friends and I sat chatting with Olga and others. She didn't drink either for her own religious reasons. She only smiled, rolled her eyes, and shook her head.

I shifted in my chair. My dress was tight and uncomfortable, and it was hot under the layers of lace and white satin.

It was a beautiful dress, but it wasn't mine. A kind woman from Olga's church, Frau Müller, loaned it to me. Her family fled Ukraine, too, and her husband was drafted in the war along the way and lost both legs. But she didn't let it cast a shadow over her.

Now that Emil and I could start our own family, I was sure of better days to come for both of us. I was married. The thought it made me chuckle. I started the day a Fräulein and ended the day a Frau. Funny, I didn't feel different.

I spun the silver ring on my finger and stroked its smooth metal. It was another symbol of his love. He took the British coins he earned to a jeweler and had them melted down into wedding rings.

Yes, he had his faults, as every man did, but our love was real. And our life together had officially begun.

I gave Emil a knowing glance and he came over.

"Let's get out of here," I said.

He grinned from ear to ear and bid his friends and some family members goodbye.

Someone arranged a room at a local Gasthaus, and Emil was eager to get me there. But it was I who helped him up the narrow stairway as he clung to me with one arm draped over my shoulder and another holding our overnight bag.

He sang as we stumbled up the stairway, *"Ja, ja, ja, ja,*

weisst nicht wie gut ich dir bin!"

He had a beautiful singing voice, but I laughed. The old German song told of love and how good he was for me, and I joked he wasn't much good to me drunk.

Inside the room, he gained his composure and removed his suit coat and shoes, then sat at the edge of the bed, looking at me with anticipation. He wasn't as drunk as I thought after all. Just happy.

He patted the mattress and motioned for me to sit next to him. I removed my veil and draped it across a small chair in the corner.

"It was a perfect wedding," he said as I sat on the bed next to him.

He leaned in for a kiss, his lips landing solidly on my cheek. I didn't want to point out the obvious absence of my family. I couldn't let thoughts of Mutti's cruel boycott ruin my wedding night.

"It was beautiful," I said.

I could agreed with that. I felt like a fairytale princess in my long, white gown, and the weather couldn't have been more perfect. I needed to look on the bright side.

"Can you help me unbutton my dress?"

He smiled. "I thought you'd never ask."

I turned around. One by one, he fumbled with the long row of buttons, his eyes trying to focus.

I was free.

I removed the billowing layers and dug in our overnight bag to find my new cotton nightgown.

Emil removed his pants and turned back the covers. He leaned against the pillow, his arms behind his head as his eyes stayed fixed on me.

I felt self conscious in the dim light and stepped behind a wood-paneled dressing screen. A large mirror stood in the corner and I examined myself as I slipped on the nightgown. It had a deep neckline and narrow shoulder straps, perfect for a warm summer evening. And it had just enough pink lace trim to suggest it was more than ordinary. I smoothed it over my form and turned to the side.

It bulged slightly over my abdomen and I tried to suck in my stomach. But it was hard to keep from showing anymore. It wasn't how I imagined my wedding night would be—five months pregnant with a tipsy groom. But everything would turn out now that we were married. Wouldn't it?

I stepped from behind the screen to present myself to my new husband.

His eyes were closed.

"Emil," I called softly, but he had fallen solidly asleep.

I walked around the side of the bed and sat beside him, brushing his hair away from his face. I traced his features as I watched his rhythmic breaths. The love was so deep it caused an ache in my soul. This was the man I would grow old with, who I would start a new family with after my own mother rejected me.

At the thought of family, the baby kicked. A tear spilled down my cheek. I vowed I wouldn't cry on my wedding day, but it was too late.

I pulled off his bow tie and laid it on the nightstand, then loosened a few buttons on his shirt. There would be no official consummation taking place, but it obviously wouldn't have been the first time. I kissed him on the cheek and pulled the covers over him. I crawled into bed.

CHAPTER 30
Spring 1949

I pushed the baby buggy down the street and around the corner. Did I have to go this way?

I suppose I could have taken the longer route to avoid walking past Mutti's house to get to where I was going, but I didn't. I was drawn there somehow. I approached the window and looked inside. There she was, putting away dishes in the cupboard. I know she saw me. She had to. Maybe she'd invite me in or swing open the door to greet me and the baby.

But as quickly as she glanced up, she looked away, pretending not to see me.

Nearly a year passed since we'd spoken. A knot formed in my stomach whenever we saw each other around our small village, like the knot I felt then as I stood in front of the window.

When the baby was born, I thought for sure Mutti would want to meet him, to hold him and lavish kisses on him, to shower him with attention and beg to babysit when given the chance. I knew she wasn't the nurturing type or one to gush over anything. But it was her first grandchild, after all.

Surely she'd break, I thought. Maybe even let Anneliesa play with him on the floor like she did with her porcelain-faced doll when she was little. The way I played with Anneliesa when she was a baby.

Mutti did whatever she could to keep Anneliesa from seeing me or letting her near the baby. But Anneliesa was a teenager now, and like most teenagers, she started making her own decisions and snuck away to see us on occasion. Werner worked in Süpplingen as a baker and would come to see us once in a while, too, maybe even bring a small dessert he made.

Yet Mutti held strong and wouldn't speak with me, let alone hold my beautiful baby boy.

But the reality is, I wasn't willing to break either. Maybe it was wrong of me, but I refused to grovel for her attention or approval. I could have walked through the door and thrust my child in her arms. I could have been the one to say I was sorry for the distance between us. But instead, the door stayed shut.

I grasped the buggy handle and forged ahead.

Waldemar was born on September 30, 1948, named after one of Emil's uncles. We thought Emil's mother could handle the birth since she had so many children of her own and helped two of Emil's sisters bring their children into the world.

But when the contractions kept coming for hours on

end without any results, I became increasingly weak from the pain and exertion, and Emil was a nervous wreck. He rode furiously on his bicycle all the way to Ochsendorf to fetch a midwife who followed him back. Groaning and screaming, I begged God to save my child and to let me live to raise him.

Finally, a few minutes after midnight, the cries of a healthy baby boy filled the room. His tears mingled with mine as I held him to my chest, and it brought a new sense of purpose, helping to ease Mutti's rejection and the lingering inner wounds from the war. I'd never felt such love toward anyone or anything. His eyes were bright blue like his father's.

Like my father's.

The buggy hit a bump in the sidewalk and Waldemar rustled under his blanket.

"We're almost there," I said in soothing tones.

I arrived at the address and looked up and down the street. A car approached. It was Doctor Rosenstiel in his new Volkswagen. Hopefully he wouldn't stop in front of the house where I stood. Anytime he drove into town, he and his new car drew a crowd of children and curious men who wanted to ooh and ahh over the black motorcar with shiny chrome trim. The last thing I needed was a group of onlookers.

Good. He kept going.

I stepped inside the garden gate with the buggy, walked to the front door, and knocked. Frau Eberhardt barely opened it.

"No one saw you?" she asked.

I shook my head.

I pulled a pair of silk stockings from my purse and handed them to her. She held them up to the light and examined them for any runs, turning them from side to side.

"They're 2.50 Deutschmarks," I said. "They're the finest quality."

"That they are," she said. "Let me get my pocketbook."

I could always rely on Frau Eberhardt to purchase my goods, and I was glad we could afford enough food. I might even buy some yarn to knit more baby socks or a sweater.

Her heels clicked through the hallway and up the stairs. It took an eternity for her to return. Of all the days for her to dawdle, when I wanted to get home early to get ready for the meeting that night. She descended with the money and I thanked her for her business. Stepping back onto the street, I grabbed the stroller and headed toward our apartment.

It's not like I wanted to deal on the black market. I knew it was illegal, but it was the only way we could get money for food, clothing, and rent. It was more a necessity than anything. Jobs became impossible to come by and the economy was worse than ever.

Before the German currency changed from Reichsmarks to Deutschmarks, we had money but there wasn't enough on the shelves to buy. Now, there enough to buy, but we didn't have the money. With the new system, any money we had in the bank was nearly wiped out. We handed over ten Reichsmarks in exchange for only one Deutschmark.

Emil's job as a translator had long been over, ever since the Rittergut no longer housed Russian prisoners. He found work in a former Nazi armament factory near the cities of Lehrte and Celle, cleaning up bombs and deactivating other explosives in an underground tunnel. The entrance to the site was an ordinary house, he told me, but beneath it was a cavernous warehouse filled with ammunition.

He'd be gone for days. Meanwhile, dark images filled my mind, of him encased in an underground bunker surrounded by bombs and the entire thing imploding in a cloud of smoke and ash, a ghastly tomb.

But that job eventually dried up, too, and he only got odd jobs here and there. So, he rode his bike to Helmstedt every week to buy smuggled merchandise from the Russian Zone. Truth be told, he'd dabbled in the black market ever since he arrived in Germany, but it became his full-time occupation now.

And mine.

He bought a pair of stockings for fifty Pfennigs, and Frau Eberhardt and others like her would gladly pay five times as much. Emil bought the items and I sold them to a select number of people in town who were good at keeping secrets. It was mostly stockings, jewelry, and other accessories. Sometimes Emil would get more expensive items like a camera, watch, or cigarettes.

The baby stroller was a perfect place to hide larger items. I'd pretend to visit a neighbor and she'd come out to greet me. Bending low to admire my infant in the stroller, she'd fawn over him and make small talk about how cute he was. Simultaneously, she examined the merchandise concealed under his blanket.

I was worried about our illegal activities at first, especially with the chief of police living in a house down the street—the house I just left. Yes, the chief of police and his wife, the Eberhardts, were my best customers.

Still, I was terrified when Emil was reported by someone in town and called into the police station for questioning. But Emil was cunning and street smart, making sure to also buy and sell items at the weekly market or a pawn shop in town, which was completely legal. It was a game of cat and mouse, and when a detective came asking about him, the shop owner or vendors at the market always vouched for him. Having Herr Eberhardt on our side didn't hurt either, and Emil was released.

Emil. We'd already had our share of fights. Fights no one won. That's what happens when both people are strong-willed and neither can admit they're wrong. The tension of having to provide for our little family in any way he could put him on edge.

Marriage wasn't the panacea I imagined it would be, but I loved him desperately, nonetheless.

At first, we lived with his mother, sister Olga, and his brother Johann. But we made enough money for a place of our own, an upstairs two-room apartment in a white brick house at Bergmannstrasse Number Three.

Home. The baby and I arrived and I left the buggy

inside the stairwell door. I checked my closet for something to wear, something different than what I wore to the meeting the night before. The navy dress would have to do.

It was Olga who invited me to the unusual church services held in town—revival meetings, as she put it. For the last few nights, practically half the town showed up in their Sunday best, singing along to the piano and listening to Pastor Goetz, a young traveling preacher. Emil didn't want to go, but I was glad to have something to do.

When I arrived, I sat next to Olga. The baby fell fast asleep in my arms to the sound of the piano and singing. When the preacher spoke, he talked about Jesus who came into the world as an innocent baby to an unwed mother and how, despite the scandal of his birth, he changed everything.

I lowered my gaze and brushed Waldemar's cheek, feeling a twinge of guilt and pain.

Did Mary receive the same scornful glances and rebuke from her mother as I had from mine at the news of being pregnant? Was she rejected, too?

I tried to think of bible stories from my childhood and couldn't remember any mention of Mary's mother. Maybe I wasn't alone. Maybe God understood.

I held Waldemar close as the preacher spoke about a Father to the fatherless, how God loved me, could heal my hurts, and would never leave me.

Never? Thoughts of Vati and his boundless love flooded my mind, and my eyes glistened with tears. Why did he have to leave me? Why did he have to die? I was a grown woman now, a wife and mother, yet inside I still felt like a lost little girl who wanted nothing more than to delight in her father's presence.

The preacher talked about the gift of grace and forgiveness.

About a loving God who was the light of the world.

Who gave the ultimate gift.

Who hung on a tree.

Who stood at the door of my heart, waiting. Waiting patiently to come in.

A memory flashed in my mind, one of Vati on a distant Christmas Eve, waiting eagerly behind a closed door.

The lights.

The gift.

The tree.

The look of delight and joy on his face when the door swung open and his waiting was over, when I rushed into his arms.

It would forever be etched in my mind. Oh how I longed to feel that kind of unconditional love again, that kind of light.

But I couldn't.

Not without opening the door.

A flood of emotion swept over me, and when the preacher asked whether anyone in the audience wanted to open the door of their heart, I raised my hand.

I wanted it more than anything.

I always believed in God, but I imagined him as a distant, mythical being, someone who watched from afar, issuing edicts and reigning down judgment. Now, he was nearer than anything I'd ever experienced before. I turned to Olga whose shining eyes met mine. She nodded reassuringly and squeezed my arm. Someone touched my shoulder. It was Frau Müller standing next to me, the friend who loaned me her wedding dress.

"Would you like to pray with me?" she asked.

Olga took the baby from my arms and I followed Frau Müller to the side of the room where we prayed.

God wasn't about to swoop in and fix my broken world in an instant. I wouldn't be instantly freed from my fearful thoughts and haunting memories. I knew that.

Life's circumstances wouldn't change. But something inside me did.

* * *

Months passed, and on a warm Monday evening, June 6th, I stood behind the Rittergut next to the river. The entire town showed up to watch. They'd never witnessed anything like it before. Two small tents stood side by side, one for boys and one for girls. About a dozen of us emerged wearing white.

When it was my turn, I walked barefoot to the water's edge and waded waist high into the crystal pool, the silty bottom squishing between my toes, the current tugging at my dress. Willow branches swayed around me like streamers, caressing the flowing water.

The sun danced on the surface and gleamed against my face, its warmth a welcome kiss in contrast to the cool waters below. The pastor held my hand tightly in his, then asked me to profess my faith.

I did.

I allowed my body to fall back, plunging to the depths of the stream. The water cascaded over me, enveloping me in its grip, swallowing the guilt and fears of my past and washing them downstream, far beyond my reach.

When the pastor lifted me, the water saturated every inch, including my soul. I exhaled and took a breath. A breath of new life.

I'd never felt so clean.

CHAPTER 31
Spring 1950

Another door wasn't so easily opened. Mutti's. It took a long time before I showed up with Waldemar in my arms. When I did, I stood outside, staring at the handle, wishing it would open on its own.

Would she answer? Would she peer out the window to see me standing there and pretend she wasn't home? My heart was pounding.

I knocked. I waited.

Nothing.

I knocked again.

Silence.

I turned to walk away when the click of a latch and squeak of a hinge cut through the air. A single suspicious eye peered out through a crack in the door.

"What are you doing here?" she asked.

I stepped toward her and the crack closed to a sliver.

Don't leave, I convinced myself. *Don't give up.*

"I, uh…" My tongue was suddenly parched. "I thought you should meet your grandson."

I held him out as if he were an offering at an altar.

A peace offering.

She stood stoic, surveying me and the baby. My arms grew tired. The door didn't budge. How was it we lived a block apart and yet neither of us would put away our pride enough to step across the cobblestones to reconcile?

Waldemar was nearly a year and a half old. She missed his first tooth, his first laugh, his first steps, his first word. I should have run to her with the thousands of questions I had as a new mother. But I couldn't change that now.

I brought the baby to my hip.

"Can I come in?"

Still no reaction. No response.

"Please?"

In the past, I wouldn't have pleaded or pressed on. Instead, I would have retreated defiantly in response to her cold reception with an "I'll show you" attitude, to show her I was in control, that she couldn't hurt me. And the chasm would have widened with each step.

But I stood my ground. If anyone was going to close the door on this relationship, it would have to be her. Not me.

The door crept open and I stepped inside. I didn't say a word. I simply slipped the baby into her arms as if it were the most natural thing in the world.

She held him as though he were a lifeless sack of flour, but as Waldemar squirmed and reached for her earring, she grasped his small hand and wrapped it around her thumb.

"No, no," she said with a surprisingly gentle tone. Her stiff grip softened and she held him close, conforming his little body to hers.

"I made some tea. Would you, uh——?" she asked with uncertainty in her voice.

"Yes. I'd like that."

She offered Waldemar back to me.

"No, you sit," I said. "I can get it."

She sat at the kitchen table with the baby in her lap, staring intently into his face as though looking for something.

Or someone.

"I think he—he has Vati's eyes," I said cautiously.

She glanced at me, startled, as though I read her thoughts. She studied his face again and swept his soft, blonde hair away from his forehead. She didn't say a word. The baby fussed and began to cry, reaching for me as I poured the tea.

"He's probably hungry," I said. "He gets a little cranky when he's hungry."

"Just like your father," she said with an unexpected smile.

She handed him to me, reluctantly, and he tugged at my blouse.

We awkwardly tried to make conversation as I fed him. It's not like we ever chatted like schoolgirls before. Not much needed to be said, I guess. The fact we sat in the same room was miracle enough.

"I—I mean, you." I wasn't sure how to tell her. "You're going to be a grandma again."

"Oh, I see."

I couldn't read her face. Was she happy? Disappointed? Maybe I shouldn't have told her I was pregnant again. Yes, too soon. She was just introduced to her first, and now the news of a second grandchild must certainly have been too much to take in.

How could I be so stupid? I tried to rush things and should have waited to tell her. But I couldn't stuff the words back inside my throat.

"Well, how… nice."

Her pained smile betrayed her true feelings, but I wasn't sure what those feelings were.

"I'm due this summer. I wanted you to know."

Her chair scraped backwards, and she stood. Was she going to tell me to leave? Instead, she bent to take a now sleeping Waldemar from my arms. She brought him to the stuffed chair in the corner, nestled him in blankets, and spoke softly and tenderly as she tucked him safely in between its thick, worn upholstered arms.

I said a simple, silent prayer as I watched.

Thank you.

For now, small steps would have to do. But we had time on our side. Time to rebuild what little connection there was or could be.

Or so I thought.

* * *

Weeks passed, and on a particularly dark night, Emil and some family members gathered in our small apartment. Cigarette smoke blanketed the air as animated voices debated the future.

"If we go back to the Ukraine, we'll be shot," said someone.

Several mumbled voices agreed.

"But can we stay here?" Emil responded. "I haven't found a decent job in three years, and I have a family to feed."

It was true. Our only source of income, the black market, was dwindling. Authorities were cracking down much harder than before and store shelves were fully stocked. People didn't have to meet in dark alleyways or sneak around town speaking in low whispers to buy what they wanted. Even if the items in the store were ridiculously expensive, most preferred buying there and not taking the risk of being arrested.

Olga and I sat to the side. Emil glanced at me and I nodded reassuringly.

"This is what we have to do," he said, pointing to a newspaper on the table.

A husband and wife with forced smiles leapt off the page. Their photo was next to an article telling about a family preparing to move to America. It was made possible by something called the Displaced Persons Act, a new law allowing persecuted refugees to emigrate from Germany to the United States.

When Emil told me of the idea a few days earlier, he was beaming with excitement.

"America is the land of opportunity, Waltraud. There's nothing for us here."

I knew he was right, and everyone spoke about how remarkable life was in America, but I struggled to match his enthusiasm. For him, traveling to yet another country, even one across the Atlantic, was commonplace, almost adventurous. He even had some distant relatives there. But for me, Germany was all I'd ever known.

For my entire life I lived within a short distance of here or there. I knew this land. I knew when swallows returned to roost under eaves and when to expect the snowdrops to emerge in spring. I knew the shortcuts to take with my bike to get to neighboring towns. I knew things, like how to get a smile out of the scowl-faced butcher when visiting his shop, and which stair tread on the way to our apartment squeaked like an injured cat under the weight of my step.

Could I possibly leave everything and everyone I knew, especially since Mutti and I were talking again?

As a refugee, Emil and his family had little choice. And because I was his wife, I had little choice either. He and his family knew they couldn't repatriate to the Ukraine, yet few in Germany were willing to hire foreigners. It left him stuck in no mans land.

No country. No job. No future.

The room felt small and I moved to open a window to let in some fresh air.

"Keep it closed," said Emil. "We don't want the neighbors to hear."

I reluctantly obeyed and Emil shared his plan with the

others.

"There's one problem," he said. "We—we need someone to go to Leipzig."

"Leipzig!" someone shouted. "You might as well send us straight to Siberia!"

"Keep your voices down!" Emil urged with a whisper as loud as their shouts.

"As if we can hop on a train and go there on a holiday," said another sarcastically.

Before the war, anyone would have jumped at a chance to visit the city of Leipzig with its cultural attractions and bustling marketplace. But now, it sat squarely in the East Zone under Russian control.

Several voices clamored for attention when Emil's broke through.

"Our papers," he said as his hand slapped the table. "That's where our papers are. They're our ticket to America."

"Why in Leipzig?" someone asked.

Olga chimed in. "They're with our uncle, Michael Czarnetzki."

Michael was married to their aunt Emma—Emil's mother's sister—and the couple immigrated to Germany in the early 1930s long before the war broke out. Emil's mother sent the family's documents along with Emma for safe keeping so they wouldn't fall into the hands of the communists.

But Emma died since—at least, that's what Michael's story was—and he still had the papers. Without them, there was no hope of America.

For months, Michael and Emil exchanged letters, writing in secret codes in case they were intercepted or screened. It was an impossible situation. Michael wasn't willing to risk his neck trying to cross the border from the east, and if Emil or any of his family members were caught crossing from the west, they would be immediately deported. Or they'd disappear without a trace.

"I'll go."

The voice was foreign, a distant echo, but it was coming from my own lips.

"Waltraud, no!" Olga couldn't believe her ears. "You know what the Russians do to women. What if you're caught?"

There was fear in Emil's eyes.

"I can't let you go," he said. "Besides, our baby."

"Who else can go?" I said. "You said it yourself. Everyone else in this room would be a dead man if they were caught. I'm the only one with German papers. They would never deport me."

I wasn't so sure of my statement, but I said it with confidence anyway.

"And they aren't going to do anything to a pregnant woman," I reasoned.

Truth is, I was barely showing and I'd have a hard time convincing anyone I was with child and due in a few months. Inside, my nerves rattled like stones in a glass jar, threatening to shatter and betray my outward confidence.

But there was something else. Amid the fear, I also felt brave, a sense of determination and exhilarated anticipation. It's something I hadn't felt since the war squeezed the light from my eyes, since Hitler sucked the life out of me and nearly all of Europe. The entire nation was wandering aimlessly in search of something.

Of what, I didn't know.

Germany was soundly defeated and with it, my sense of who I was. But ever since I walked out of that river, a new sense of being was slowly rising within me.

We talked long into the night, and by the time we were done, it was decided.

I would go.

CHAPTER 32
Spring 1950

The hazy moon cast shadows through thick trees, and several dogs barked in the distance. Every footstep was an explosion as we walked through the wilderness in single file. If the guards didn't hear the crack of branches beneath our feet, they'd surely hear my pounding heart. Or worse, the dogs would smell our fear and be let loose to hunt us down like helpless rabbits, ripping our flesh into pieces.

I doubted my decision to go, but there was no turning back. If stopped by guards, we were told not to run, but to surrender. They were prone to shooting first and asking questions later.

There were three others being smuggled with me, two men and a woman. We didn't know each other's names. We weren't supposed to. The less we knew, the better. No one said a word.

Through his dealings with the black market, Emil

knew someone in Helmstedt who would smuggle me into East Germany for one-hundred Deutschmarks. It was a lot of money, but others chipped in since they needed the papers, too.

"Walk one kilometer outside town," said Emil before I left to meet the smuggler. The sun was setting and it would be dark soon. "If anyone comes, hide in the ditch. You'll come to a bend in the road. There's a telephone pole next to a large boulder. Duck into the woods on the left side of the road. He'll meet you there."

Emil embraced me as though he were saying goodbye for the last time. "He'll get you through safely," he whispered in my ear. The catch in his voice betrayed his confidence. He released me and held my shoulders squarely.

"You have your identification card?"

"Yes," I said. "And my birth certificate."

"Good. I—I—wish there was some other way."

"There isn't," I said. Now I was the one whose voice trembled. "I'll meet you at the restaurant where we had soup for lunch."

He stroked my hair and rested his cheek on mine. I didn't want to let go, but eventually headed down the road to meet a stranger who would hold my life in his hands.

Our small group of outlaws went through the woods to cross the border. It was best that way, we were told. Other border locations were lined with sand, and guards raked it every morning to clear footprints left from people who crossed the night before. Inexperienced smugglers would get caught when they tried to take the same route again.

We approached a narrow clearing and a silhouette of crisscrossed timbers stretched out before us. The border. It was hard to make it out in the dark, and without the guidance of the smuggler, I would have stumbled right into them or mistaken them as fallen logs. My eyes adjusted. A roll of woven barbed wire spiraled across the top of the barrier. How in the world would we get through?

Holding his finger to his lips, he motioned for us to stop at the edge of the clearing. He listened, then stepped lightly toward the wooden beams.

A breeze blew through the treetops and cast a white noise over the forest, making it difficult to hear anything out of place. Perhaps it was a good thing, helping to mask the crunch of our footsteps against the previous season's fallen leaves and dried grasses.

The loud crack of a branch punctured the darkness. We stopped dead in our tracks. The girl gasped with a whimper and the man with her quickly covered her mouth with his hand. Her shining eyes were filled with terror and I thought she might go mad and start screaming in panic.

More rustling.

Should we freeze or run for our lives? We were still on our side of the border. Surely they wouldn't shoot us if we were still in the West Zone.

Could they?

A high-pitched snort shot through the trees followed by the beat of hooves running in the opposite direction.

Deer. Thank God.

We all took a deep breath. If there were guards patrolling the area, there's no way a herd of deer would have been bedded down or grazing young saplings nearby. They would have been long gone, and from the looks of it, the guards were, too.

The smuggler motioned the all clear as he pulled out a pair of gloves from his pack. He reached for the wire and separated it strand by strand. It obviously was cut beforehand, and this wasn't the first time he'd crossed here.

One by one, we scaled the beams and crossed to the other side. He meticulously braided the barbed wire back together as though it had never been cut. We walked for a long while until we reached the edge of the woods and he motioned for us to stop again. Lights from a small town flickered in the countryside a couple kilometers ahead.

"Here are your train tickets," he whispered. "And five Marks to hand to the train attendant. Discretely, now. Like this."

He folded the money under the ticket and demonstrated in the blackness, handing each of us our passes with the money tucked beneath his clutched hand.

"The train leaves in the morning. Make sure you get into town before sunrise."

He spoke in rapid succession, rattling off instructions as though he'd said them a hundred times before. He had.

"Find the main road and follow it to the train station, but stay out of plain sight. Don't stop anywhere or speak to anyone. Don't sit next to each other on the train. I'll meet you back here next to this pine tree tomorrow night after dark. God speed."

And just like that, he disappeared into the night.

We got to the train station before dawn and stood separately, waiting to step onto the platform. The announcement came, and people started boarding.

The man taking tickets gave me a strange look. His face was long and bony, wrapped in leathery skin, and his eyes squinted as though the sun were beaming down. But the skies were overcast with dark clouds rolling in, and it looked like it might rain.

I nervously handed him the ticket with the folded money tucked underneath. I didn't even notice his sleight of hand or where it went when he handed the ticket back to me, but the money was gone.

"Guten Tag," he said with a tip of his hat and a creepy, half-toothed smile.

I nodded and squeezed past him to find a seat by the window, holding my rucksack in my lap. One of the men from the group was already seated a few rows ahead of me. He didn't look out of place, and I hoped I didn't either.

But then the girl who whimpered at the sound of the deer came down the aisle and stared at me with those same terrified eyes, as though they'd be stuck that way forever. I looked away, pretending to peer out the window. She couldn't have been more obvious. If something went wrong, I had no doubt she would be the reason.

Others filed in and the train started moving. I sat for a

long while, drifting in and out of a half-wake state. It had been a long night, but sleep wouldn't come. I rummaged in my sack for the small loaf of bread I packed, picking off small chunks and eating them as discretely as I could. I was past the morning sickness, but didn't dare eat anything too rich, especially with the moving train.

A withered old man with a scraggly white beard sat next to me. His suspenders pulled his worn, baggy pants nearly to his chest. He stared my way and wet his lips, his eyes fixed intently on the bread in my hand, as though it were a ghostly vision. I'd seen that look before many times during the war.

It was hunger.

"Here," I said, and broke off half the loaf.

His eyes moved from the bread to meet mine with skepticism and suspicion.

"I'm not very hungry," I said, gesturing for him to take it.

It wasn't far from the truth. My stomach was turning from all the nerves.

"It's a shame to let it get stale."

He sheepishly accepted my gift, and it made my heart glad as he savored each bite. Was this what life was like now for everyone across the border? Or was he only a poor old man I happened to sit next to by chance?

We were pulling into a stop at a train station when he turned to me.

"You're not from here, are you?"

I froze.

"What? What do you mean?" I'm sure he sensed the

panic in my voice.

"No one on this side shares their food. It's everyone for themselves."

What had I done? I didn't follow the simple rule to not speak with anyone. Was he an informant? A hungry man might do anything for a slice of bread. Would he turn me in? I sat motionless as the train came to a stop. He stood. He was going to tell someone. I knew it.

Instead, he bent low.

"Be careful. Don't speak to anyone."

I nodded slowly, acknowledging the same words the smuggler told me. This time, I would heed his advice.

The old man hobbled off the train. The crumbs sat mockingly on my skirt, evidence of my foolishness. I swept them to the floor and put the remaining bread back in my bag. When a middle-aged woman boarded the train and sat in his place, I didn't make eye contact. I didn't say a word. I wouldn't speak to another soul until I got to Leipzig.

I turned away from her and leaned my head against the window, looking out at the war-torn town as the train pulled away from the stop. I found it hard to believe there were still half-bombed-out buildings left standing after five years. Some of them looked lived in.

I had entered another realm, a half-lit dream where everything looked drab and lifeless. If I didn't know better, I'd have thought the train windows were made of clouded glass, casting drab shades of gray over the entire landscape. Or maybe it was the rain clouds. But I sensed it was something more. It made me sad to think we were once one people, one nation. But now there were two Germanys, two worlds.

After hours on the train, Leipzig came into view. As the train slowed, I barely believed my eyes. I'd never seen a train station so immense and palatial. The concourse alone would have taken up half of Beienrode.

Stepping onto the platform, a web of arched metal soared above, some portions perfectly symmetrical while others were tangled and twisted with big gaps revealing the clouds—remnants of a bomb strike years earlier, no doubt. I had to catch myself from staring at the awe-filled wonder of it and drawing attention. With so many people bustling along, no one noticed me, though. Good. It would be easy to blend in with the crowd.

It felt good to escape the stuffy train car to stretch my legs and catch some fresh air. I searched for a street sign and dug in my rucksack for the piece of paper with the address. I studied the hand-drawn map.

Walking through Leipzig with its tree-lined streets reminded me of Braunschweig—the way it was before all the bombings. Like many larger German cities, it didn't escape unscathed, but it wasn't hit as bad. And they didn't use incendiary bombs to burn it to the ground.

A knot twisted in my stomach. Try as I could, I couldn't forget the bombing of Braunschweig and the bodies in the mass grave. The face of the dead girl with braids would forever be carved in my memory.

I shook it from my thoughts. I needed to stay alert. Concern over being discovered by the Russians or East German Stasi police was eerily familiar, like when I encountered a Nazi SS officer or Brown Shirt during the war. I hoped to never have to feel that kind of fear again. But I did. I was sure my every step was being watched. Vati's words came to mind—*Listening ears are everywhere.*

I looked behind me. Nothing. I kept walking.

How was it, by some chance of fate, I ended up on the right side of the border where, despite the hardships, there was freedom. Freedom to move about. Freedom to say what I believed. Freedom to think.

I didn't fully realize how oppressive it was living under Nazi rule until I wasn't. I couldn't get back home soon enough, to get out of this dismal place.

But first, I had to complete my mission.

A blister on my heel throbbed and my muscles ached, but I still had several more blocks to go. What I wouldn't give for a hot bath and a soft bed. But from the look of the run-down row houses, I'd be lucky to get another piece of bread. I hoped Emil's uncle was hospitable, unlike the women who passed me by, keeping their eyes low and their children close. Or the elderly women who leaned their elbows on windowsills, peering out through tattered curtains, keeping a watchful eye on the stranger roaming their neighborhood.

I arrived at the address and climbed the stairs to find the right apartment number. The soft tap of my knuckles echoed along the barren walls. The click of a lock came from the end of the hallway. In front of me, a man barely opened the door. A suspicious glare studied me with eyes too small for his head. Everyone gave suspicious looks.

"What do you want?" His gruff voice spoke low.

"I—I am Waltraud. Emil's wife."

The corner of his mouth twitched and his eyes shrank further as he opened the door only enough to look down the hallway. Empty.

"Get in."

I slipped through the narrow opening.

"Were you followed?"

"No, I don't think so," I said. "I hope I'm not any trouble. I—"

"Sit down."

I sat at the kitchen table and took in my surroundings. It was a cramped two-room apartment on the third floor and everything looked tired. The same thread-bare curtains I saw along the way hung on their windows, only they were closed in a vain attempt to keep the outside world in its place. The housing shortage in Leipzig was similar to every other city in Germany, regardless of which side someone was on.

His wife barely looked at me from the stove where she was frying something putrid. It was the familiar suspicious glance, and I felt uneasy. Who was this woman who mysteriously took the place of Emil's aunt? No one was sure what happened. We only knew his aunt disappeared and their only son, a teenager at the time, left home, never to return or speak to his father again.

She didn't acknowledge me, and the tension between her and Michael filled the room. It was because of me. She didn't want me there. I could tell. I wouldn't have minded a cup of tea or even a glass of water, but I wasn't about to ask.

Michael grumbled as he rummaged through a cupboard door. He slid aside some mismatched plates and pulled out a wooden box.

"You're sure no one saw you?"

He glared at me. He didn't want me there either.

I didn't dare tell him about the close call with the man on the train who knew I was from the west. I wouldn't make the same mistake again.

"I came straight here."

"Hmph," he grunted, dismissing my assurances as though I took a tour of the countryside and strolled through the park feeding pigeons on my way.

"I can't believe they sent a woman."

I straightened my back and sat silent. He was condescending and crass, put off I was there. Emil's mother mentioned he was a stern and controlling man, but I wasn't expecting such a cold reception.

The lid of the box flipped open and he removed some rolled up papers tied with string and others folded in quarters.

"These are the ones," he said as he unfolded several thick pages and slid them in front of me. "They're of no use to me."

"Thank you."

My expression of gratitude was met with a scowl. Was he angry because he resented our hopes of going to the United States while he was stuck in East Germany? Or was he an embittered old man, the type who snarled at children playing in the park or wagged a threatening finger at anyone with a different opinion? I sensed it was the latter, and I understood why his only son didn't stick around.

I held the papers gently, for fear they'd disintegrate at my touch like an ancient scroll. The edges were torn and the pages stained, but it felt like recovering priceless crown jewels or discovering a missing renaissance painting. And here it was, all along, in a cramped apartment tucked away in a box, guarded by a bitter, old stranger who couldn't wait for me to leave.

I knew they were only paper, but they were heavy in my hands, like lead. Perhaps it was the weight of what they meant. I held the destiny of myself, my children, Emil and his entire family in my hands.

CHAPTER 33
Spring 1950

I settled into a seat on the train and looked out the window, thankful I was on my way back. It was going to be another long day, but at least I could rest. I kept my bag close, afraid to leave it out of my sight.

The night in Michael's apartment was long and awkward, and I couldn't stomach whatever it was his wife cooked up. She and Michael got in a fight, yelling back and forth about whether or not I should stay there overnight. It's like I wasn't even in the room. I sat silent at the table, awaiting my fate.

Thankfully, Michael won and I didn't get tossed on the street. By the defeated look on his wife's face, I had a feeling Michael always won.

Could I blame her for wanting me to leave? A neighbor could easily report a stranger was staying with them, and they'd get in trouble for harboring someone who was unauthorized to be there.

Watchful eyes made it hard to spit or clear your throat without being dragged to the police station for questioning. Michael himself reminded me of a staunch Nazi who would turn on someone without blinking. I barely said a word all night for fear he'd find a reason to change his mind and kick me out.

From the looks of it, it didn't take much convincing for him to ease right into the Russian way of doing things when they took over from the Nazis.

Different rulers. Same rules.

The train ride seemed longer. Anticipation, I suppose. Or maybe it was my aching back from sleeping on the kitchen floor the night before. I adjusted in my seat, unable to get comfortable, unable to sleep. I stared out the window.

The rain clouds were gone and gaps of blue poked through, allowing rays of sunshine to stream down over the countryside. The fields were alive with new growth after the spring rain, a patchwork of every shade of green. The world looked more vivid than it did the day before, and the same towns I passed didn't look as depressing.

My mission was nearly complete and I considered the bright skies a sign the rest of my journey would go smoothly. I'd be home that night. Granted, it would be too late to tuck Waldemar into bed, but not too late to nestle against Emil in the safety of his arms and the comfort of my own bed.

I arrived in the border town and exited the train. It would be a few more hours before dark, so I decided to find a place to eat or have a cup of tea. It was a small town, but surely there must be a Gasthaus or even a bakery. I strayed from the train station and turned the corner.

A big mistake. A border policeman was headed straight toward me.

How could I be so foolish to walk the streets like a common citizen? There must have been dozens of strangers who showed up unannounced every week to catch a train, all of them waiting for their chance to cross the border one way or the other. Surely the East German police knew it.

I stuck out like a sore thumb with my red hair and newer clothes, let alone the panic settling on my face. I didn't dare bolt. Nor did I dare freeze in my tracks. Either would raise suspicion. But what if he asked for my papers? How could I explain why I was there?

Stay calm, I convinced myself. Look normal. Take a deep breath.

I was resigned to be stopped and interrogated when a man hobbled across the street in front of me, stopping to speak with the officer. He reminded me of someone, someone I——. Could it be? It was the man from the train who I gave bread to the day before.

Dear God. He's going to tell the authorities about me. He's going to point me out and lead him straight to me.

Instead, he and the officer walked in the opposite direction. I stood dumbfounded as the man glanced back with a wink. Was he a man or had I entertained an angel in disguise?

I didn't spend time pondering it. I made my way off the street and headed for the edge of town, watching to make sure no one followed. I'd find a place to hide until nightfall. It didn't matter how hungry I was. I'd lost my appetite anyway.

The sun crept behind the horizon. My legs were stiff and cramped from crouching behind bushes, and pins and needles pricked my feet. Feeling slowly returned and I headed toward the edge of the woods, practically sprinting across the fields and fence rows. The moon and stars gave barely enough light and I stumbled several times in unseen furrows. I feared I might step right into a fox hole and break my ankle. The silhouette of trees traced the night sky. A single pine tree pointed to the stars.

Almost there.

The man and woman from the group were hiding behind the trunk of the tree and I joined them. Another figure emerged beside us. We all made it.

The strange hoot of an owl lofted through the darkness. It was the smuggler's call, alerting us of his presence.

Just as we had the night before, we followed him in single file. The forest held an eerie silence and a chill settled in the air, signaling a late spring frost. The smuggler was more nervous than he was the night before and he walked slower.

He stopped. Stepped. Then stopped again.

He stood for a long time, and I swear the hiss of our frosty breath carried to the watch tower standing several kilometers away.

"Why aren't we moving?" whispered the girl whose nerves were on edge the day before, and she was even more skittish today.

"Shhhh!" the man with her reprimanded her.

I didn't see the smuggler's face, but I imagined he was furious at her, wishing he never allowed her to come along. I wished the same.

The forest was too quiet. Too still. It didn't feel natural.

The budding branches of the oaks and elm trees were holding an awful secret, waiting for the right moment to blurt it out with all its ugly consequences.

A shadow crawled from behind a tree and a beaming light blinded my eyes. A booming voice shattered the silence.

"Halt!"

The girl shrieked. She ran. A tree branch swung back, slapping my cheek. A flashlight followed her. A shot rang out and she crumpled to the ground in a heap of sobs and wailing.

"Don't shoot! Don't shoot! Oh my God! No!" She screamed over and over. She wasn't hit. The soldier merely shot into the air as a merciful warning to not run.

The rest of us froze with our hands held high, and dogs barked in the distance. I'd felt fear before. Fear when the bombs fell. Fear when the foreman raged at me at Pflichtjahr. Fear when the SS officers nearly caught me helping the English soldiers. But as the glint of the soldier's rifle reflected off the beam of his flashlight, there was a level of intense terror I'd never experienced before.

I thought for sure my legs would give way beneath me, or my thrashing nerves would betray me. I was caught in their snare in a foreign land where I didn't belong, where anything could be done to us without anyone ever hearing of it. We might disappear into thin air, never to be seen or heard from again.

The soldier lined us in a row, shining the intense light into our faces one by one. I shielded my eyes with my forearm, only to have him thrust it away with the barrel of his rifle.

"Hands above your head!"

My arms shot up and I turned my face to the side. Was he going to execute us on the spot without a trial?

Was this the end of my journey here on earth? Was this how Vati met his end, lined up and shot by the Russians and left in the forest to rot?

Instead, the soldier marched us back to the open field, prodding and poking with his rifle when someone stumbled or he thought we weren't going fast enough.

"Don't get any stupid ideas," he said as he forced us toward the watchtower.

I wasn't about to put up a fight. There were stories of how soldiers shot someone in the leg or heel if they tried to make a wrong move, leaving them a cripple, or letting them slowly bleed to death.

When I found myself alone in an interrogation room, my mind whirled with scenarios of what would happen. Would I be strip searched? Raped?

I remembered stories of those who took their own lives rather than fall into the hands of the Russians to be raped and brutalized at the end of the war. I once knew a girl who was defiled by the Russians. She hid her younger sister to save her from the same fate. Is that what awaited me?

I was encased in concrete. No windows. No furniture besides two wooden stools and a crude table. Paint was peeling off the walls and it was cold and musty, reminding me of cramped, wartime bomb shelters. A spider crawled across the floor and disappeared under the door. He didn't want to be stuck in there either.

Claustrophobia set in and I paced back and forth despite my exhaustion, a million thoughts going through my head. Would they keep me forever?

They confiscated my rucksack when I arrived and, with it, my papers and all the documentation I got from Michael. It was all for naught. Tears streamed down my face at my hopeless situation.

Outside, a slamming metal door rang through the hall and heavy footsteps approached. Someone fumbled with a key in the lock. The door swung open.

"Well, Fräulein," the warden said. "Or is it Frau?"

I was afraid to speak and looked at him red-faced, waiting for his next move.

"Well, which is it?" He sat at the table and motioned for me to sit across from him.

"Frau. Frau Tomtschik," I said, my voice cracking with each syllable.

I lowered myself to the stool in slow motion. I sat

upright, my hands in my lap, my heart in my throat.

"We're off to a good start then," he said as he studied his clipboard. "Your papers say the same. If you continue to be honest with me, you might get to go home."

"Yes, sir."

"What happened to your face?"

I reached for my cheek, feeling the crusted blood.

"A tree branch," I said.

"So, it's not from my officer? They're known to get a little rough now and then when people don't cooperate."

"I've been cooperating."

"That's what I like to hear." He handed me a handkerchief and I wiped the dried blood from my face, being careful not to make the cut start bleeding again.

"Now, tell me, what's a young woman from—" he looked at the papers on his clipboard. "Beienrode. Yes, that's it. What is a young woman from a small village across the border doing this far to the east? Did you get lost?" he said with sarcasm.

I should have rehearsed what I would say if I were caught. I didn't dare mention Michael. I had no doubt someone would show up at his door the next morning to interrogate him and he'd tell them exactly what they wanted to hear to save his own neck.

"Well?" He waited. "Who are the people with you on tonight's stroll through the forest?"

"I don't know," I said truthfully.

"You don't expect me to believe that, do you?"

"We didn't speak to each other. We were told not to."

"I see. So you don't know them?"

"No. I only met them yesterday. Some of the others might be together, but I can't know for sure. I'm alone."

"We have them each in separate rooms right now for questioning. We'll see if your stories match up. And the leader?" he asked.

"I don't know his name. Someone else arranged for me to meet him on the other side. I—I just gave him the money to get me across and didn't ask questions."

"How much?"

"One-hundred Deutschmarks."

His eyebrows raised, as if calculating how much the smuggler had taken in on a single night.

"A lot of money for a young woman. Where did you get it?"

"I was saving up."

"For what?"

I thought hard about what to say.

"Do you have family? Across the border?"

I dared to ask the question, hoping against hope his heart would be moved. Surely he had one.

He was German. I could tell by how fluently he spoke. He only had a hint of the thick Russian accent I heard coming from the mouths of other soldiers when I was taken to the room. Maybe I could appeal to his heritage, his recollection of a time when Germany was one country. How is it we were now enemies?

"I'm the one asking the questions here," he said. "Why are you here?"

"Family," I said. "It wasn't so long ago we traveled back and forth to see each other for no reason at all other than to be together, never imagining we'd be separated like this."

He nodded.

"Now, we can only wave from across rivers or electric fences, unable to hug one another or even shake a hand. We can't exchange Christmas gifts. Can't attend someone's wedding. A woman has to hold up her baby to show him to her parents who will never hold their grandchild, never hear them say Opa or Oma. Why did I come here? Family."

While it wasn't the whole truth, it wasn't a lie either. I meant every word I said. I knew families who were separated by raked sand and barbed wire. He didn't need to know the only family I had in the East Zone was a sour old man who I couldn't wait to get away from.

"You're quite sentimental, Waltraud."

I prickled at him calling me by my first name.

"Now, tell me about these papers."

He pulled the remaining documents from a leather satchel. I stared, thankful they hadn't been incinerated.

"They belong to my husband."

"So why are they with you?"

"You know how it was in the last days of the war. The chaos. Trying to stay one step ahead of the bombs. One step ahead of the, the—"

"The Russians?" He read my mind. His intense gaze made me uneasy.

"He lost his papers. I came to get them back."

"So the truth comes out. From who?"

I sat silent.

"Well?"

"An uncle. In Leipzig."

"Leipzig? You've had quite the adventure." To my astonishment and relief, he didn't press for any further details about this mysterious uncle.

"Why didn't your husband come? Why is he sending a woman to do his job?"

It was a slight against Emil, as though he weren't man enough to risk his own life and, instead, risked mine. But this man didn't know how brave Emil was, what he endured, how he'd do anything for me and his family.

But he couldn't do this.

"I have my papers," I said. "He doesn't. I can prove who I am. He can't. What would you do if he were the one sitting in this room without any proof of his right to be in Germany—on either side. I think we both know."

The warden studied the documents in silence, then tucked them back in his satchel.

"Come with me." He stood and opened the door, motioning for me to exit.

"What about my papers?"

"I'll put them in safe keeping."

He walked me down a long corridor, his keys jingling from his hip with each step. He stopped in front of a door with metal bars and fingered through the keys on the ring, then opened the lock.

"You'll stay here."

The metal door opened with a long, drawn-out screech. Inside, a single wooden cot sat against a dingy concrete wall with faded yellow paint. A bucket sat in the corner for relieving myself, the stench of urine already in the air. A shelf against the wall was bare except for a bowl of broth and a piece of bread.

"There's food for you there. I'll be back with more questions later after I speak with your friends."

"They're not my—"

The door rattled shut behind me. It was dark and cold. What time was it? How many hours had passed since we were apprehended, since I was placed in the interrogation room? I lost track. All I could think of was Emil waiting at our meeting place as each hour passed, growing more frantic with each chime of the church bell in town.

Eleven. Twelve. One. Two. It must have been close to morning, maybe even daybreak. But the windowless walls of the prison gave no clues.

I removed my shoes and pressed my swollen feet against the cold floor. It was soothing to the touch. I felt the rim of the soup bowl. Cold. The piece of bread was small and stale, but I forced myself to choke it down. I hadn't eaten since, since—I couldn't remember. I hadn't slept. Of that, I was sure.

I climbed onto the cot and sat with my back against the wall and my knees to my chest, pulling the thin, scratchy blanket around my shoulders. Despite my exhaustion, sleep wouldn't come. There wasn't even a pillow.

I leaned back, closing my eyes, trying to pray, trying to speak to a God who I was sure had abandoned me. Agonizing thoughts squeezed at my heart.

How long would I be held here?

Would Emil eventually give up hope?

If too much time passed, would he find someone else?

Would my son grow up and not remember my face, my voice, my touch?

What would happen to the child inside me?

I was convinced I would spend the rest of my days in a cold, lonely prison.

Wasn't Paul the apostle in prison? Didn't the ground shake and the prison doors swing open at the sound of his praise, releasing the shackles from his feet? I tried to recall the lyrics to a hymn, but words failed me.

Before I knew it, I was with him, strolling through ancient Roman streets. No words were said, but I had a peace I couldn't explain. He guided me toward the city gate and smiled as he walked away. I eased into a run, effortlessly floating above the dusty road toward an indescribable joy, an indescribable light, a light so bright I could barely look upon it.

The beam of a flashlight hit my face. Keys jammed into the lock of my cell door, jolting me awake. The prison door swung open. Was I still in a dream? How long had I slept? Throughout the night, I was dragged out of the cell for more interrogation, then in, then out again. Or was that a dream, too?

"Out!"

It was a Russian guard. In a daze, I scrambled to put on my shoes, then followed him back down the corridor to the interrogation room.

"Come in. Sit down," said the warden.

I did as I was told and the door shut behind me. I still

felt disoriented.

"You were able to rest?"

"Not exactly," I said.

"Well, next time we'll be sure to put you up at a Gasthaus in town."

He was pleased with himself over his little joke. I stared blankly, uncertain whether to say another word.

"But there won't be a next time. Will there?"

"No sir."

"Frau Tomtschik, do you know what the others said about you? The others you were caught with in the forest?"

"I hope they told the truth like I did."

"Well, it's hard to know, isn't it?"

I sat silent.

"Frau Tomtschik. Your friends claim they don't know you either. Don't know why you crossed the border. Don't know the smuggler."

I was relieved, thankful they didn't crack under pressure and make up some wild story to get out of trouble. But it didn't change the fact I still sat across from a prison warden.

"It all sounds a little too convenient to me. I'll give you one more chance to tell me the truth."

"I haven't told any lies."

"Ah, but you're holding something back, aren't you?" he said with a stare.

"I don't know what else to tell you. There's nothing more. I only want to get home to my son. He needs me." His stare softened.

"He's about a year and half now. Likes to play with wooden blocks and gets into everything. Blonde hair. Blue eyes. The perfect boy."

I felt guilty appealing to his superior Aryan mentality. I'm sure it still lingered. But I knew no other way to gain his sympathies.

"Do you have any children?" I asked.

"None of your business."

I sat, silent.

"Two sons," he finally said, looking at the papers in front of him, pretending to make a note.

"My second is due this summer."

He craned his neck over the table to look at my stomach.

"You don't look it."

"I know, but it's true. I swear to you. I'm not some infiltrator, some spy. I'm just a mother who wants a better life for her children. Just like you. Just like all Germans. It shouldn't matter where the border is."

He sat silent for a long while, then reached to the floor and raised his satchel to his lap. One by one, he pulled out my identification papers, then those from Michael and placed them on the table with my rucksack. I held my breath, afraid to hope.

"Gather your things. My guard will take you to Checkpoint Alpha in Helmstedt and release you there."

My head spun. Released?

"But it must be understood," he said. "You are never to step foot across the border without authorization again."

When I emerged from the prison, another day was coming to an end. My eyes adjusted to the sun now low in the sky. Had I been in the prison for one night or two? I lost all sense of time.

An officer instructed me to climb into a truck and he drove me to the border crossing where a long guardhouse stood beside the road. A smaller hut had a red star on top and a hammer and sickle on the side. There was another truck ahead, and the girl with terrified eyes was ordered out and escorted to the white, wooden border gate. Once through, she bolted down the road and disappeared. The other two men and the smuggler were nowhere to be seen.

Several men roamed about in long military uniforms and hats. The officer stepped out of the truck and showed one of the border guards his orders to release me.

He returned. "Get out."

He motioned for me to walk through the gate and stood behind me with his rifle slung across his chest, as though I might try to sneak past him to get back in. Such a ridiculous notion. I never wanted to step foot inside the East Zone again.

I walked to the other side. The ground. The trees. The clouds. The birds. The people. They were all the same on one side of the gate as they were on the other, yet worlds apart. I clutched my rucksack to my chest and ran into Helmstedt, a free woman.

The town was growing still as evening approached and I was tempted to find a Gasthaus for the night, but I wanted nothing more than to get home, even if it took hours to get there by foot. Maybe my bicycle was still where I left it tucked behind the restaurant, the one where Emil and I had lunch, where we were supposed to meet. I decided to check.

I rounded the corner, and I couldn't believe my eyes. There he was, sitting alone at a table outside with his bike propped against the wall. Emil. Had he been there the whole time?

Even from behind, he looked older and lost in some sad way with his wrinkled coat draped over his hunched shoulders. He kept searching down the street in the direction where I was supposed to have returned. He raked his hand through his hair and leaned against the building. My legs felt like they might dissolve with each quickened step.

"Looking for someone?"

He spun around, his face etched with anguish, his eyes bloodshot from worry. A waterfall of desperation released into a tide of relief as he bolted from his chair and wrapped me in his arms. Our bodies shook and I wept in his embrace.

"Oh my God, my God!" he said over and over again, kissing my cheeks, my hair, my shoulder, my hand.

It was as though he wanted to confirm I was real with each touch of his lips, not an apparition that might vanish into thin air.

"I thought I lost you. I thought—" He couldn't bring himself to speak his deepest fears. "I've come every day. When you didn't come, I—"

His face grimaced. Again, he stopped short, unable to speak the unthinkable.

"What happened?" he asked.

"We were caught. We were so close, and then—"

"Are you okay? They didn't—"

His mind was spinning with disturbing thoughts of torture and profane abuse.

"Your cheek." He tenderly touched it with his thumb and searched my eyes.

"No. No. They didn't hurt me."

The torment lifted from his shoulders and I tried to conjure a weak smile as I patted my rucksack.

"I have the papers," I said.

"Those stupid papers."

He shook his head and held me close again, stroking my hair.

"I've been cursing those papers," he said. "They're why this happened. I should have never let you go."

He grasped my face in his hands and our teary eyes met. "It's you I need."

I wanted to stay in the safety of his arms forever, but I had to get home to my boy, to hold him in my arms and never let go.

"Can we go home?" I said.

I wanted nothing more.

He retrieved my bike, and we made our way toward a prism of colors. The sunset cast a luminous glow across the landscape and made every blade of grass glisten like emeralds.

I told the story of the last few harrowing days as we

rode side by side down the dusty road toward an indescribable joy, an indescribable light.

CHAPTER 34
September 1951

M uch time passed since that terrible yet glorious day, and life became a whirlwind of planning, filling out forms, writing letters, visiting government offices, filling out more forms, and waiting.

Each immigrant family needed to find someone living in the United States willing to sponsor them, someone who would take responsibility for the family for the first two years to help them get accustomed to a new land and find a job.

Emil's second cousin, a man named John Bieber whose family immigrated years earlier to a state named Wisconsin, agreed.

Some of Emil's family already made the trip and settled in the city of Milwaukee. Their letters told of the abundance and how easy it was to find work, and our anticipation grew.

At first, a church in Idaho was eager to sponsor us,

and we almost agreed, thinking we'd visit his family on weekends. We had no idea how expansive America was—so unlike Germany where you could travel from one region to the next in a couple of hours by train, a half a day at most. In America, it would take days to travel one way. So we decided on Wisconsin. It would take time to get used to saying such strange names.

Our daughter, Monika, was over a year old already. She was born July 29, 1950, and was so tiny people thought she was premature. Anneliesa liked babysitting Waldemar, but was thrilled to have a niece, a little girl to play with or dress up. Werner worked as a baker and we'd visit when he came to town.

Any gains I had with Mutti were erased when I told her about our plans to move to America. I was helpless to do anything about it and tried to put myself in her shoes. Maybe she felt abandoned or forgotten. Or maybe she was trying to hasten the inevitable, creating a separation sooner than later instead of waiting for an ocean to do it.

In the year since Monika was born, our housing allocation increased again, and we lived in a three-room house with an attached shed that once held a blacksmith shop. Having a house to ourselves, albeit small, was a luxury. There was a yard for the children to play in and a garden where I could plant flowers and vegetables.

It was good to get my hands in the dirt and watch things grow, rekindling my connection to the earth, the land, and nature. I was happy there, yet a sadness overshadowed me as I knelt and held the soil in my hands, the soil of my homeland, a home I might never see again. I softly wept on my knees, tears splashing on the ground. I surveyed the fields and distant woodlands, engraining them in my mind.

Our house stood on the edge of town between the tiny stone church and the Schunter River. They were sacred places to me, marking two of the biggest decisions of my life—one a commitment to Emil in marriage and the other my commitment to God. And there I was, living in the middle, having made another decision, a commitment to leave everything behind.

Before we could leave, all four of us went to a government office in Hamburg for medical testing and immunizations. We were only supposed to stay twelve days, but it stretched to fourteen. Emil did all right, but the children cried with each shot. For a long time, they'd scream and run away anytime someone wearing white approached for fear of more shots, whether they were a nurse or not.

When they poked and prodded to draw blood from my arm or give me a shot, I fainted. There were sixteen shots in total for each of us and I grew concerned my innate aversion to needles and seeing blood would prevent me from passing the physical. If I didn't, we'd be denied access to America. But I finally completed the shots, and we returned to Beienrode two weeks before we were to board the ship.

We gave away any furniture we had and packed two large travel trunks with our remaining belongings. What little savings we had in the bank were withdrawn and used to buy baby clothes and some things we thought we might need for our new life—coats, warm boots, some blankets. We were warned of the winters there.

The new German government was happy to see millions of refugees leave to ease the housing and supply crisis, but they didn't want their money to go with them. Germany feared a mass exodus of money would strain the economy. We were penniless but were assured we'd receive a stipend once we arrived in America.

Most of Emil's family, including Olga, Johann, and their mother, were also making arrangements to make the trip. I knew I would see them again, but the goodbyes were hard.

I rarely met with old friends like Liesa, Trudi, or Papa Schulz anymore. We mostly stayed in touch through letters. Still, the thought of getting on a ship and sailing across the sea had a finality to it. I missed them all the more and regretted not doing a better job of staying in touch. But life and trying to survive during and after the war took its toll on many relationships, and we each went our separate ways.

Mutti wasn't speaking to me again, and I only had Werner and Anneliesa as my close family.

"I will miss you and those babies," said Anneliesa through tears. "I wish I could come with you."

"I'll write often, and send you pictures from America," I said. "Maybe I can come visit, or you can come stay with us."

We both knew how unlikely it was, but pretended it was true. As a German citizen, she couldn't move to America. The only reason I could go was because I was married to Emil, a refugee.

"Have you told Mutti when we're leaving? Has she asked about me?"

"I told her."

"So, she knows?"

"Yes," she said.

"She knows I'm leaving on Sunday and might never be back? And she still doesn't want to see me? Not even the children?"

Her silence was telling. My heart, heavy.

"She's not the one leaving."

Anneliesa's words stung, but I knew she was right.

"Maybe you should try one more time," she said. "I don't know. Maybe she'll at least say goodbye. She still has the picture of you on her bureau." She smiled. "Next to Vati's."

Tears threatened to spill from my eyes, imagining Mutti gazing upon a make-shift shrine of photographs depicting the images of those she lost, whether real or imagined.

Me and Vati.

I wanted to push the thought of him out of my mind. He'd been gone for years, yet the loss still crept up on me and pierced my soul without warning. Most of my memories of him were from another lifetime when I was a young girl or barely a teenager, yet he made me who I was and remained my constant companion, if only in my memories.

Would he have wanted me to go, to close the door and never return? To leave the Fatherland he cherished so deeply? The Fatherland that betrayed him and all of its people? If I left, would his memory stay behind? Would I lose all sense of him, of who I was, and where I came from?

"He would be proud of you," Anneliesa's voice brought me back. When did she become such a grown-up, sharing words of comfort and wisdom, able to see into one's thoughts? And how could she know? She barely remembered him.

"I wish you could have known him," I said.

"I do." She reached for my hand, squeezing it gently. "You kept him alive for me all these years."

Tears tumbled down our cheeks.

"Maybe it's time you let him go," she said.

I nodded and sniffled quietly. We hugged, and I sensed Vati's presence along with a far greater Father assuring me he was all right, and I and my family would be, too.

The next day, I showed up at Mutti's house with my children unannounced, knowing Anneliesa would be there to let me in.

"I know you don't want to see me," I told Mutti. "But you should at least say goodbye to your grandchildren."

It wasn't a happy reunion, only a sad goodbye, and Mutti wished me well. It was the best I could hope for under the circumstances.

When I got up to leave, I hugged her, but it was like my arms were wrapped around a cold pillar of stone.

"I'll write often," I said as I pulled away. I looked her in the eyes. "I love you."

She flinched and brushed imaginary crumbs off her

skirt.

* * *

With our luggage and tickets in hand, our little family arrived at the port in Bremerhaven on the North Sea on Monday, September 17, 1951. The cool, fall day greeted us with overcast skies. A wind blew across the waters and merged with the damp air, blanketing everything in a dewey layer of mist. The briny taste of saltwater touched my lips and the smell of the sea mingled with the tangy whiff of body odor from the mass of people around us.

A former Navy transport ship, the U.S.S. General R. M. Blatchford, stood tall and stretched before us, a large vessel of riveted steel and welded metal, ready to set sail to New York.

Men held their hats to their heads with one hand while carrying suitcases in the other, each marked with American addresses in large letters. People pressed in on either side, jostling each other to move ahead and calling to others in a cacophony of languages. Little hands gripped tightly to their mothers' skirts, and the cries of frightened infants rose above the crowd.

They were all eager for a new life. A new hope. I wished I were so sure. It was a chaotic dream, as though I were outside myself, observing from afar and not part of the throng. Yet I was filled with every sensation and emotion imaginable. There was something in the air, an excited anticipation and unchartered trepidation I'd never experienced before.

"Move along. Move along," someone said.

This is really happening.

Monika was getting heavy as she clung to me from my hip, and so was the suitcase tugging on my arm. Emil and Waldemar led the way with another trunk in tow.

"Ticket." The voice was distant. "Ticket!"

He was speaking right in front of me.

I handed him my boarding pass. Legs unsteady, I stepped onto the ramp and ascended toward the belly of the ship, fully aware my feet no longer touched the land where every footstep, every breath, every single heartbeat of my life was spent.

Until then.

I looked back to the shore, taking in one last glimpse of my homeland. Germany, with all its faults and hideous scars, was a familiar and ragged old friend who I thought I could never part ways with, who wove the intricate story of my life and intertwined it with its people and those I loved.

But, a new chapter was beginning.

Tears welled in my eyes, blurring the landscape and casting over it an ethereal swirl, threatening to wash it from my memory.

I turned to face the ship and stepped aboard.

EPILOGUE

The boat swayed in the choppy waters, and my stiff fingers held tightly to the railing as I looked across the dark bay.

There she stood, tall and proud, her golden torched flame towering above the waves, her steely gaze a symbol of strength and freedom.

She was beautiful, this Lady of Liberty.

A virtual palace emerged from the sea like Atlantis, its spires pointing to the heavens. Its beautiful stonework and massive archways contrasted against the New York skyline with its glass towers and skyscrapers.

Ellis Island was beautiful, too.

Wooden pillars lined the dock, and lawn and trees stretched beyond. The journey took a lifetime and my legs were shaky. Emotions piled up inside me with each step. It felt familiar, like being introduced to an old friend.

"Here, let me help you off the boat," a voice said.

I grabbed Monika's hand and stepped onto solid planks, thankful for sound footing beneath me. I never did have very good sea legs.

"Step this way," another voice called and I followed.

We walked through the tall arched doorways of Ellis Island and into the baggage room, then ascended up the grand staircase. I stopped several times to catch my breath and rest my weary knees, but I was determined to reach the top.

When I did, I stared in awe. The cavernous expanse of the registration hall with balconies all around and the soaring tiled ceilings—they rivaled those of a cathedral. Light streamed through the windows with a reverent stillness and illuminated the flag with stars and stripes.

It was just as I remembered it.

Except the flag held forty-eight stars then. Not fifty.

"Are you okay, mom? Mom?"

I buried my head in my hands, my shoulders trembling, my tears flowing, unleashing every memory over the last fifty years. I was anguished with the sorrow, the joy, the hope, the pain. The beauty of it all melded together into a lifetime of stories telling of so much loss and so much love.

My story.

Monika touched my shoulder, "Are those tears of joy or tears of sadness?" she asked.

"Both."

I took a deep breath and pulled myself together, reliving every step. We had long since parted ways with the tour guide and I recalled the chaotic scene, pointing to where the lines formed for each nationality, the desks where we answered questions and got processed, the medical testing area, and the stairway to the left that led us back to our luggage and out the doors to board a ferry.

I stepped onto the red polished tiles and sat on a bench to take in the wonder of it, sweeping my fingers across the wood worn smooth. Maybe it was the same bench where I sat on that remarkable day more than half a century earlier.

"I thought I'd never come back here," I said. "It hasn't changed one bit."

Monika hugged me close. When we sat together on a bench in this great hall the first time, I was the one holding her. Now, she held me.

I wished Emil could have been there to see it. He would have remembered, too, how we were separated for the weeklong sail across the sea, arriving on the weekend, and having to wait on the ship until Monday morning when the office opened. The mass of people. The chorus of different languages. The train ride to Milwaukee.

But he was gone now, taken by cancer years earlier.

We worked hard, very hard, to make it in the United States. And we did, despite starting with twenty-four dollars to our name, the amount we were issued when we arrived at Ellis Island. To anyone looking from the outside, we achieved the American dream.

We eventually had five children, a home, food on the table, and a car in the garage. But those who got close saw the cracks, the tumultuous years, the flaring tempers, the times when I was sure we'd never make it and I swore

I couldn't go on. But we never gave up.

I couldn't. My very name means strength.

Monika and I walked slowly back to the boat full of tourists. I stopped again, holding onto a railing to catch my breath. This old body was failing me. I looked back one last time, then stepped aboard and sat to rest my aching feet.

These feet.

They had taken me where I never imagined I'd go, and to some places where I never wanted to return. From cobblestone streets to prison cells. From a wretched grave to a cleansing river. From the Fatherland to a foreign land.

And all the while, these feet were leading me. Leading me home.

AUTHOR'S NOTES

The events in this book are true as told to me by my mother, Waltraud. She had an incredible ability to recall memories in vivid detail. Through the years, I secretly recorded many hours of stories and recollections from her life in Germany.

The main characters are real people with real names, and the cities and villages hold the same cobblestone streets she walked. Some of the conversations and surrounding circumstances are as I imagined them to be based on who I knew her to be. Chances are, they were much more extraordinary than I painted them. That's because she was extraordinary, and anyone who knew her would agree.

Some may ask why I wrote the story from her perspective. It's because I wanted to create the sense she was speaking the words to you much like she spoke them to me.

Much happened after she and Emil left Germany. Life in America was hard, especially during those early years when she didn't know the language and didn't have any of her own family members to confide in.

She and Emil accomplished a lot together, but some of the wounds lingering in my father's own heart were never healed, making life difficult at times.

Emil's entire immediate family and many of his other relatives eventually immigrated to the United States with the exception of his sister, Martha, whose husband didn't pass the physical examination. Sadly, she was murdered in Germany in the mid 1950s and her killer was never found.

Not until they came to America were Waltraud and Emil made fully aware of the extent of atrocities committed by the Nazis, and they struggled to come to grips with such a horrific part of their German heritage. When they viewed photos in an American magazine depicting the Holocaust, they wept openly—an especially unusual emotion for my father to show outwardly.

In addition to Waldemar and Monika, Waltraud and Emil had three more children including Erika, John, and me, Tamara—"*Tammy.*"

Emil and Waltraud worked in Milwaukee for a time, but my father wanted to farm the land as he and his family did in the Ukraine. Through the years, they owned several farms and eventually settled permanently on a farm near Bear Creek, Wisconsin.

Waltraud and her mother were estranged for more than twenty years. They reconciled through letters and, in

June 1973, Emil and Waltraud purchased a plane ticket for her mother. She flew to America to visit the family while they lived on a farm in Bowler, Wisconsin, where she met the rest of her grandchildren.

Waltraud visited Germany for the first time in 1979. It would be the last time she saw her mother who died a few months later following a serious car accident. Werner died in 1982 at the age of fifty, also from a car crash.

Waltraud traveled to Germany several times since to visit family including Anneliesa, who died at the age of seventy-six in 2012. I joined my mother for three of those trips where we walked the small towns and backroads, and I documented more stories from her childhood.

Then, in the stillness of a cool summer afternoon on June 12, 2020, my beloved Mutti, Waltraud Emma Marie (Michaelis) Tomtschik, age ninety-three, arrived at her heavenly home—the true Father Land—where she met Jesus, her savior, face to face. I imagine an embrace with Him saying, "Well done my good and faithful servant," before giving her a grand tour of a beautiful garden prepared just for her, with bluebirds and abundant flowers in colors she's never seen.

I imagine, too, she had a joyful reunion with my father, Emil, catching up on all that happened since he departed over twenty-seven years earlier.

Waltraud remained on her farm and lived on her own until her final days. But she didn't fade away. Instead, she lived life fully by spending time with family, traveling, volunteering, serving at her church, holding sleepovers, expanding her passion for flower gardening, and knitting hundreds of slippers, socks, and other handiwork to give away to those she loved.

Her sharp wit, spunk, laughter, hospitality, and love were overflowing.

There will never be another like her.

I miss you, mom. I hope the way I've told your story makes you proud.

Until we meet again.

Waltraud Emma Marie (Michaelis) Tomtschik
May 26, 1927 – June 12, 2020

Waltraud, Age 16 (Summer 1943)
The photo Waltraud sent to her father, photographed by Trudi

ACKNOWLEDGMENTS

Thank you to those who helped my mother's story come to life and who have encouraged me through this labor of love.

To my siblings, Waldemar, Monika, Erika, and John who helped capture our mother's story and are a part of mine.

To my husband, Paul, for his love and support.

To friends and family too numerous to count who've always believed in me, offered feedback, given insights, and cheered me on along the way.

To the God in whom my mother instilled her hope, and mine.

— GERMAN TRANSLATIONS —

Auf Wiedersehen — goodbye

BDM (Bund Deutsche Mädel) — mandatory female branch of the Hitler Youth for girls ages 14–18

Bürgermeister — mayor

Berufsschule — trade school

Entschuldigen Sie, bitte — I beg your pardon, please

Deutschmarks — German currency after the war

Feuerwehr — fire department

Frau — married woman "Mrs."

Fräulein — young unmarried woman

Gasthaus — a rooming house with restaurant

Guten Tag — good day

Hakenkreuz — swastika

Hausfrau — housewife

Herr — Mr.

Jungmädel — mandatory female branch of the Hitler Youth for girls ages 10–13

Luftwaffe — Germany's air defense military branch

Mutti — mom or mommy

Oma — grandma

Opa — grandpa

Osterfeuer — Easter fire

Pfennig — penny

Pflichtjahr — compulsory year of service for teenage girls at age 14

Reichsmarks — German currency during World War II

Rittergut — a large estate and farmland belonging to a baron

Schreckliche — terrible

Sieg Heil — A Nazi salute meaning "hail victory"

Sportplatz — sports field

Sprengbombe — incendiary bombs

Tante — aunt

Tanzen — dance

Vati — dad or daddy

Wehrmacht — Nazi armed forces

Gustav Michaelis (Vati), Waltraud's father

Werner, Emma (Mutti), Waltraud & Anneliesa (circa 1939)

Anneliesa, Werner & Waltraud (circa 1941)

Waltraud & Emil's wedding (June 5, 1948)

Emil, Waldemar, Monika & Waltraud (1951 in Hamburg)

Waltraud & Emil (1985)

Waltraud with her five children
Front: Tammy, Waltraud & Waldemar
Back: Erika, Monika & John

Author Tammy Borden & Waltraud, her mother

ABOUT THE AUTHOR

TAMMY A. BORDEN

Tammy is a professional copywriter
turned novelist, compelled to document the
unforgettable story of her mother's life growing
up in Nazi Germany. She lives with her husband
in East Central Wisconsin and carries on her
mother's love of handiwork, gardening, and
nature. Tammy is also the author of a memoir
sharing her own life's journey,
A Perennial Life—Finding Purpose in Every Season.

TammyBorden.com

Did you enjoy Waltraud's story?

Please share about it with others through conversations
and social media, and leave a review on Amazon,
Goodreads, and other book-lover platforms.
Help support independent authors.

Thank you.

Scan the code to view on Amazon.

Made in the USA
Las Vegas, NV
27 April 2024